TEN MINUTE MISCONDUCT

S.L. STERLING

be her boyfriend for the wedding and get Hugo off her back. I figure it's helping her out but for me it's the perfect opportunity to convince her I'm not the same guy I used to be.

I want her to know I'm the man she deserves and I'm going to put everything on the line to get her to be mine.

About the Book

Lorelai Anderson got under my skin years ago and I'd never been able to get her out.

When I found out she had a crush on me I turned into the biggest dick around. I did what I did to keep her away. I knew I wasn't the man she needed, and her brother agreed.

Then I left town to play hockey which was both a blessing and a curse.

When I got signed to the Dominators and returned to Vancouver, I suppose I got what I deserved. Not only did Lorelai hate my guts, but she had a boyfriend. So, I kept my distance from her, until her friend started dating one of my teammates. I had no choice but to come around. It got worse when I got the invitation to her brother's wedding. There was no way I could back out.

As my luck would have it Lorelai and I end up on the same flight to Hawaii and that's when I find out she is very single. I also find out that her ex is going to be at this wedding and despite having a new girlfriend, the cheating jerk is harassing her to get back together with him. When she breaks down in tears, I do that only thing I can think of. I make a split-second decision to

Ten Minute Misconduct

Copyright © 2024 by S.L. Sterling

All rights reserved. Without limiting the rights under copyright reserved about, no part of this publication may be reproduced, stored in, or introduced into a retrieval system, or transmitted in any form or by any means (mechanical, electronic, photocopying, recording, or otherwise) without the prior written permission of both the copyright owner and the above publisher of the book. This is a work of fiction. Any references to historical events, real people, or real places are used fictitiously. Other names, characters, places, and events are products of the author's imagination, and any resemblance to actual events or places or persons, living or dead, is entirely coincidental. Disclaimer: This book contains mature content not suitable for those under the age of 18. It involves strong language and sexual situations. All parties portrayed in sexual situations are consenting adults over the age of 18.

ISBN: 978-1-989566-77-0

Paperback ISBN: 978-1-989566-84-8

Harcover ISBN: 978-1-989566-85-5

Editor: Brandi Aquino, Editing Done Write

Cover Design: Thunderstruck Cover Design

TEN MINUTE MISCONDUCT

BY

S.L. STERLING

©2024

Chapter One

Lorelai - Two Weeks Before the Wedding

Knox Evans is and always will be the most obnoxious man I've ever met, I thought to myself as he lay on my treatment table.

"Don't try to hide it, Lorelai. I know you enjoy grabbing my ass every chance you get."

I clenched my teeth as I worked to stretch his hip and glutes, while he looked up at me with that shit-eating grin on his face, which I wiped off by forcing the stretch a little too far. He winced a bit, and I immediately backed off.

"Sorry about that." I moved him into the next position.

I'd been the lucky recipient of taking on Knox as a

patient while Stacy was off for a little while. To say I was counting the days until her return was an understatement.

"Ow!" Knox cried as I dug my fingers into his hamstring. "What part of injury don't you get?"

"What have you done to yourself? This didn't feel like this three weeks ago," I replied, easing off the pressure a bit.

"Guess you could say it might be from lack of stretching after helping two people move into their new condo. Which reminds me, I still haven't gotten an invitation for a drink yet." He sucked in a breath as I dug my fingers into the tight muscle a little gentler this time.

I bent down and pulled out the tube of heat rub, placed a dollop in my hand, and began rubbing the cream into the back of his leg and glute.

"Who ever said you'd get an invitation for a drink?"

"You did," he said, meeting my eyes. "And I quote, 'Thank you so much, Knox, for helping me move all my stuff into my new room. I think we will have to have you and Dylan over for a drink to celebrate.'"

I rolled my eyes, placed the cap back on the tube of rub, and handed it to him. I actually remembered saying those words too, but I'd be damned if I were going to let on. After all, after he left that night, I'd had to move all the boxes by myself into my real room because I'd been too stubborn to agree with him when he'd suggested I take the room with the large floor-to-ceiling windows.

"Apply this tonight after a hot shower, and after practice tomorrow morning. You need to make sure you are taking care of this, otherwise it's not going to get better. I'd like to see you again, but there won't be time, so I guess we will pick up where we left off after the wedding. Just make sure you're stretching," I said, checking my schedule and adding him to the first appointment I had available after we were back. "Ten on the twenty-fourth?"

Knox sat up and hopped off the table, making his way to the door.

"Got it. You know, if you want to see me more often, all you need to do is ask." He winked.

Again, I rolled my eyes, said goodbye, then grabbed my cell phone from my desk, checking my messages. I was midway through an email when my door opened again, and Knox looked it.

"What?" I questioned.

"Let me know what night to pop over for that drink, princess."

It was only a matter of seconds after the door shut that I felt like I might explode from annoyance and took off out of my office.

I marched down the hall toward Aurora's office. If I didn't have time to calm down after my appointment with Knox before my next appointment, my poor patient would suffer the wrath. I pushed her door open without even thinking of knocking.

"What on earth!" she yelled as she looked up at me from the report she was working on. "Don't you think you should knock first?" she questioned, turning her eyes back to the paperwork in front of her.

"I'm going to scream!" I cried, making my way over to her treatment table, hopping up and lying back.

"What is going on now?" She sighed, flipping the paper over and continuing to write, not paying much attention to me at all.

I'd not exactly been the most approachable person for the last little while, and I knew I'd been driving Aurora crazy because I hadn't wanted to talk. Truth was, I was irritated about many things. The main problem was my brother and soon-to-be sister-in-law and their upcoming wedding. First, when the wedding invites arrived, Aurora had promised to be my plus one. She took that back only a few days later when her boyfriend Dylan had asked her to be his plus one instead.

I didn't blame her; they are so in love it's disgusting, and it really shouldn't have surprised me she'd choose him instead of me. I'd have done the same thing if I had someone.

That wasn't even what had made me truly angry. One night, I'd been over helping Candace, my soon-to-be sister-in-law, with some wedding things. She'd asked me to go over the dinner seating chart to make sure she hadn't missed anyone who'd confirmed to attend the destination wedding. As I was cross-referencing, I came across my ex's name on the completed seating chart.

I finally asked Candace about it since my brother had promised he'd drop Hugo from the wedding party, but he hadn't. In fact, he'd made him one of his groomsmen instead. I was so upset when I'd gotten home, I couldn't even talk about it, and I'd been harboring this information and these feelings for days.

Until now.

"You will not believe this!" I cried, burying my face in my hands.

Aurora continued to write out whatever treatment plan she was working on and let out a sigh. "I'm not a shrink, you know. That table was ready for my next appointment."

"Could you please just listen?" I cried, shoving my fingers into my hair.

She looked up and put her pencil down, inspecting me.

"Okay, what's up?" she asked, getting up and

coming around to the front of her desk and leaning against the edge.

"It's bad, terrible, and I'm doomed."

"What is? Why are you doomed?"

"My brother, the idiot that he is, invited Hugo to go to his damn wedding, making him one of his groomsmen, even after he promised he wouldn't even invite him. I'm going to have to spend a week in Hawaii with my ex-boyfriend. Do you know what that means?"

"Uh…it means you'll be spending a week in Hawaii and your ex-boyfriend will be there as well." Aurora shrugged.

"No, what it means is that he is going to continue bugging me for another shot with me. I just know it. I didn't tell you, but there was a message on my phone the other night from him asking me if we could talk, and he left another message again this morning."

"Did you call him?" Aurora asked.

"Are you crazy? No, I didn't call. I deleted it instead, but still."

"So just ignore him."

"Easy for you to say Miss I'm in a Relationship with Someone Great."

Aurora looked at me and shook her head before gathering up the paperwork she had been working on and shoving it into a file.

"Why aren't you saying anything?"

"Because, as always, you are overreacting."

"You know, I remember when you were insane before you got together with Dylan. I listened to you. I helped you."

Aurora shrugged. "That is true. So how was your day?"

"Don't get me started," I said through clenched teeth. I had one more appointment left and then the weekend was here.

"That bad?"

"Yes. It was that bad."

Aurora laughed. "You know, you are acting like you had to treat Knox today or something." She giggled, shoving her file into her filing cabinet.

"It was hell, and you hit the nail on the head. Stacey's off for a bit, and I was the lucky recipient of his case."

"Stacy is going to be off for a bit, so you may as well get used to it. There is talk that she was overloaded with clients anyway, so you just might be the lucky winner of treating Knox Evans for good."

"Even my best friend…" I cried.

"Is that why you are down here, because he was your last appointment, and you need to blow off steam?"

Aurora had tried to get me over this hatred I

carried for Knox Evans. She figured that perhaps he'd grow on me, but she was wrong. There would be nothing in this world that would change my feelings regarding Knox Evans.

She walked over to me and placed both her hands on my shoulders and waited until I met her eyes.

"It's going to be okay, you know. If you want, message Hugo and tell him he'll need to get through me first before he gets to you. He'll also have to get through Dylan."

I studied her eyes, seeing the sincerity in them.

"I just can't believe my brother would have invited him. Especially after…well, after I found out the truth about the end of our relationship."

"I know, but they were friends' way before you two ever dated," Aurora said, once again defending my brother. "There was only so much that Candace could do."

"He cheated on me. With my cousin! Candace shouldn't need to do anything. He should have been automatically uninvited and banned from the family."

The memory of finding out flooded my mind as Aurora met my eyes, sorrow filling them. It was then we heard a knock on her door and Dylan popped his head into the room.

"Hey, ladies."

"Hey," Aurora said, making her way over to him,

placing a kiss on his lips, ignoring the fact that I was in literal breakdown mode.

"What's going on?" he asked.

Aurora shut the door behind him and looked at me.

"Hey, Dylan," I muttered.

"Are you okay? You look a little messed up."

"It's the end of her world." Aurora giggled as I flopped back on her table and began pouting again.

"What is?" Dylan asked, sitting down on the chair in the corner.

"My stupid brother and this damn wedding," I said, burying my face in my hands, trying to shut the world out, even for a moment.

"Don't you worry your pretty little head. We will get you through it," Dylan said, placing his hand on my shoulder, no doubt trying to comfort me.

"I don't think it's possible to get me through it," I mumbled.

"Hey, they don't call us the dominators for nothing." He winked and grinned. "No one messes with us. Now, when you ladies are finished here, lets do dinner."

"Sounds good, I'm in." I said, running my hand through my hair, trying to let go of everything.

"Great! Knox and I have a craving for that new pizza place."

Chapter Two

Lorelai

"Are you sure you'll be okay getting to the airport alone?" Aurora asked for the hundredth time as she wheeled her suitcase to the door.

"For the millionth time, yes. I'll be fine." I shoved a book into my carry-on for the flight.

"I still don't understand why you switched flights at the last minute. We would have been seated together."

"No, you'll be with Dylan," I muttered, knowing full well that she'd traded seats with Knox, which would have forced us to sit together. I shoved a slice of green pepper into my mouth and looked over at my friend. "Besides, I told you, I had some things to finish up for work, and this will enable me to make sure that I get those finished before leaving."

"You're on vacation, Lorelai." Aurora said, frowning. "You deserve this time. Besides, you've been busting your ass ever since we got hired, working late, taking on more patients than you probably should, working weekends. A handful of days off won't hurt anything."

Ignoring her, I made my way over to the fridge and grabbed a soda just as a loud bang caused me to jump. I looked up as Aurora opened the door to our condo. Dylan poked his head around the corner, a huge grin on his face.

"Ready to go there, sexy?" he asked, stepping inside and immediately meeting Aurora's lips.

Their infatuation with one another was enough to make me ill. I rolled my eyes and went back over to the stack of books I'd set aside and ran through them again, looking for another one to read while he examined her lips yet again. There was no way I was going to make it through the next few days if I had to watch these two the entire time.

"Sure am," she whispered. "Oh, and I packed your favorite bikini and the items I brought home the other night that were in the brown paper bag."

I felt my stomach turn and swallowed hard as I tried to ignore their public display of affection. This was another reason why I'd changed my flight. There was no way in hell I could sit on a flight for six hours and listen to these two go at it. They had no shame.

"God, I can't wait," he said, devouring her mouth once again.

"Get a room, would you?" I barked, shoving another sappy romance novel into my bag, which would probably make me hate my life even more than I already did.

"Hate to break it to you, but we are." Dylan winked, taking hold of Aurora's bags and pulling them into the hall.

"Alright, you're sure you'll—"

"Yes, I'll be fine. I will see you tomorrow at some point," I said.

Aurora came over and stood beside me, studying me.

"What?" I demanded.

"Love you. I'll see you tomorrow. Safe flight okay." She wrapped her arms around me.

I weakened at her embrace and almost instantly returned her hug. "I'm sorry I'm such a grump," I muttered.

Aurora let me go and placed her hands on my shoulders. "It's okay, I understand. You're going through a lot right now. Just know that it will all work out, okay."

I nodded, fighting back the tears that were threatening to fall. I hoped she was right, but I seriously had my doubts. She let me go, smiled, and then headed out of the condo.

Once she was gone, I took a moment to take a deep breath. I'd been so excited for my brother and for Candance, until the other day when I was going over the final list of confirmed guests. It was there I saw Hugo's name, along with a plus one.

Yet another reason I'd changed my flight was because I knew most guests were on the flight leaving in a little under three hours, so aside from not wanting to watch Aurora and Dylan go at it for the entire six-hour flight, I also didn't want to be on the same flight as my ex and his new love interest.

Not when I was flying solo because I was completely unlovable.

I hung my head and wandered down to my room, checking over my suitcase one more time, adding in two more bathing suits before I zipped it up and wheeled it to the door. Then I grabbed the plate of leftovers from the fridge, along with another soda, and made my way into our shared office. I sat down behind the desk and started finishing the reports I knew needed to be submitted before I left.

I WOKE WITH A START, the room slowly coming into view as I tried to figure out where I was. I laid there staring at the wall, and then lifted my head and glanced around the room. My computer monitor was on, and when I looked down at the pile of papers that I'd fallen asleep on, I noticed a puddle of drool.

"That's attractive," I muttered to myself as I wiped my cheek with my shirt.

Somehow, I'd drifted off while working on the last report I had to submit. I stretched, my body stiff from laying the way I was, and glanced at the clock on my desk.

It was almost two in the morning. Alarmed, I shot up from the desk and grabbed the phone, quickly calling a cab. Then I scurried into my room, stripped out of what I was wearing, and changed into yoga pants and a T-shirt, quickly grabbing my sweater from the closet.

I rushed into the bathroom, brushed my teeth, washed my face, and ran the brush through my hair, pulling it up into one of my clips. I was going to be late; I knew it. I'd miss my plane and then what would happen? They advised to be at the airport two hours ahead of time, and I'd be lucky if I made it there with an hour and a half left to spare.

The cab raced through the streets. Lucky for me, there wasn't a ton of traffic at two in the morning, and I'd met the cab right when it pulled up outside the condo.

It seemed luck was on my side as I sailed through security. I guess it helped when you only took carry-on luggage. It skipped through the nightmare of checking bags. Once through, I stopped and grabbed a coffee and bagel and then made my way to my gate, where I got to sit down for twenty minutes before they started allowing passengers to board the plane.

I shoved my bag in the overhead bin and my other bag down on the floor in front of my seat and took my seat beside the window, glad I'd upgraded to business class. There was way more room this way.

I slipped my sweater on and pulled my neck pillow and headphones from my bag, along with my book. I had no idea if I'd be able to stay awake, but figured I'd get comfortable now as opposed to doing it when the plane took off.

I'd just gotten situated and opened my book when I heard a familiar voice.

"Well, I'll be damned. It's princess!"

I took a deep breath before lifting my head to see

Knox Evans standing in the aisle, bag in hand. God wouldn't be that cruel to me, would he?

Of all the seats on this plane, please don't be sitting with me.

He chuckled, threw his suitcase in the overhead bin, and then placed his other bag on the seat beside me. He reached over his head and pulled his sweatshirt off. My eyes immediately fell to the bare skin of his stomach as his T-shirt lifted.

"What do you think you are doing?" I said, my jaw clenched as he sat down beside me, shoving his bag between his legs.

"Uh, same as you. Taking my seat."

I frowned and looked around at the rest of the seats in the upgraded section. He had to be in the wrong seat. Only my hope faded as I looked around and noticed the last three seats were now being taken. I let out the breath I was holding.

"Is this some sort of joke?"

"Nope, don't think so, princess. You are going to get all the Evans charm for the entire flight. Consider yourself lucky. Girls would kill to be in your position." He winked, showing me his boarding pass and pointing to the selected seat.

"I don't understand. Dylan said you were on the other flight."

"That would have been true, but I had some things I had to take care of and would have been crunched for time. Which leads me to ask, why did you change your flight? Last I heard, you were on that flight as well."

"I too had things to take care of," I said, feeling irritated, so I turned my attention back to my book and tried to focus on what I was reading. Only I could concentrate because Knox was staring at me.

"What?" I finally demanded.

"Oh, princess, put a smile on that face of yours. Life isn't so bad. We are on our way to one of the most beautiful destinations in the world."

"It's four in the morning. I'd be happier if I were sleeping in my warm bed at this hour."

"You know, you need to learn to embrace this early hour. It's honestly the best time of day!"

"Says you. I like my sleep. Now, I wanted a quiet flight, and I take it from the look on your face that won't be happening now, will it?"

"That depends on you."

"On me? How would it depend on me?"

"Well, you are the only one who is starting any conversation here. I was simply sitting here looking out the window."

I closed my eyes and took a deep breath. Nothing had changed. He was the same old Knox. Same as he'd been all those years ago that night in the bar.

Aurora always wondered why I hated him, and I'd

made up a stupid half-assed excuse, but it was far more than the reasons I'd given her about him teasing me about the crush I had on him. In fact, that hadn't happened at all. I'd just made it up to get her to stop asking me because the truth was far too painful for me to want to remember.

I stared at the page in front of me, pretending to read while the memory of the night Knox became my mortal enemy flashed before my eyes. I swallowed hard to remove the lump that now sat in my throat.

It was Phil's birthday, and I'd gone with him, Knox, and a couple of other teammates to a bar to celebrate. I'd had one too many celebratory drinks for being the designated driver, which is what happens when you try to keep up with a pile of hockey players.

I'd had a crush on Knox for a while now, and when I stumbled off to the bathroom, I'd decided that it was time to grow up and tell him how I felt. I stayed there until I was certain I had enough courage to confront him, and when I finally returned to the bar, it was like the universe was helping me along. Knox was there alone.

"The guys went out to get some air," he said, sucking back his beer as I leaned up against the bar. "You want another?"

I nodded and smiled. More liquid courage was exactly what I needed. I was close enough to him as I stood there that I could feel the heat coming off his body and I could smell the scent of his cologne. I couldn't remember a time in the last two years that he hadn't worn this cologne. In fact, every time he was around, my hormones were in overdrive.

"Where did you say Phil went?" I questioned.

Knox turned his blue eyes on me and smiled. "He wasn't feeling too well. The guys took him outside."

I nodded as our eyes locked. Knox was older than Phil by three years, which put him almost ten years older than me.

As I stood there looking at him, I wondered what his lips tasted like and I zoned out, thinking about what they would feel like against mine. I'd heard he was an amazing kisser and wondered how true that statement was.

I jumped when the bartender placed two more drinks on the bar in front of us.

"Drink up," Knox said, nodding to the glass.

"Trying to get me drunk?" I asked, looking up at him.

"No need to try. I think you are drunk."

I closed one eye and thought for a second. "Maybe just a wee bit," I said, holding my index finger and thumb together, giggling.

He kind of chuckled. "Is that why you're looking at me weird?" he questioned, lifting the bottle to his lips and taking a mouthful of fresh beer as he watched me.

When he lowered the bottle, that was when I made my move. I placed my fingers under his chin, turned his head toward me, and kissed him. The instant our lips met, I felt a heat roll over my body. I wanted to live in that feeling forever, only it was over before it even started.

He pulled away and stood up. The look on his face wasn't

what I'd imagined it would be when I'd played this night over in my mind.

"Lorelai..."

"I really like you." I sort of moaned.

"That's nice, but—"

"So was that kiss," I said, hoping he'd take me in his arms and make me his. Only when I took a step forward, Knox took a step back.

"It's enough, Lorelai. Stop making a fool of yourself. I'm not even the slightest bit interested in you. You aren't my type," he barked and took off, leaving me standing there alone.

Immediately, I could feel the tears burn, and as I watched him walk away, the pain of rejection ran through my body. Don't make a fool of myself? Was that what I'd done?

Embarrassment flooded me and I turned around and ran from the bar. I never wanted to see him again.

"Earth to Lorelai! God, she zones out like this all the time." He chuckled.

"Is she okay? I can get some help if you think she needs it."

I looked over at him to see him shrugging his shoulders, nodding his head toward the flight attendant, who held out a bottle of water to me.

"Did you want water?" he repeated.

I blinked, tried to laugh it off, and took the bottle of water. The same feeling of embarrassment flooded me again. Ignoring it, I opened the water and drank down half the bottle, trying to calm myself after revisiting that horrible moment in time. I could feel that same pang of rejection every time I thought of Hugo, along with every relationship I'd ever been in, which hadn't been that many. It had been just enough to confirm to me I'd probably spend the rest of my life alone.

"Get a grip, would you?" Knox whispered in my ear.

I inhaled deeply, as that familiar scent of his cologne hit my nose. I stopped breathing and closed my eyes and held my breath as I tried my best to figure out how the hell I'd ever make it through not only this flight, but the next few days.

Chapter Three

Knox

Lorelai sat beside me, texting at a furious rate as a bout of turbulence hit. I grabbed my seatbelt, quickly doing it back up, and then glanced over at her. I hated this part of flights, and even I should be used to it by now, I wasn't.

"Did you put your belt on?"

She ignored me, muttering to herself about how this wedding was going to be the shit shows of all the shit shows.

I smirked to myself as I hit her arm, causing her to almost drop her phone. She glared at me.

"What did you do that for?"

"You should do up your belt. The sign is on." I grinned.

She let out a sigh. "I don't undo it, therefore I don't need to worry about it. You can also stop worrying about it and leave me be. I'm a grown woman, perfectly capable of taking care of myself," she grumbled, going back to the crazy texting.

This wasn't exactly how I'd imagined this trip starting out. I'd actually changed my flight because I'd found out from Dylan that I'd be sitting beside Lorelai on the other flight. I hadn't wanted her to be uncomfortable the entire flight, so I figured changing my flight time would be best. Yet, here we were. It's funny how things always come back to bite me in the ass, regardless of what I do.

She let out an irritated sigh, continued typing, and then shoved her phone into the back of the seat in front of her and closed her eyes.

"Is something wrong?" I questioned.

She shook her head but then mumbled under her breath something about how this wedding was going to be the death of her. I sat there quietly, but then curiosity got the better of me.

"Why would that be?" I questioned.

"What?" She frowned.

"Why would this wedding be the death of you?"

She shook her head. "If I were actually speaking to

you, then you'd have a right to ask, but since you like to listen in to my private conversations with myself, then here is your answer. It will be the death of me because it's just the way it is. There are already issues. The shit show is already beginning. Plus, I am going to be forced to be around Hugo every single second of pretty much every single day. That's why!"

I could already see the tension not only on her face but in her shoulders when I looked at her. "Well, I can understand things going wrong. That's just par for the course with any wedding, destination or not, but I don't get the Hugo part. Why would you find it an issue to be around someone you're in a relationship with?"

"Can you not keep up?" she said, throwing her head back and closing her eyes.

I frowned and shook my head, wondering what the hell she was talking about. It wasn't as if we spoke to one another daily, and we never talked about anything personal. Hell, I was lucky she was civil during my treatments, now that she was looking after me while Stacey was off sick.

"I'm not exactly sure what it is I'm supposed to be keeping up with?"

She gave me the death glare before speaking. "Knox, in the last few months that you've been around, has there been any sign of Hugo?"

I thought for a moment. Every time I'd seen her had been with Dylan and Aurora. We were always at some event for something, or when we'd helped them move into their new place. I thought Hugo should have been there, but I never gave it much thought that he wasn't. I figured the guy was working, however, come to think of it, I hadn't heard her speak of him, which was odd, but I really gave it little to no thought.

"Have you even heard me mention him?"

"No," I said, shaking my head.

"Well, genius, that is because we broke it off. Or he broke it off. We are over, finished. Have been for a few months now, practically a year. Yet my stupid brother didn't honour my wishes and ask him not to come to the wedding like he promised he would. So now, I get to see my ex-boyfriend parade his new piece around in front of me, while I am left in the dirt picking up the pieces. I'm also incredibly single, which will only make him think I'm not over him."

I wanted to be sad for her, however, inside I was cheering. Ever since that night she kissed me in that bar, I'd wanted to be with her, but for the sake of my relationship with her brother, I knew better. So, I avoided the complicated mess that it promised to become and shoved her away.

I could still remember the look in her eyes that night as the words of rejection flew past my lips. My words had been harsh, and I hadn't meant one of them. In fact, the memory of that kiss had haunted me for years. When I'd finally gotten up the nerve to approach her, she was in a relationship with Hugo and she seemed happy, so I bowed out and internally wished them all the happiness in the world.

Well, not entirely true, but I'd like to think I did because I'm a decent human being. Anyway, I'd thrown my chance away with her and I focused my energy on others, not giving her one more single thought until this second.

When she'd first started with the Dominators, I'd thought about asking her out again, but stopped because I was certain she was still involved with Hugo. Her lack of interest in anyone, including me, said it all.

Just then, her phone went off. She grabbed it, typed a response, put her phone back, and then buried her face in her hands, her shoulders shaking.

"You know what? I think you could use a drink. What do you say?" I questioned as she lifted her tear-filled eyes to mine, then immediately looked away from me.

I hit the button for service and waited for the flight attendant. Almost immediately, she appeared, and I ordered us a drink without giving Lorelai a chance to turn it down.

I held out the can of tonic and a small bottle of gin for her, along with a glass.

"What's that for?" Lorelai questioned. "Trying to get me drunk so I shut up?"

Clenching my teeth together to stop myself from saying something I'd probably regret, I shook my head.

"It's a peace offering and something to help you cool down. I also think you need to shut that phone off and ignore the fact that Hugo will be at this wedding and focus on being in one of the most beautiful places in the world."

"He's already starting, though."

I frowned, not sure who she was talking about. "Who is? Your brother? Aurora?"

"Hugo! Like I said, can you not keep up?"

"That's who you were talking to? Why would you be talking to him?"

Lorelai unscrewed the tiny cap from the small bottle and dumped the contents into her glass, adding the tonic after.

"He wants us to talk," she said, using air quotes to emphasize to *talk*.

"Talk about what?"

"Who the hell knows? He called me not too long ago and left a message, but I didn't call him back. I have nothing to say to him."

"Makes sense. Yet, I'm confused. Why are you

talking to him now? And why does he want to talk to you if, as you put it, he has his new piece there with him?"

Lorelai took a sip of her drink and rested her head against the back of her seat. "I don't know."

"Do you have things you want or need to say to him?"

I studied her face as I waited for her answer, secretly wanting to know the truth. Did she not get closure? Did she need closure? I was confused why this was bothering her so much, if she didn't want to be with him anymore.

"No, I have nothing to say to him."

"Then ignore him."

"I have been, but I also don't want him messaging me the entire trip, either."

"Lorelai, don't you know that it's better to ignore him than to give in and answer? That alone will only keep him coming back. Either ignore him or tell him straight up that you have nothing to say and tell him to stay away from you during the trip because your boyfriend will get angry."

"That would be lying, and I don't do that."

"You did when I met you."

She frowned. "What are you talking about?"

"'Hello, I'm twenty-six,' when, in fact, you were only twenty."

"That was different."

"How was that different?" I questioned.

She took a drink and smiled. "It just was. I was young and stupid. Now I refuse to do those things."

"You shouldn't be, not when it will benefit you."

"Is that what you do?"

"Depends on the situation at hand." I shrugged.

"Do you know what I feel like doing?"

"What?"

"I'm this close to getting a return flight back home when I land and saying to hell with it."

"I get that, but you know you can't."

"I know. If it weren't my brother's wedding, I'd do exactly that." She sighed, taking a drink. "That way I wouldn't have to watch them slobber all over one another."

It bothered me that she was so bothered about Hugo being at the wedding with his new girlfriend, so I ran through things that may help her face whatever demons were going through her head. A series of thoughts floated through my mind, and I sifted through each one of them.

"He's just such an ass, and he hurt me so bad, I'm at a loss." She sighed.

"What would be an ideal situation for you to face this situation?"

Lorelai thought for a moment and then shrugged.

"What is it that bothers you about the most about the upcoming situation?"

"That he has someone that he's moved on with and I'm here, alone."

"So, don't be here alone." I shrugged.

Lorelai looked at me as if I had two heads. Then a smirk fell on her lips. "Okay, so who am I supposed to be here with then? You?" She chuckled to herself. "God, that is just hilarious," she murmured before rolling her eyes.

"Why not?" I shrugged.

"Oh, my god! You can't be serious." She downed the rest of her drink while I signalled for another two.

"I'm totally serious!" I said, smiling up at the flight attendant, who brought over two more drinks and placed them on my tray while I tapped my credit card on the machine.

"First, no one in their right mind would ever believe that we are together."

"Why not?"

"Really! You really have to ask? Are you telling me that my hatred of you doesn't speak for itself? Or the fact that you can't stand me doesn't show through."

"Oh, it speaks volumes, but it's not something that we couldn't deal with." I shrugged, ignoring her thoughts of me while dumping the two little bottles of alcohol into each glass before the mix.

"Nice try, but it would never work."

Here I'd figured I'd come up with a way to mend fences between us, and she wasn't having any part of it.

"I think it would. I can be very convincing if I want to be."

"Oh, I'm sure you can." She rolled her eyes.

"Well, that's okay. Don't say I didn't offer. Good luck with Hugo and all that!" I said, holding my glass up for her to clink hers to mine. We each took a drink, and I pulled the magazine I'd brought to read from the back of the seat and opened to the article I'd left off at. I could feel her watching me.

"Wait, were you actually serious? You'd do that for me?"

I said nothing to start, but then finally nodded. "If I knew it would make things better for you, yes. We could do this. No one needs to know the truth. It would be our secret."

Her eyes met mine as she sat there. She didn't say a thing, then her phone vibrated, and I watched her eyes fall to the screen, irritation lining her face once again.

"We could pretend like we just started dating, in secret. That way, there would be little to explain to anyone. Give me your phone."

"What? Why?"

"Trust me, just give me your phone."

I quickly took her phone and began typing out a

message. When I was done, I didn't hit send. Instead, I passed the phone back to her.

"Read it. Then send it," I said. "Change nothing."

She met my eyes and slowly took her phone from my hands. She looked down at the screen and read what I'd typed, then she looked up at me.

"Now hit send," I urged.

I watched as her thumb hovered over the send button. She was about to press it, pulled her thumb away, and looked at me again. This time I simply nodded, and that was when she glanced back at her phone and hit the send button.

"Now, turn off the phone and put it in your bag and forget about it."

She did as I suggested, and then she sat back and took a sip of her drink.

"Do you really think this is going to work?" she questioned a few moments later.

I nodded. "Considering you just told Hugo that your boyfriend was getting irritated as hell that he was interrupting your cuddle time and for him to be forewarned when we land, I do. Now, we just need to come up with a convincing plan."

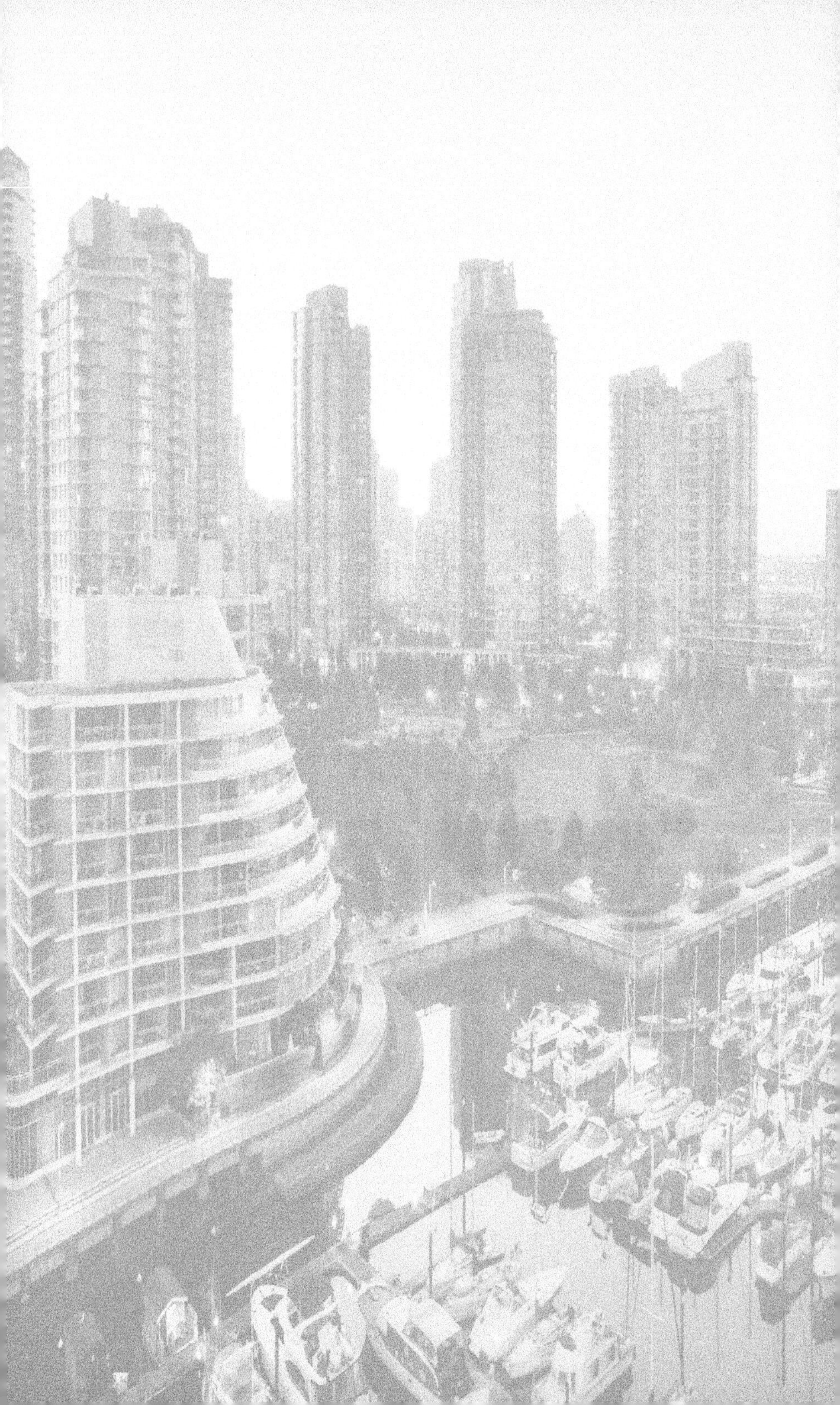

Chapter 4

Lorelai

I STOOD off to the side while Knox went into the washroom, thankful he had already secured us a luggage cart. I pulled my phone from my bag and turned it on. I had gotten a little sleep on the last half of the flight, and I was mortified when he woke me up to find out I'd drooled on his shoulder.

While I waited for him, I figured this was the perfect time to send a text to Aurora. Ignoring the slew of texts that were waiting for me from Hugo, I opened a new message and began typing.

> Lorelai: Landed okay. You awake?

I stood waiting for a moment and then saw the three dots bouncing up and down.

Aurora: Yes.

Lorelai: Am I interrupting anything ;)

Aurora: You'd like that wouldn't you... sadly no, Dylan went out for a run with Phil

Lorelai: I need to tell you something

Aurora: Okay, oh, before I forget, Hugo is looking for you.

Lorelai: That's nice. He can go to hell.

Aurora: Okay then....little angry are we

Lorelai: You don't know the half of it. Anyway.

Aurora: Okay, so what do you need to tell me

Lorelai: I can't face him alone. So, promise me this goes nowhere else, but Knox and I are fake dating. Just for the week, just because of Hugo.

There was nothing, no dots bouncing, nothing. I

imagined Aurora passing out from shock at that last message. What if she had hit her head? What if she was bleeding all over the floor? What kind of friend was I. As worry crept up inside of me, that was when I saw the dots bouncing around.

> Aurora: How many drinks did or have you had? How many did I have? I could have sworn you just told me you and Knox are fake dating.

> Lorelai: …yep…I did…

> Aurora: Cut the crap.

> Lorelai: Just please don't blow our cover, just go with it.

> Aurora: I'll have to let Dylan know. I'm sure he'll roll with laughter when he finds out.

> Lorelai: Let him know whatever you want. Tell him not to blow our cover either or he'll have to deal with the wrath that is Lorelai.

> Aurora: Okay, okay, I promise, we won't blow your cover, but you are going to have to fill me in on how this happened.

> Lorelai: Let's just say it was because of Hugo and his incessant texting and Knox and his want/need to control most things.

> Aurora: Uh, what happened on that plane? I'm concerned now.

> Lorelai: An asshole texting me, a few too many drinks and something I'll probably regret for the rest of my life. Got to go, he's coming. See you soon.

I shoved my cell phone back into my pocket just as Knox exited the men's room and walked over to me.

"Need to go? I can watch our stuff now."

"I'm good."

"It's a half hour drive to the resort."

"I know, I'm good. Let's go," I said, pushing the cart toward the exit.

I stepped out the front doors of the airport and walked over to the first cab I saw. I pulled my bags off the cart and shoved them into the open trunk of the taxi and went to climb in without even so much as a goodbye to Knox, but he stopped me when I tried to close the door.

"What do you think you are doing?" I questioned, looking up at him.

"Uh, taking a cab to the resort." He smiled, climbing in.

"Not this cab!"

"Yes, this cab! People are going to know we flew in together, and if this dating charade is actually going to work, we need to make it believable. We need to at least pretend to be happy around one another, especially in public."

"What?" I frowned. He was crazy. There was no way in hell we'd be able to do this. "You aren't serious? You can't be!"

"Yes, Lorelai, I'm being serious. What would people have thought if you and Hugo went into separate cabs when you were dating? I told you, if this is going to work, we need to make it believable to the outside world."

I shook my head and slid over, feeling completely defeated. What sort of nightmare did I get myself into?

Knox climbed in and shifted his large body into the backseat beside me. I'd never realized just how big he was until now, his body right up against mine. If the scent of his cologne hadn't driven me crazy enough on the flight, it certainly was going to now as the heat from his body enveloped me.

There once was a time not all that long ago I'd have killed to be this close to the man, but not now. I'm not the same naive girl I once was.

Knox gave the address to the Emerald Treasure Resort and Spa to the cab driver, and the next thing I knew, we'd pulled away from the curb.

Thankfully, it was a quick thirty-minute ride. The moment I saw the resort, my spirits lifted. As the cab came to a slow roll, I touched the doorhandle, ready to push the door open, when the driver came to a full stop.

"Wait!" Knox said, putting his large hand on my upper thigh.

"What? Why?" I cried, feeling irritated as I glanced down at his hand and shoved it off my lap.

"Would you stop!" he gritted. "I can see your brother. Who knows who else is in the lobby. So, just wait before you go jumping out the door," he said, opening the door. He didn't hesitate. He turned back toward the cab and held out his hand for me to take.

He was an excellent actor, probably a better actor than a hockey player, and even though I thought this was stupid, I played along.

Knox pulled out his wallet and paid the cab driver while I stood off to the side with our luggage as my brother approached us.

"It's about time the two of you arrived. You guys catch a ride together?" he questioned, furrowing his brow.

I was about to divulge our secret to my brother

because letting him think this charade was true made my stomach turn, but Knox beat me to it.

"We did. I didn't want to say anything earlier, but this was why I changed my flight."

I looked up at Knox in confusion.

"Man, we've gone out on a few dates together, and we both talked about it and changed our flight so we could be alone without being asked a million questions about us on the flight. We've tried hard to keep this hush-hush and knew this time would come where our secret would be out."

Phil looked over at me. Even though he wore a soft smile, I could see the questions in his eyes.

"Surprise," I said, smiling, as Knox pulled me into him and gave me a sideways hug.

Phil looked at me again. "That makes perfect sense. I will say I'm a little shocked seeing the two of you together, though."

"I'm sure you are," I said as Knox let go of me and grabbed his bags and headed off toward the front desk with Phil.

I grabbed my bags and followed behind, and that was when I spotted Hugo sitting at the lobby bar. I tried to ignore him, pretending I hadn't seen him, but when I glanced back over, I realized he hadn't taken his eyes off me, even though his new girl was sitting right beside him, her arm draped across his lap.

I ripped my eyes away, but when I glanced back over, I noticed he looked angry. While Phil took my bags and moved them off to the side with Knox's bags, anger filled me. That was when I grabbed Knox's arm.

"What is it?" he questioned, looking at me.

"Stop me, or else I'm going to walk over and punch the ass in the face," I muttered.

Without reaction or even looking up, Knox pulled me against him and stepped in behind me. He wrapped his arms around me, his hands resting on the flat of my stomach, his thumb softly rubbing the bare skin of my tummy. "Ready to check in, gorgeous?" he whispered as he placed a kiss on the side of my neck.

My body flooded with a rush of heat and all I could do was nod as we started walking in the direction Knox was leading me in.

"Just so you know, I saw him. Don't worry, I got you," he whispered into my ear as we approached the front desk.

Knox pulled out a chair and guided me to sit down at the front desk while we waited for the clerk to get off the phone.

"You know, the more I think about it, it doesn't surprise me that the two of you got together," Phil said to Knox as if I weren't even standing there. "I always figured the two of you would finally come to your senses and date at some point."

"Same here." Knox chuckled while I frowned. "Just took us a little bit to realize our senses."

Why would he say that? Knox had put an end to the idea of us way back when, and I'd hated him ever since. I also hated the fact that we were going to be lying to everyone here, and when we got back home, we'd have to come up with some stupid reason why things didn't work. Our friends and my brother would be sad for us. All this craziness seemed like way too much work for what it was worth. I could handle Hugo; we didn't need to hurt the people we cared about because of him.

"I was basically just waiting for someone to pass the puck in my direction so I could score," Knox replied.

Phil chuckled. "I won't lie. I am a little relieved you two are together. It helps solve a huge issue, actually," Phil said, looking over at me.

"What huge issue?" I questioned, standing up.

"Funny thing, actually." My brother gave me his crooked smile, which meant whatever he was going to say meant he wasn't sure how I would take it.

"What's a funny thing?" I asked again, concern growing inside me.

He gave a nervous laugh and leaned in closer to the two of us.

"There was a mix-up and the hotel shorted us a

room on the block that we reserved. I guess something happened with the reservations, and they miscounted the final numbers. I figured this would be a totally awkward conversation, but I guess we have the awkward all figured out."

I thought for a moment. I was tired but almost sure my brother was trying to tell us we were going to have to share a room together. Then I shook that idea out of my head and smiled before I got angry for no reason.

"What do you mean?" I questioned.

"I mean, they are short a room, but it totally works out. You guys won't have any issues sharing a room together. Here is the key to your suite," he said, grinning and handing a key to Knox. "I got them yesterday."

Knox looked down at the two keys placed in his hand and glanced at me. I was trying not to freak out as I glanced at Knox first, and then looked at Phil.

"You are joking, right?" I questioned.

Phil frowned. "No. I'm not. There isn't anything else the hotel can do, they are full. Besides, you two went to all the trouble of taking a separate flight so you could be alone. Surely, you don't want to be apart the entire vacation. Now you don't need to run across the resort in the middle of the night to be together at night. You'll both be comfortable in a shared room."

I felt my cheeks heat as I clenched my teeth. I wanted to die.

"No need to be embarrassed, sis," Phil said, punching my arm.

I tried to smile as Knox put his arm around my waist.

"She's just not used to us being public yet is all. I was going to try and get us a room together when we got here anyway. We'd talked about it on the plane, but it looks like that problem has been solved. I love it when things work out in my favor. Isn't that right, sweetie?"

I felt like I was going to be sick, but I clenched my teeth and smiled before nodding. It had been solved alright, and I'd been right, this wedding would be the death of me. Now I just needed to figure out how to get out of sharing the room.

"Okay, well, you guys are probably exhausted. I'll let the bellhop know to take your luggage up to room 5302, and I guess I will see the two of you down in the bar in a couple of hours. Take your time, you two lovebirds. I'm sure you'll want to take a nap." He winked.

Knox chuckled and pressed a kiss to my cheek, which I immediately wanted to wipe off.

"See you in a couple of hours," Knox said to Phil as he slipped his hand into mine and we took off toward our room.

I STOOD out on the balcony of our room, looking down at the resort as Knox dealt with the bellhop. I felt sick to my stomach. There was no way I'd be able to share a room with him, I thought to myself as I turned and looked toward the small sofa in our room.

I'd taken a moment to check and see if there was a pullout bed there while Knox had checked the bathroom out. It wasn't a pullout bed, and when Knox returned to the room that was when I noticed the bathroom didn't even have a door. It was just an extension of the room. I stared down at the crowd of people around the pool, my brain about to explode.

"Well, our bags are here. You can start unpacking. Figured you could have the right side of the closet," he said, coming out onto the balcony and sitting down.

"Where are you going to sleep?" I questioned, turning and looking over at him. That had been on my mind since I realized the small couch wasn't a pullout.

A confused look came over his face. "Uh, the bed."

"Oh no. No way," I gritted.

"What do you mean, no way?"

"You can't honestly expect us to share a bed?"

"Why not?"

"What do you mean, why not? We aren't actually dating, you know. Behind the closed door of this room, we are strictly Knox and Lorelai, not fake couple Knox and Lorelai," I said, crossing my arms in front of me.

Knox chuckled. "Afraid you'll fall for me?"

I rolled my eyes. "There is no way in hell that would ever happen, so you can drop your ego down a few notches."

"Ouch!" he said, covering his heart with his hand.

"So, where are you sleeping?" I asked again, this time looking toward the small couch.

He glanced over his shoulder in the direction I was looking and then looked back at me. "Uh, I'm 6'2", I won't fit on that!"

"Not my problem!" I shrugged.

He stood up and started moving toward me. I backed up to the door and felt my body hit the glass as he approached me. He placed his hand on the door above my head and looked me directly in the eyes. "I think you've forgotten who is helping who here?" he said. "The least you could do is let me share the bed. After all, I'm the one with the bad hip, remember, and you were the one who told me I needed to take care of it or else your treatment wouldn't work. I'd say sleeping on a four-foot couch, all cramped up, isn't what you meant by taking care of it."

He was so close to my face I could feel him

breathing as his eyes stared into mine. I hated it when he threw my words back at me.

"Fine! You can have the left side of the bed. I sleep on the right. I don't want to hear it either."

Knox shook his head and tsked. "Bad hip." He shrugged.

"No, the left side or the couch. Take your pick."

"So bossy!"

I squinted my eyes at him, feeling irritated.

"Better be careful, princess, bossiness turns me on." He winked as he stepped back and leaned on the railing.

I huffed as I stared at him, and then turned around and headed into the room. If I thought I'd have difficulty before making it through this trip, now it would be a miracle if I made it.

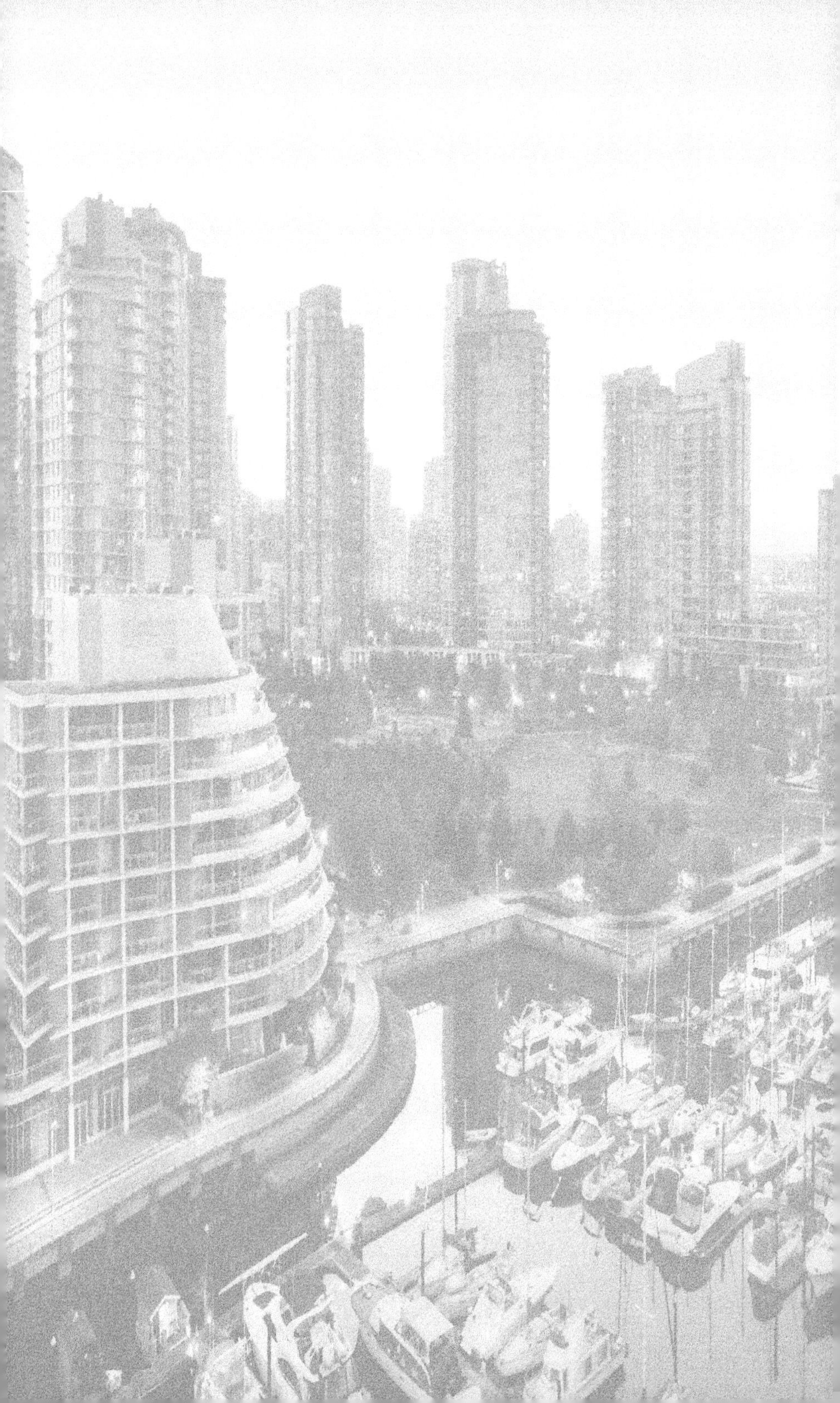

Chapter 5

Knox

I FLOPPED down on the king-sized bed and turned on the TV just as Lorelai came into the room. She glanced over at me with disgust and, without saying a word, made her way over to her bag and started hanging her dresses in the closet.

We'd spent most of the day apart. She'd gone down to the beach with Aurora, Candace, and some of the other girls that were part of the wedding party, while I hung out with the boys.

I'd come back to the room early and showered and gotten ready for dinner. I figured it would ease some tension if one of us got ready early. As she paraded back and forth in front of the TV, hanging up each dress she brought, I could barely pull my eyes from her bikini-clad body.

"You seem on edge. What's wrong?" I questioned.

"Do you seriously have to ask me that?" she asked, hanging up the next dress with force, only to have it fall to the ground.

I watched as she bent to pick it up, then she glanced at me, scowling.

"You seem upset."

"Really? How can I not be?"

"Look, I've had enough of the attitude, okay? I'm helping you out, so I'm sorry if the little kiss on the cheek was a little out of line for my fake girlfriend, but like I said, if this is going to work, it needs to be believable, and you've got no choice but to loosen up a little," I said, flipping through the TV channels.

"It's not that!"

"It's not? Could have fooled me. You've been uptight ever since that happened."

"I told you this trip was going to be the death of me."

I frowned and shook my head. "Not sure what you are alluding to their princess."

"Stop with the princess, okay? I was supposed to have a separate room, and now, because of some hotel booking error, here we are," she said, opening her arms and waving to the room. "The bathroom doesn't even have a door!" she squealed.

I turned my attention from the TV to her, looked toward the bathroom, and smirked. "Don't worry, I won't look…much."

"It just would have been better to have our own rooms."

"I hate to break it to you, but I was supposed to have my own room as well. I was also looking forward to putting it to some use because I planned on getting a little something this weekend, but that went out the window for me with the news of sharing a king-sized bed with you!"

"Oh my god, you are impossible!"

"I'm just stating facts there, princess! You're just moping around because you won't be able to have quality time with your vibrator. I get it!"

Almost immediately, her cheeks went red, and I thought for a moment her head was going to pop off. She glared at me and then turned away.

"You'd only hope that I wanted to spend some quality time with my vibrator," she bit out.

"Sure would. I like to watch. You could always put a show on for me." I winked.

Lorelai just glared at me, before grabbing her toiletry bag.

"I'm going to go take a shower and get ready for

dinner. Enjoy your alone time. Just make sure you're finished before I get out of the shower, and make sure you don't leave any mess behind. I have to sleep in that bed as well. Also, if I catch you even so much as glimpsing into the bathroom, you are dead."

I smirked as she gathered some other things from her suitcase. She was too much.

"I'm all dressed for dinner," I admitted, looking down at myself.

She shrugged as she walked by. "Dressed or not, that doesn't normally stop a man from getting himself off."

She made her way into the bathroom area, and I couldn't help but smirk as I adjusted the pillows behind my head. I'd be willing to put a thousand bucks down to say there was a vibrator in her suitcase, but I knew if I valued my balls, I'd dare not look.

I'd actually deserved every single word and every glare she'd given me. I had to prove to her that somehow I wasn't the same ass I was all those years ago. I was wrong to have put her down the way I had the night she expressed an interest in me. If I really wanted another shot at her, I had to cut the crap.

At the end of the show I was watching, I glanced at the clock. She'd been in the bathroom the better part of an hour, and I hoped she was just about ready or we'd be late. I shut the TV off and sat up and called her name.

"What?" she barked.

"You about ready?"

"If you're worried about missing dinner, go on. I can catch up."

I wasn't worried about missing anything. I'd hoped she would have been ready faster so we could go down and have a couple of drinks together, because I figured this apology I was holding might go better for me in public with alcohol.

"It's not that. I um, wanted to talk to you about something," I said.

"Just say whatever it is you have to say."

I took a breath. It would be better if she were standing here in front of me while I said it, so she could see that I meant it.

"I'm waiting," she called.

I closed my eyes. "Look, I just wanted to apologize for the way I acted all those years ago."

"What are you talking about?" she questioned, still not in front of me.

It felt like my heart was going to fly out of my chest as I sat there. I didn't know why I was struggling so badly with this. Perhaps it was because I didn't know if she even remembered that night. She was pretty drunk, and chances were she either didn't remember or she thought the entire thing had been a dream.

"Knox? Are you going to continue or make me wait?" she said.

When I looked up, Lorelai stood before me, looking at me with confusion. My heart almost stopped as I looked at her. Her hair looked different. Normally, it was pulled back in a ponytail or clip, but now soft curls framed her face and her long hair fell over her shoulders. Her red painted lips matched her ruby-red dress. She looked sexy as hell.

"Are you going to tell me what it is you wanted to say or what?" she asked again, this time with annoyance.

"When you kissed me that night in the bar…."

Her cheeks now matched the colour of her dress as she stared at me. "Never bring up that night up to me again. That was one mistake I not only regret, but one I'd never make again, and besides, it doesn't matter what you said to me all those years ago."

"It wasn't the truth, what I said," I confessed, her coconut-scented body spray hitting my nose as she passed by.

"You were being nothing but honest," she said as she made her way over to where she'd laid out her shoes and slipped her feet into a pair of black heels. She walked over to the mirror and smoothed her dress down her body, then reached up and wiped above her lip.

"I wasn't honest, and it wasn't the truth," I said, standing up, my voice barely audible.

"That may be what you believe now, but I saw the look in your eyes. It was the truth then, and honestly, Knox, it's okay." She turned and made her way over to me, wiping away some crumbs that must have fallen on my shirt when I had a couple of chips earlier. "There, that is better," she said as she looked up at me and gently smiled.

The look in her eyes nearly gutted me. She could try to tell me it was okay, but there, hidden deep in her eyes, the truth reflected.

"I pushed you away that night because you were Phil's little sister, and I knew back then I'd probably lose my friendship with him. Not only that, but you didn't deserve to be with a mentally fucked-up guy like me. You deserved better."

Lorelai frowned and glanced at me before she stepped away and put on her earrings.

"What exactly do you mean by fucked-up? I just want to know, since I am sharing a room with you, after all."

"Lorelai, it's not a shock that I don't have a clue how to make a relationship work. I mean, my dad left my mother, and any of the other marriages she was in lasted less than two years. I didn't want to take a chance that I'd fuck things up with you, so I pretended to be the bad guy and I pushed you away."

Lorelai shook her head. "Knox, please, let's just put it behind us. It really doesn't matter. I'm different now, and until you brought it up, I'd forgotten all about that night. Now let's just get through these next few days, and then you'll be free of me. You can go back to your life, go get some, and the pair of us can stop playing this ridiculous charade."

"No."

"So then, what you are saying is the truth?" she said, crossing her arms in front of her.

"Yes. I fucked up, and I'm sorry. I'm going to do whatever it takes to prove it to you this week, and I am going to make damn sure your ex knows just exactly what it is he gave up when he walked away."

She stood there, staring at me. I couldn't tell if she believed me or not. I wanted her to say something, anything that acknowledged what I'd just said. Only instead of commenting, she grabbed her small clutch purse, shoved her lip gloss and key inside, and made her way over to the door.

"We are going to be late."

I watched as she walked out of the room, head held high, and disappeared out of sight.

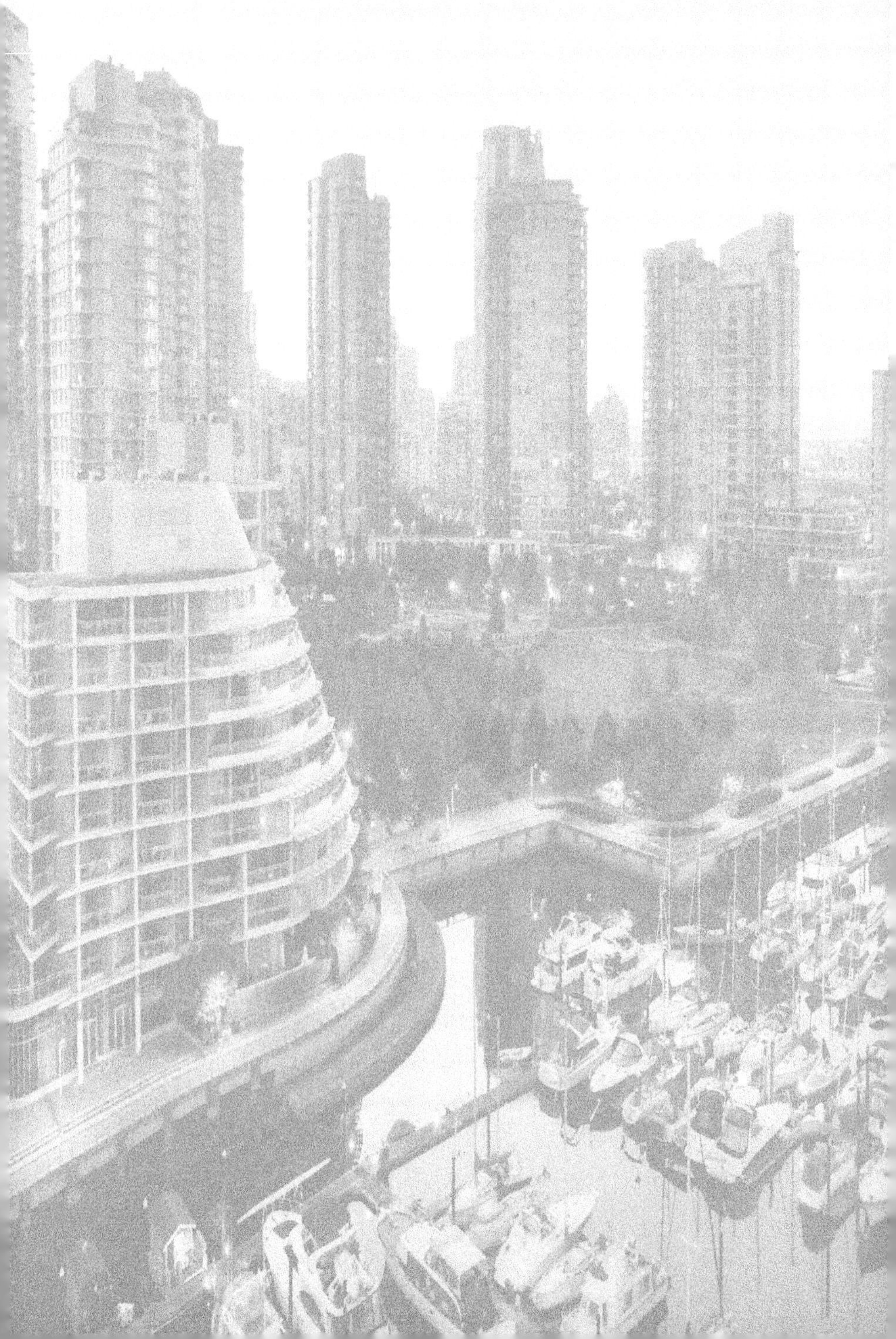

Chapter 6

Lorelai

DINNER WAS INTERESTING. We'd barely said a word to one another, and once we left the restaurant, I walked at a quick pace, knowing that Knox was right behind me. It would only be a moment before he caught up to me. Truth be told, I just wanted to be alone.

Ever since we'd left the room and throughout dinner, the only thing on my mind had been his apology. I didn't even know what had made him think of that night, or why he was apologizing. I'd figured he'd forgotten all about that night—or rather hoped he had.

I'd been thankful we were at a table with Dylan

and Aurora for dinner. The two of them had kept the conversation going. It helped that they knew all about the charade we were putting on. Now we had to mingle with people. I was already feeling good from the drinks at dinner, but the more I drank, the more I thought about that night so many years ago.

How dare he bring up that night up to me.

"Can you please slow down?" I heard Knox call out from behind.

We were the last two to leave the restaurant, and I was rushing so I didn't have to be alone with him. I just wanted to be surrounded by people and laughter and to have my mind taken from my memories.

Instead of waiting for him, I sped up and ducked into the first public washroom I saw. I just needed to get away from him for one second. I needed to compose myself from the garbage he'd spewed at me back in the room.

What kind of crap was that? Was he trying to get me into bed? He was sorry for the way he treated me that night all those years ago. Right. Did he think I was only born yesterday? I remembered the look of disgust on his face that night.

I also remembered the words I'd heard him whisper to me right before my brother made his way back over to us. They certainly weren't the words of someone who meant the opposite.

I placed my clutch down on the counter and looked at myself in the mirror. It had taken me months to rebuild my confidence after that rejection. It was the only reason I could attribute to the fact that I couldn't hold on to a relationship and why each and every one of them failed. The memory of that night, the insecurity it had burned into my brain, had made me allow every guy I'd been involved with to walk all over me.

There was one man I wasn't allowing that from, and he stood right outside the bathroom door. "Knox Evans will not walk all over me," I mumbled to my reflection.

"We are going to be late for drinks!" Knox yelled.

I hung my head, then looked at my reflection, straightened my dress, re-applied my lip-gloss, and then pulled the door open and stepped out. Knox stood across the way, the sleeves of his white linen shirt rolled up and his arms crossed, giving me an amazing view of those powerful forearms. His eyes ran the length of my body and then met my eyes.

"Let's go. We can't be late," I said, taking off toward the bar.

He grabbed my arm, stopping me.

"We can't go in there with this type of tension between us. People will think we have been fighting."

"That's good, because we have."

"Would you stop? We are supposed to be in a new

relationship. All I wanted to do was let you know I was sorry. That's it."

One look into his eyes and I knew if I let my guard down, I'd be done. I'd be putty in his hands.

I took a deep breath, pasted a smile on my lips, and nodded. "Okay, fine, thank you for the apology. Now, can we?"

I pulled out of his grasp and headed toward the bar where I saw Candace. We'd hung out all afternoon, but I hadn't said a word to her about Knox and I, and I knew the questions were coming since Phil had probably mentioned something. I took a second to compose myself.

"Hey!" I said, putting a fake smile on and praying no one could tell the difference.

"Oh, I am so glad you are here. Aurora said you were tired, and she wasn't sure you'd be coming," she said, wrapping her arms around me.

That was my girl, covering for me. I smiled as our hug ended. "I wouldn't miss this. I might be tired, but I can sleep later."

"I doubt that." Candace laughed, giving me a knowing look as she glanced over my shoulder.

I was sure she was looking at Knox, and my stomach turned at her insinuation.

"Are Dylan and Aurora here already?" I questioned.

"Yep." She pointed up to the balcony where I watched them kiss before he whispered something in her ear and pointed to something while they looked out over the ocean toward the sunset, drinks in hand.

"Great!" I said as Knox came over and placed his hand on the small of my back.

"Hey, Knox. You know, I was saying to Phil that this is quite the surprise," Candace said, looking between the two of us. "The two of you really kept this on the down-low."

"Well, you know me. I don't like to jinx anything." I smiled.

"My little secret keeper," Knox said as he placed a kiss on my cheek. "We weren't sure how or when to bring this public because I wasn't sure how Phil would take it when he found out," Knox added. "Would you like something to drink, princess?"

It was like nails on a chalkboard every time he called me that. Did I want a drink? Right now, I wanted anything with alcohol in it. Yet, I composed myself and looked up at him. "Why don't you surprise me? You know what I like."

"Sure do. Candace, what are you drinking?"

"Oh, I'm good with this." She smiled and watched as Knox made his way over to the bar.

I wanted to kick myself. Knox knew absolutely nothing about me, so I could only imagine what he would bring back. Why didn't I just tell him what I wanted? Ugh, and again with the kiss on the cheek, really.

Normally, the thought of him putting his lips on me would have made me want to be sick, never mind the real thing, but something strange had happened the first time he'd done it. I'd felt butterflies fluttering in my stomach, which was what had made me angry. The same had happened after he'd apologized when I'd brushed the crumbs off his shirt back in the room, and again only a few minutes ago. I had to keep reminding myself that all this outward display of affection was only for show. It wasn't real.

"So, when did this happen?" Candace questioned.

"When did what happen?" I questioned, looking back at her.

She gave me a questioning look. "Uh, you and Knox? I never saw that coming in a million years."

It was then I'd remembered divulging to her one night over drinks just how much I detested Knox. Now I needed to backtrack. We'd not really discussed the facts of how we'd gotten together, so I swallowed hard and prayed that she didn't ask me too many questions.

"It just sort of happened." I shrugged.

"I see. It wouldn't have anything to do with the fact that—"

"Here's your creamy coconut margarita, princess!"

Knox said, handing me something in a tall fancy glass, the rim coated in toasted coconut shavings. He slid his arm around my waist and pulled me back against him.

I frowned as I studied the drink. How did he know coconut was my favorite? Was he somehow stalking me, and I was oblivious?

"Is something wrong? You love coconut anything." Cadence added as Phil stepped up beside her, and then Dylan and Aurora joined us.

"No, not at all," I said, taking a sip. "Not used to the rim coated in toasted coconut. Normally, it's that sweet one."

"So, what did I miss? What were you gals talking about?" Knox asked.

"Oh, I was just wondering how this came about between the two of you." Cadence said. "It didn't seem like that long ago Lorelai was—"

"Talking about how much I liked you," I said, looking over at Knox and smiling.

Cadence frowned. "Yah, that's it."

I could tell from her expression she wasn't buying this as I swallowed my mouthful of coconut heaven.

"Well, I was telling Phil earlier I always knew Lorelai had a crush on me, and when I found out how her ex fucked things up, I figured I'd give her time to process things before I swooped in and swept her right off her feet." He pressed another kiss to my cheek while I sucked down the rest of my drink, emptying the glass.

"Want another one?" Dylan questioned while Aurora looked my way with a small smile.

I nodded as I handed the glass to Dylan and noticed the room was kind of on an angle.

"I'm just glad they finally came out with it," Phil added.

"Me too!" Aurora chimed in as more people gathered up beside us.

"Me three!" I added. "It was hard enough keeping this secret. The man always wants to have his hands on me. It was almost impossible at work." I giggled and then let out a tiny hiccup, which caused me to giggle more. "That and he is horny all the time," I said in a low voice to Cadence.

Aurora gave an awkward laugh, then grabbed hold of my hand, giving me a funny look, which only caused me to laugh a little more.

"Could I speak with you over here," Aurora said, nodding her head off to the side.

I looked at Aurora just as Knox wrapped his arm around my waist and leaned into me.

"What do you say we head upstairs and watch the sunset before it's gone?" Knox asked me.

I looked around as more eyes fell on us and

nodded. "See what I mean?" I added just as Dylan returned, handing me my drink.

"Go enjoy. It's beautiful," Dylan said.

Just as we were about to walk away, Aurora grabbed my hand and pulled me into her. "Watch how much you drink. You're pretty roasted," she whispered, giving me a squeeze, letting me know once again she wouldn't blow our cover. "Be careful."

I let out another hiccup and tapped her cheek with my hand. "It's fine. You guys coming?" I questioned with begging eyes.

Aurora nodded, but Dylan shook his head.

"We will be up soon, just going to mingle with some people down here for a bit."

Knox guided me over to the stairs and whispered, "Drink up," as we made our way up to the upper level and over to the railing.

"Would you like another?" he questioned, nodding to my almost empty glass a few moments later.

Whatever was in these was strong, and it was apparently no secret that I was already feeling a little tipsy. I smiled. "Are you going to have another?" I questioned.

I might have felt a little drunk, but I wanted to make sure I wasn't partying all alone.

"I think I will." He held up his almost empty glass.

"Okay then, make it a double." I giggled.

He slipped the empty glass from my hand as he met my eyes.

"I think a single will be good for you." He winked and then left me standing there, making his way over to the bar where he placed the two glasses down, then leaned against the bar, waiting his turn.

I could barely tear my eyes from him. As I stood there watching him, I realized just how good-looking he truly was and how somewhere deep inside of me I wished he could really be mine.

I now knew for real that I was drunk. I probably shouldn't have any more alcohol, I thought to myself as I watched him talking with the bartender as he made our drinks, laughing and joking. I realized how confident he was with himself. He spoke to others at the bar as well, including them in the conversation and laughing with others.

When the bartender placed the drinks in front of him, he slipped him a few dollars and then grabbed our drinks and turned my way, but not before I could turn and pretend like I hadn't been ogling him the entire time he was over there.

"Here you are," he said, handing me my glass and winking. "One double."

He raised his glass to mine, clinking them together, and we both took a drink as his soft blue eyes met mine. How I wanted to get lost in them, I thought, then looked at his lips. How I wanted them to kiss me again. Heat passed through me as my mind took over.

"Look at that!" he whispered while he nodded toward the sunset.

I turned a bit, tearing my eyes from his, and looked out over the water as the sun dipped just below the water. The sky was many shades of pinks and purples, and it was then he placed his glass down on the edge of the railing and rested his hands on my hips, pulling me back against him.

I leaned back and looked out over the water, drinking more of the coconut goodness.

"Beautiful, isn't it?" he whispered again, his hand moving over the flat of my stomach, his thumb rubbing against my skin.

I nodded, breathing in the scent of his cologne and feeling the warmth of his body against my skin. My mind wandered, thinking of what it would be like to be with Knox. I loved the way my body responded to his touch, and I wanted him to touch me more.

I lowered my hand to my side, placing it on the side of his muscular thigh. God, I'd drank way too much, I thought to myself, as my hand rested on his leg. I needed to stop these thoughts now.

"Want to dance?" he quietly asked as the DJ finally started playing some music.

I hesitated for a second and then nodded as he

tried to take the glass from my hand, but I shook my head and drank down the rest of the contents before placing it down. He then pulled me out to the dance floor where, almost immediately, the song changed to something slower.

He pulled me into his arms, and together we rocked to the music. I was feeling almost too relaxed in his arms and closed my eyes as I rested my head against his chest. Again, I felt that funny flutter in my stomach as we swayed to the music. When I opened my eyes again, I saw Aurora and Dylan next to us, swaying to the music as well. She smiled in my direction and that was when I felt Knox press a kiss to the top of my head before he let me go.

"Let's get some more drinks," he told Dylan while Aurora approached me.

"You two looked very comfortable," she whispered as Dylan and Knox walked over to the bar.

I nodded. "It's just for show, remember?" I said, moving over to the railing and looking over the water. "It's not real."

"Sure, of course, but the two of you are playing it well," she said. "Even in front of Hugo and his new piece." She nodded over to the side.

I looked over my shoulder to see Hugo sitting there watching me. When had he gotten up here? I'd been so lost in Knox that I hadn't noticed him. He was watching me intently as we stood there.

"God, he makes me so angry," I gritted. "He just thinks he's entitled to everything." I thought back to his text message about wanting to talk to me about getting back together while on this trip with his new girl.

"Just keep playing it up. I think it's sweet that he is helping you with this."

"You would think that," I bit out. "However, you don't need to walk down the aisle with him, locked arm-in-arm."

"He's a good guy, Lorelai. Maybe just give him a chance to redeem himself."

"Whoa, who are we talking about here?" I said, spinning around to face her.

"Knox! Who were you talking about?"

"Hugo, the ass," I replied, glancing over in his direction to see he was still watching me. "He's been staring at me since we came up here, hasn't been able to take his eyes off me."

"Well, don't look at him, drink your drink instead." Aurora said, grabbing me and turning me to face her. "He'll only think you are interested in him when you should only look at your boyfriend," Aurora said through clenched teeth.

Aurora smiled as Dylan and Knox returned, handing us both our drinks. Knox didn't hesitate. He didn't even miss a beat; it was like he knew what was going on the entire time he'd been gone.

"I got you," he whispered in my ear as he slid his arm around my waist. Without another moment wasted, he cupped my cheek with his hand and brought his lips to mine.

My breath hitched, and I felt my legs get weak as his tongue parted my lips, washing through my mouth. The entire world fell away as his lips danced against mine. My hands gripped his biceps, and I was thankful his arm was around me, holding me, because as the kiss continued my entire body became weak as he delivered the most mind-blowing kiss I'd ever experienced. Exactly what I had wanted.

The minute he pulled his lips from mine, the world came crashing back down and I realized we were in the same spot we'd been before, and even though all eyes were on us, it seemed like we were the only two there.

It was then he guided me out onto the dance floor for another slow song, leaving Dylan and Aurora to watch our drinks.

At the end of the third song, he delivered another one of those mind-numbing kisses as Hugo and his new piece danced beside us. When the next song started, we went over and joined Dylan and Aurora when Hugo approached us.

He looked at Knox and then at me and tried to

take my hand. "Lorelai, can we talk for a moment—alone?" he questioned.

Knox immediately stepped in behind me and wrapped his arms around me in a protective embrace. "You can say whatever needs to be said right here, buddy. No need to take her over there."

I did not know what was happening. My head was fuzzy from the alcohol, my body was on fire from that kiss, and here I stood in Knox's arms, my body feeling at home against his, as my ex-boyfriend begged to talk to me. I was so confused.

When Hugo didn't answer, Knox placed a kiss on the top of my head, then murmured something I couldn't make out to Dylan and Aurora.

I watched as Hugo and his new girl walked over to the seating area and took a seat. Immediately, his eyes were on us, watching our every move. I needed out of here.

Dylan and Knox let out a laugh at something Dylan had said, and then they announced they were heading back to their room for the night. They both waved good night, leaving us there on the rooftop patio.

I closed my eyes, resting my head back on his chest. His hands gripped my hips as he gently kissed my cheek.

"Why don't we go back to our room?" he whispered, placing another tender kiss on my neck. "I think you might need some rest."

I met Hugo's eyes across the room. I felt like I was doing something wrong, but instead of letting it get to me, I turned in Knox's arms, raised up on my toes, kissed his lips, murmured a yes, and let him guide me over to the stairs and back to our room.

THE MOMENT we were out of eyesight from anyone at the wedding, our hands fell away from one another, and I trailed slightly behind Knox, back to the room. We were both quiet, which I was thankful for. My mind, however, was anything but quiet.

The kiss from earlier ran through my mind. Easily it was the best kiss I'd ever had, and I wanted to feel it again so badly, but this was only for show. This wasn't supposed to be anything, yet my body betrayed me.

We approached our room, and I waited while Knox used his key to open the door. He held it while I stepped inside, and the second my shoes were off and the door closed, he grabbed hold of my arm and pulled me into him, delivering another one of those earth-shattering kisses he'd delivered earlier.

My body and brain betrayed me as my fingers fiddled with the buttons on his shirt, opening each one of them until I'd pushed his shirt from his strong shoulders, letting it fall to the floor. I relished the feel of his warm skin against mine.

His lips not leaving mine, his fingers found the zipper on the back of my dress. Cool air brushed my skin as he unzipped it, his large warm hands gently removing my dress from my shoulders, his fingers tracing my arms as he slid the fabric off my body.

Wrapping his arms around me, he guided me to the bed and pulled me down with him. I looked up at him as he looked down at me, his hand cupping my cheek again as he brought his lips to mine.

I closed my eyes as he kissed down my neck, pushing the cup of my bra off me, his tongue running around my nipple before he sucked it into his mouth. He continued kissing his way down my body, running his tongue around my belly button as his fingers danced along the band of my panties.

My body had been on fire all night. I didn't want to admit it to myself, but from the moment he apologized, I'd wanted to kiss him, and here we were for real. He placed a kiss on the flat of my stomach, and I let out a gentle moan, loud enough that he heard it, and he repeated that kiss.

"I want you out of these," he said, his voice barely a whisper.

My eyes closed, my body humming with anticipation. I wanted nothing more. "Just rip them off me," I murmured.

It was then I heard his deep chuckle. "Do I see a bit of a dirty girl in you?"

I felt my cheeks heat as I looked down and met his eyes.

"It's okay, I like it." He grinned, then I felt his powerful hands grip the edge of my red lace panties, and with a couple quick rips, they were off me. He took hold of my leg and placed it on his shoulder, his head diving right between my legs.

I closed my eyes and ran my fingers through his thick hair. Within moments, I was shaking as his large hands gripped my ass while he lapped and sucked at my centre relentlessly.

I couldn't control myself, and seconds later, all I could hear were the sounds of my moans bouncing off the walls of the room.

"That's it, baby," he whispered before running his tongue through my centre again.

I opened my eyes a little and saw him get up on his knees, quickly shedding his pants.

"You ready for more?" he murmured, meeting my

lips with his as he reached over and opened the nightstand on his side of the bed.

The tremors of my first orgasm were still running through my body as I watched him rip open the condom wrapper and sheath himself before placing my legs over his large thighs.

Placing a hand on either side of my head, he bent down and kissed me again. He reached between us, lining himself up at my entrance, and gently pushed himself a little inside me, breaking our kiss.

Inhaling deeply at his intrusion, I gripped his wrist, biting my bottom lip and closing my eyes.

He backed out a little, then inched forward a little more.

"Relax," he urged, kissing me again as he slipped inside a little deeper. He clasped his hand with mine and kissed me again, slow and deep. The instant our lips connected, my body relaxed, and he slid in a little farther, almost to the hilt.

He stretched me and filled me in ways I'd never been before, and once he was fully seated inside of me, I closed my eyes and surrendered to the feeling of being held in his arms as he buried himself deep inside of me.

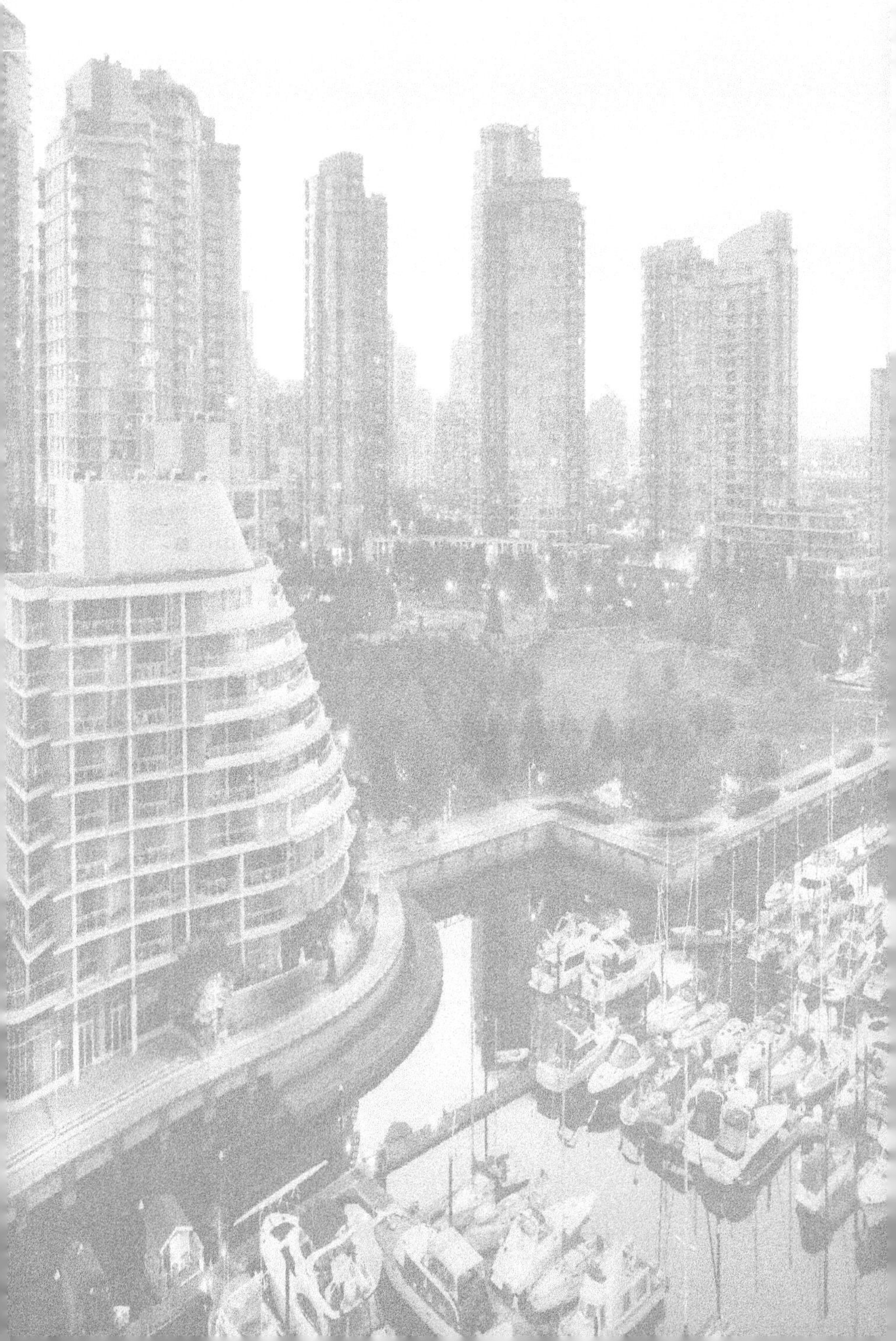

Chapter 7

Knox

THE ROOM CAME into view as I opened my eyes. Sun was coming through the curtains, causing my head to start to ache. We'd both drank so much. I wiped my hand over my face as the events of last night danced through my mind.

I stared up at the ceiling, replaying what I remembered, when I felt a hand move down my chest, finally resting on my hip. I looked down to see Lorelai, sound asleep, her arm wrapped around my waist, her head on my chest.

The events of last night had been unexpected.

When I'd gone in for that first real genuine kiss, I'd expected her to slap me. Instead, she nearly melted on the spot. I'd loved it so much. So, I went in for another and another after that, then we returned to our room. I hoped that the time it took to get back to the room, things would cool down. My plan had been to come back to the room and put myself into a cold shower while she passed out.

Then we got *into* the room.

The instant her eyes met mine, I knew I was done. My cock ached, and the tension buzzing between us was palpable as she stood in front of me. All I wanted was to hold her in my arms as I gave her everything, I had in me to give.

The second the door to our room was closed, I couldn't hold back. I had to take her, and so I took my chances.

My cock stirred at the memory as she shifted and rolled away from me, pulling the sheets up over her shoulder. I glanced at the clock, wondering if I had time to have her one more time before I had to leave to meet the guys for our golf game. The last thing I wanted to do this morning was leave before she woke up, but it didn't appear I'd have a choice. I'd be late if I did anything other than get up, so I slipped from the bed, showered, and then took off toward the lobby to meet the guys.

I sat in the back of the van with my head against the window, trying to grab a couple more winks before we hit the golf course. The girls were spending the day at the beach and then were heading to the spa while we were out hitting the greens. It looked like a perfect day for it too, not a cloud in the sky.

"Knox, you awake back there?" Dylan yelled, startling me.

"What…yeah, what's up?" I asked, sitting up and stretching.

"Late night, huh?" He chuckled.

Phil turned and looked at me, and then I noticed Hugo glaring in my direction. He'd be lucky if he made it through today without being harmed. Something about him I really didn't like.

"No later than you," I said, punching the back of his seat.

We pulled up to the course and the pile of us climbed out of the van and all sat down while Phil checked us all in. Lucas, Clay, and Dylan all sat down, each of them looking my way.

"What?" I questioned.

"We want the goods." Clay smiled.

"Yeah, spill it," Lucas added.

I grew uncomfortable as Hugo stared at me. I wasn't sure how much I really wanted to divulge in front of him —or Phil, for that matter. The guys and I had shared our fair share of locker room talk, but this was his sister I'd been with last night. I didn't want to show disrespect to her by sharing intimate things with the guys.

"Okay, guys, carts are coming," Phil said, sitting down.

"You must be interested in how the hell your sister started dating this asshole." Clay laughed as he looked at Phil.

Phil shrugged. "Not really."

"So what the hell is the story?" Lucas questioned.

"No story. There isn't anything to tell. We didn't go public with it right away. We wanted to give our relationship time to breathe, and we both agreed that bringing our relationship out in the open to other's attention might not give us a chance."

"So you're hiding her?" Clay chided. "Afraid big brother here may beat you?"

"No, you ass, it's exactly as I say."

"How long have you guys been seeing one another?" Lucas asked. "I swear we weren't out that long ago, and you weren't holding off looking at the ladies. In fact, I swear you just took that brunette home less than a month ago."

"Oh yeah, that night at the club in Boston. Fuck, I remember now." Clay added, "That was one hell of a night. Phil you'd of died if you saw the tits on her."

"Like either of you'd remember. You two were so fucked up that night. For the record, I took no one home, and besides, I'm not dead, man. I can look, same as she can."

The guys all laughed.

"See, he covered his ass there." Phil chuckled. "When it becomes more serious, that is when you have to stop."

I rolled my eyes and looked off toward the course, then turned back to Phil. "As if you don't look." I winked, trying to make light of a conversation that was really bothering me.

"Like you say, buddy, I ain't dead and neither is she."

We both laughed, and then I turned to grab a bag of clubs, which was when I noticed Hugo glaring at me. I wasn't in the mood for his shit and was happy to see two golf carts pull up. Dylan, Phil, and I climbed into one and took off, while Clay, Lucas, and Hugo climbed into the other, following us. I hoped that this would be the end of the conversation, but by the time we were out onto the fifth hole, the guys started with the questions again.

Dylan handed each of us a beer, which we quickly opened, did a cheer to Phil, and drank back the contents of the first beer of the day. Hugo started us off, and while we all waited for our turn, that was when Phil turned to me.

"You know, I hate to bring it up again, but I have to admit, I'm glad you guys got together. Somehow, I always felt you guys would be a good match, even if I said something different. You're good for her," Phil added as Hugo came up beside us. "No offense to you, Hugo," he said, smacking him on the shoulder as he went to take his turn.

Dylan bumped my shoulder as Hugo looked my way and gave me a smug smile.

"Hey, none taken, Phil. I sort of knew we'd never work out."

Phil turned and looked at Hugo with a questioning glance. "How's that?" he questioned.

Dylan stepped in front of me, stopping me from doing something stupid when I heard his answer. He could already sense that my patience was thin. Phil looked at the pair of us.

"Oh well, you know."

"No, we don't know, so you best elaborate," I bit out.

"No need, because if you don't already know, you soon will." He chuckled to himself.

"What the fuck is that supposed to mean?" I questioned, glaring at Hugo.

"Lorelai, shall I say, has always had a wandering eye," Hugo said, pulling his phone from his pocket, reading a message that must have just come in.

I clenched my jaw as I glared at him. I didn't realize I was clenching my fist until I heard the can in my hand crinkle. Dylan punched my shoulder, trying to tear me away from the situation, but I ignored it. There was no way he or anyone else was going to deter my attention in this moment.

"You're up!" he shouted.

I continued to ignore him as I stared at Hugo. "That's interesting."

"What is?" Hugo asked, looking up from his cell phone as if he hadn't been part of the conversation at all.

"She has a wandering eye. She isn't the one who cheated."

"Oh no," Dylan muttered as Clay, Phil, and Lucas turned their attention to me and Hugo. "Guys, you've got to help me here," Dylan begged.

"I'm staying out of it," Clay mumbled.

"Same here," Lucas added.

"Oh, come on, Knox, it didn't take rocket science. I could see her watching other men a mile away, every fucking chance she got!"

Our eyes locked, tension rising between the two of

us as we stood there staring at one another. All I wanted to do was wipe that stupid grin right off his face, but I was doing everything in my power not to start a fight. I'd been known to fight on the ice, but never off it, but in this case, it might be worth it.

I stepped forward, getting into his space. "Don't say another fucking word. There is no way in hell you are going to stand there and paint her as the bad guy when all she ever was to you was loyal."

"If that's what you think, then you are going to be in for an enormous surprise."

There it was again, that stupid, arrogant grin.

"Is that why you are trying so hard to get back with her?" I gritted, taking another step forward.

"Hey, I just wanted to talk to her, let her know there wasn't a chance in hell that I'd give up Molly."

"No…don't fucking lie to me. I saw the fucking texts! She wants nothing to do with you," I said, lunging forward.

"Whoa, come on, Knox, calm down," Dylan said, stepping in front of me and placing his hands on my pecks, pushing me back.

"Get out of my way," I gritted, looking down into Dylan's face. We stared at one another until he got the hint and moved out of my way, allowing me to take another step toward Hugo.

"Why the hell would I want to go back to that trash?"

In under a minute, I went from mad to furious. I took another step, cocked my fist back, and went to punch but stopped when Lucas, Clay, and Dylan all grabbed my arm. Almost immediately, Phil was in my face.

"Okay, we are going to take a time out," Phil said, looking directly at me while the guys pulled me in the opposite direction of Hugo. "You are both here for my wedding. Let's try to act like adults. Now, this conversation has gone on long enough and is now over. Besides, you are talking about my sister, Hugo," Phil said, looking over at Hugo while holding me back.

"Fine. I'm sorry," he said, holding his hands up and heading away from us.

When Dylan, Lucas, and Clay knew it was safe, they let me go. Phil made his way over to Hugo.

"It may be over, but how about you tell that to the child on the other side?" I yelled as he and Hugo shared a few words.

"Come on, Knox, chill, man," Dylan said, leaning against the golf cart while I took a moment to cool off.

"I will not tolerate that asshole talking dirt about Lorelai. She doesn't deserve it, man. If he starts again, I don't know if I'll be able to hold back."

"Just try. What's it going to look like if the groom's

sister's boyfriend beats the shit out of one of the best men?"

"It will look like he fucking deserves it," I gritted, pacing around to cool off. "Would you tolerate that if he were talking about Aurora?" I questioned, crossing my arms across my chest.

"Not on your fucking life."

"Then don't tell me to calm down. One hit, that will be all it takes. He won't have a fucking clue what hit him."

AS THE DAY continued to pass, I'd never been more thankful for something to hit. I launched the ball into the air on the last hole and completely lost sight of it as Dylan joked about that, which I kindly reminded him not to bring up again.

I was feeling pretty good by the time we hit the end of that hole, and I was happy that we'd made it to the end of the course without another incident. I didn't want to be the one responsible for ruining Phil's wedding. I didn't want to do that to Lorelai.

I unloaded my golf bag, headed to the washroom while the guys unloaded theirs, and once I returned, I leaned up against the wall, waiting while the other guys took their turn in the washroom.

Hugo was the first one out, and he sauntered over with a cocky grin. "You made the right choice."

"What?" I questioned with disgust that this guy would even have the balls to start another conversation with me.

"I said you made the right choice. That piece of ass isn't worth ruining your career over."

What the actual fuck was he talking about?

"What do you mean by that?"

"Well, you know, taking care of the situation. Only one hit, you don't think I'm stronger than that?" Hugo said, shoving his hands in his pockets, rocking back and forth on his heels.

I closed my eyes and took a deep breath, then looked over to see Dylan step out of the men's room. He looked up, took one look at my face, and hightailed it over to where I stood.

"What do you say, boys?" he questioned. I knew he was trying to change the focus of whatever was being said, but I didn't want to let it go.

"One more word. That's all I can handle. One more arrogant, bullshit word out of his mouth, and he's mine," I said quietly to Dylan.

"Come on, make it your best shot," Hugo said, holding his arms out to the side, approaching me.

Phil jumped in front of me, pushing Hugo away. Then he turned and glared at Dylan.

"What?" Dylan shrugged as Phil gave him the same look.

"How about you guys take the big guy and go get a drink?" Phil said. "Let's get things cooled off before someone kills someone."

"Alright, let's go," Dylan said, standing.

"No, he wants one fucking shot. Let me give it to him."

"One shot. Okay, how about we will go buy him one?" Clay added. Lucas and him stepping in beside Dylan provided a wall between Hugo and me.

I'D TAKEN off the moment we arrived at the resort and headed back to the room. I just needed some time to be with my own thoughts without disruption and hopefully calm down. I rounded the corner to see our room door open.

I paused, not sure I was ready to face Lorelai after last night. After all, I wasn't sure how she'd react to me leaving her this morning without so much as a goodbye.

I watched her as she stood there, typing away on her phone, looking a little distraught as she shoved things into her bag between messages. Then she placed her phone down and sat down on the edge of her bed and wiped at her eyes.

Was she crying?

Had I done this to her? Made her cry?

Then her phone rang. She looked up, and that was when I ducked back around the corner, out of her line of sight.

"What do you need?" I heard her question.

"No, he isn't back yet. I'm ready though, and I will leave him a note letting him know where we are having dinner."

I listened some more, poking my head carefully around the corner.

"No, Aurora, nothing happened… Please let it go…I'm positive. I'm telling you; he isn't here. I haven't seen him anywhere. Now I am going to put my shoes on and come meet you guys… Tell Dylan to call him if he wants to know where he is… I'll meet you guys shortly."

I watched her hang up the phone and then scribble something on a piece of paper before grabbing her bag and heading out the door. I waited, listening to the heels of shoes click on the pavement as she walked away from where I was hiding.

When I was sure she was gone, I made my way to our room and opened the door. Shutting it behind me, I made my way over to the note she'd left and read it.

Not sure where you are, but we are having dinner at the Italian restaurant tonight. I hope I'll see you there. If not, I understand.

I frowned at the last part of her note. What would she understand? I guess I'd royally fucked this up by leaving this morning. I knew I had.

Instead of getting changed and making my way to dinner, I dropped her note back where I'd found it and took off out of the room, making my way down to the bar.

I'D WATCHED her from a distance all night. Dylan and Aurora kept her occupied, but it was when they left her alone to dance that I saw the look on her face.

She turned around and looked out over the water, sadness creeping into her eyes as she finished her last drink. Then she made her way over to them, whispered something to Aurora, and left the patio.

I finished my drink, then followed behind her, making sure to keep my distance. When I knew she was safe back in our room, I took a seat down on one of the pool loungers, keeping an eye on the light in our room. When it finally went out, I gave it another full hour before I decided it was safe to go back to the room. I wanted to make sure she was asleep because I didn't want to face the look of rejection I'd seen in her eyes earlier.

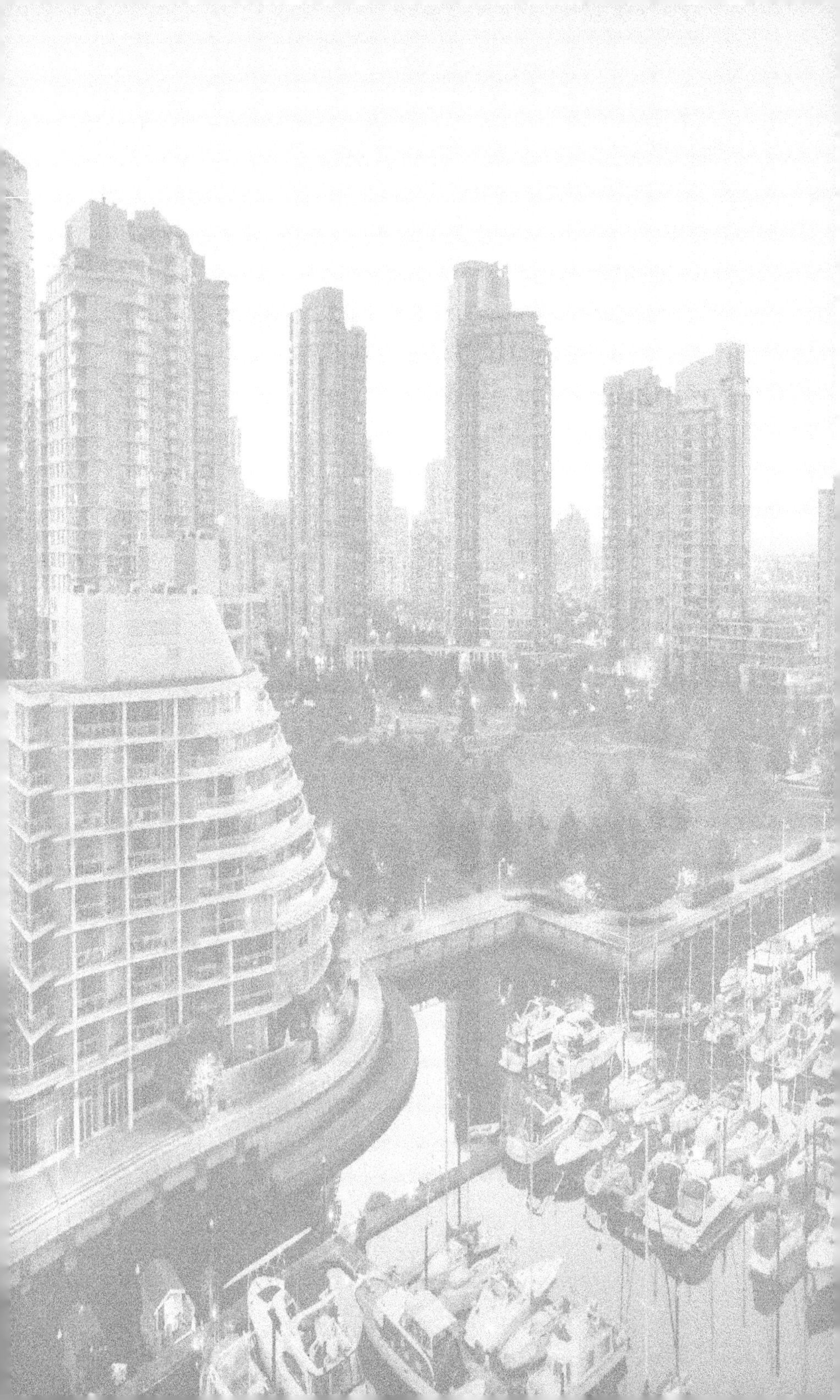

Chapter 8

Lorelai

IT WAS the morning of the wedding and I'd just finished having my makeup done. I slipped out of the chair and headed into the room where Candace and the other bridesmaids were busy laughing and getting dressed. I walked over to where my dress hung and pulled it off the hanger, my mind a million miles away from what was going on today.

"I have not steamed that dress yet," Aurora said. "Hang it back up."

"What?" I questioned, barely able to make sense of what she'd said.

"I said I haven't steamed it yet. I'm getting to that

one next," Aurora repeated, looking at me with questions in her eyes.

I knew I'd been acting off since yesterday when I woke up after the night I'd shared with Knox only to find he'd left without so much as a murmured goodmorning. It only made me more upset when he'd not come to see me after golf, he hadn't shown up for dinner, and when he finally returned to the room, it was well after I'd been asleep. He was gone before I woke this morning as well. Not even a note left. I didn't even know if I had a right to be angry or bothered. It was nothing but drunk sex.

"Sorry," I murmured and took a seat down on the couch. I watched as she finished the dress she was working on and moved over to mine.

"That fucking Hugo," Candace said, coming into the room in a rush, an angry look on her face.

Immediately, I looked up from my phone where I was checking to see if maybe Knox had messaged me, to see Candace standing there looking as angry as a wasp.

"What did he do now?" Aurora questioned.

"What hasn't he done?" she said, flopping down into one chair.

I frowned as Candace made eye contact with me, but quickly looked away.

"What did he do?" I asked, swallowing hard.

The room was quiet as we all waited for Candace to speak.

"I will not ruin my day by telling you. All I'm going to say is that you are lucky you got out of that relationship when you did. I never thought I'd say it, but I am glad you are with Knox. He may have a cocky exterior, but underneath that is a man with a heart of gold," Candace said, doing her best to calm herself.

"That he does," Aurora quickly agreed as she looked over at me, waiting for me to agree.

I swallowed hard. "That he does, and I'm lucky to be trying to make it work with the man," I said, wanting to slap myself silly for leading my soon-to-be sister-in-law to believe that I was together with Knox.

"I just can't believe Hugo would actually have the balls to behave the way he is," Candace said, shaking her head. That was when the worried look fell onto her face and her eyes filled with stress.

All the girls turned and looked my way, except Aurora. She kept on steaming my dress, which made me wonder if she knew something I didn't.

"If he ruins my wedding, I swear…" she muttered.

"He won't," Aurora assured her.

"What did he do?" I questioned, catching Candace's eyes.

Aurora and Candace exchanged a look with each

other before Candace murmured, "You should tell her."

I frowned and looked at Aurora. "Tell me what?"

Aurora cleared her throat and then let out a deep breath, still not saying anything.

"I don't think now is the time," Aurora said to Candace, completely ignoring me.

"No, she should know," Candace said.

"Would one of you please tell me what is going on?"

Aurora and Candace exchanged looks again, and then Aurora turned and looked at me. "Did Knox mention anything to you about yesterday?"

I shook my head, completely worried about what could have possibly happened on the golf course.

"Hugo was all up in Knox's face, egging him on. Dylan said it was quite the morning and afternoon. He was just being his usual asshole self."

"Great," I muttered, feeling slightly confused why Knox wouldn't have at least taken two minutes, pulled me aside to let me know what had happened.

"Don't dwell on it. Here is your dress. Go get in it," Aurora said, smiling at me as she handed me the dress.

I was about to go into the washroom to change when I stopped. I looked over my shoulder to see the two of them whispering to one another.

"Did they get into a fight?" I questioned.

Aurora once again glanced at Candace before turning to me. "Do you think Dylan would let that happen?"

"I guess not. I just don't want someone showing up with two black eyes."

"He may have wanted to hit him, but Dylan and the guys stopped him. Nothing to worry about." Aurora said, once again glancing at Candace.

I wanted to smile; I wanted to be happy, but I couldn't. If what they were saying was true, and Dylan had to stop Knox from hitting Hugo, then I feared Knox was taking this fake relationship a few steps too far and it needed to end now, before someone got hurt.

ONCE I'D DRESSED, I stepped out of the bathroom and did a twirl while faking a smile.

"Ah, you look amazing!" Candace cried.

"No, you look amazing!" I said, stepping forward and circling around the bride-to-be. "You are already glowing. What are you going to be like after the wedding night?" I asked.

"Oh god, stop," Candace said, blushing. "Oh, before I forget, could you do me a favor?"

"Absolutely," I said, ready for my assignment.

"I forgot the jewellery back in our room."

"No problem. I'll run back and get it," I said, almost to the door.

"Nope, Phil said he was sending one groomsman over with it. I was hoping you could meet them downstairs?"

"Sure thing." I smiled, silently praying he wouldn't send Hugo.

I left the chatter and giggles of the girls and made my way downstairs. I stepped out of the building into the tropical sun and immediately began looking for some shade. I was about to make my way over to a tree when I heard a whistle behind me.

I whipped around to see Knox heading my way. Even the way he walked was annoying. In fact, everything about him annoyed me.

"Hey, princess."

There it was, the nails on the chalkboard, I thought as his eyes travelled the length of my body.

"Candace called for this," he said, stepping closer to hand me the bag that contained the jewellery.

"Yep, she did," I said, taking it from him and going to head inside. "Thanks for bringing it over."

"Figured I'd lend a hand. That way, you wouldn't have to see Hugo." He winked. "He was halfway out the door when I volunteered.

I turned away and went to pull the door open without another word, only I felt his hand on my upper arm. "Everything alright?" he questioned.

I stopped. No, everything was not alright. Did he not know how he'd made me feel, leaving me the morning after we'd…

"What is it?" he questioned.

I tried hard to bite my tongue, but it was useless. I whipped around and glared at Knox.

"The girls told me what happened yesterday during golf, since you didn't."

Knox nodded. "I didn't think it was something I really needed to tell you. However, if you want to know, he was in my face, and I didn't like what he was saying about you."

I blinked hard, he didn't like what he was saying about me, but it was okay that he'd said nothing to me the next day at all after giving me one of the best nights of my life.

"Thanks, but believe it or not, I have a mouth," I said, crossing my arms over my chest.

"Not when you aren't present, you don't."

"I don't need you to defend my honor, Knox."

"Hey, I'm not defending your honor. I was simply putting him in his place."

I stared at him, at those blue eyes I had gotten so lost in just two nights ago, believing there might be a little something more between us than there clearly was.

"Don't bother," I muttered.

"Hey, wait a second. You were the one who cried on my shoulder when he wouldn't leave you alone, remember?"

"Consider it a moment of weakness," I bit back.

Knox stared at me with confusion lining his face. "What is the matter with you?"

I stared back, studying the look on his face, not backing down for a moment. Did he truly not understand why I was upset?

"Nothing," I said, my jaw clenched.

"No, it's something."

"Let's just stop the charade, okay?

"What charade?" he questioned, studying me.

"Knox, don't be stupid. There really isn't any need to keep pretending we are something when people aren't around us. We are just Knox and Lorelai."

"Pretending what? I was at a golf game with people who think we are together. Was I supposed to just stand there, let the guy talk smack about you and not say anything? It's not the way I roll, princess."

"This isn't the way I roll, either. I don't go for the hot-headed men," I said, getting into his face.

He gave me that shit-eating, ego-driven smirk. The one I hated. "No, you go after guys who treat you like shit, and I hate to break it to you, princess, but I'm not that type. If you are with me, then you are mine, and I'll defend you until the earth stops spinning, hotheaded or not. So, if we are doing this, then get prepared. Hugo will go down."

"Says you," I bit back, clenching my jaw.

Without another word, I turned around and marched inside. He seriously was the most infuriating man I'd ever been around, and I could not wait for this wedding, this facade to be over with and for my life to get back to normal.

I WATCHED as my brother and Candace shared their first kiss as a married couple. The crowd cheered, and as they made their way down the sandy aisle, I smiled and then turned, meeting Hugo's eyes. He'd been staring at me the entire wedding, and I'd had to do everything in my power not to let him know I knew it. How the hell I ever saw anything in him I'd never know, because looking at him now made my stomach turn.

Once Phil and Candace made their way down the aisle, the entire wedding party was to follow. I glanced up to see Hugo standing there waiting for me. He held out his arm out for me to take, a smile on his face. Reluctantly, I slid my arm through his, my stomach turning at the thought of him touching me again.

We stepped out into the aisle and began making our way toward Candace and Phil when Hugo leaned over to me. The cologne he wore was the same as when we dated, and I seriously had to swallow hard to stop being sick. I couldn't believe that at one time I'd thought it smelled good. His lips skimmed my ear as he whispered to me.

"Best tell your boy to rein it in." He then smiled at the crowd.

"What?" I questioned, looking up, only to see Knox watching us. His eyes were dark as he studied the two of us.

"I said, you best tell your boy to rein it in. He has a temper," Hugo repeated.

I didn't falter. I tore my eyes from Knox and smiled at Hugo, pretending to laugh at what he said, then I rested my head on his shoulder. When we got to the aisle Knox was sitting in, I glanced up at him to see his reaction. His eyes met mine. They were filled with confusion and something I'd never seen before, jealousy. I didn't care; I wanted to prove a point. What that point was now, I didn't know.

His eyes were glued to me as we continued past

him and down the sandy aisle. When we were at the end, I slipped my arm from his and went to walk away, but before I could get away, he grabbed my hand.

"Just one more chance. That's all I want."

"Let me go," I whispered and pulled my hand away, making my way over to the girls.

When I got over to them, I turned and looked back toward the crowd of guests, and that was when I saw Knox still looking my way, a questioning look on his face. He knew Hugo had said something. He also had seen me rip my hand away and the glare on my face at what he'd said. I was no longer fooling him like I thought I was. I knew he could tell, and I knew I was going to have to answer his questions about it this afternoon, but right now, I had to look happy for the photos.

AFTER THE SPEECHES and toasts had been given, we'd eaten and soon after people began dancing, I moved over to where Dylan, Aurora, and Knox sat.

"Everything okay?" Aurora asked, glancing between Knox and me.

I'd avoided Knox after the wedding, and we still

hadn't spoken to one another. He'd tried to get me to talk with him after we were finished with the pictures, but I marched right past him, following the girls. I knew I was being childish. If I had a problem, I should have just owned up to it like an adult.

"Yep," we both said in unison, neither of us looking at the other.

I could feel the tension between us, like usual, only this time the energy felt different.

"Am I sensing a lovers' quarrel?" Dylan said, grinning at Knox, then Aurora.

Knox let out a breath, muttered something under his breath, and stood up. "I'm gonna get a drink."

He walked away without even so much as looking my way or offering to get me a drink.

"I'd like one," I said, loud enough that I knew he heard me.

"Fine," he barked back at me.

I glanced at Dylan and Aurora just in time to see Dylan take her hand in his and place a kiss on it.

"We are going to go dance," Aurora said, smiling as she allowed Dylan to lead her to the dance floor for the first slow song of the evening.

I watched them as they moved to the dance floor where he wrapped his arms around her and placed a kiss on her forehead.

God, they really were in love, I thought to myself, then I looked over at Knox.

Regret boiled inside of me as I sat there, watching him over at the bar. I'd been a complete bitch to him all day because I'd been angry. No matter how angry I was, all I needed to do was talk to him. Instead, I'd watched him all evening, wishing I could have taken back my words from this afternoon.

He glanced over his shoulder at me. He looked sexy as hell in the white linen pants and light-blue linen shirt he'd decided to wear today. They both hugged him in all the right places.

The one thing missing this time was that sexy grin of his. His glance didn't linger either. Instead, he turned back toward the bartender and then struck up a conversation with the woman who stood beside him. Alarm bells started ringing immediately as they smiled at one another. I wanted to scream, to cry, to get up and go tell him I was sorry.

It was then a drink dangled in front of my face before it was placed down on the table, causing me to jump.

I whipped around to see Hugo standing there, a grin on his face.

"What do you want?" I bit out. He was looking to start shit. I already knew it.

"You looked thirsty, so I brought you a drink. I also

wanted to come over and see how things were going. Looks like you and Loverboy are on the outs." He nodded over to where Knox was now facing the woman he'd been smiling at.

"Why are you trying to cause shit, Hugo?" I questioned.

"Not causing shit. I just want to make sure you are happy in your newfound relationship, because that smile you gave me earlier told me otherwise."

I studied his eyes for a moment and then glanced at the bar to see Knox watching us over his shoulder.

"No, you are trying to stir up shit, Hugo. Stop trying to start things with Knox at my brother's wedding, for fuck's sakes. It's not the place."

"Wow, such big dirty words for a pretty girl. Is your new man wearing off?" he questioned, placing his hand on my thigh.

"Get your hand off me," I said, my voice elevating as I swatted at his hand.

He looked down at his hand and then into my eyes.

"Wow, you never used to push my hand off you before," he said, this time gripping my thigh a little higher and tighter than before.

I clenched my jaw together as I tried to pry his hand off me while I scanned the room for Aurora and Dylan. Panic set in when I couldn't see them, I needed help. I looked over toward the bar and it was then I saw Knox making his way across the room. If looks could kill.

In seconds, he arrived, holding two drinks, one in each hand, staring at Hugo. I felt Hugo release my thigh, as Knox continued to stare at him, but ignore him at the same time. He set the two glasses down on the table and then held out his large hand to me.

"Come with me," he barked, his face serious.

When I didn't immediately jump up, he met my eyes.

"I said, come with me."

I placed my hand in his and followed him out to the dance floor, where the song that was playing ended and immediately a slow song played. He didn't say a word. Instead, he pulled me right into his arms and held me close against his body like it was his job to protect me from Hugo.

"Everything okay?" he whispered as he placed his head against mine.

I nodded, not wanting to stir the pot. I knew Knox had a temper. I'd seen him fight once on the ice, because once was all it took. The other players didn't mess with him again after that. I knew Hugo was only trying to provoke him, and I also knew that Hugo didn't stand a chance if Knox got his hands on him.

"What did he want?" he questioned, holding me tight as we swayed to the music.

I swallowed hard. "To see how things were going between us," I quietly answered.

"What was your answer?" his deep voice asked.

I swallowed hard as he pulled me tighter into him. The feel of my body against his was distracting and comforting all at the same time. When I didn't answer him, he chuckled.

"So, he wants to see how it's going, does he?" he said, glancing over my shoulder toward the table.

I knew immediately then that Hugo was probably sitting there watching us, or perhaps he started dancing near us with whatever her name was. Whichever it was, I soon forgot all about it when I caught the look on Knox's face.

He looked down into my eyes and cupped my cheek. "He wants to know how it's going. How about we show him?"

Before I could protest, his lips were on mine and he delivered another one of those passionate and breathtaking kisses, only this one was better than before. I wasn't sure if I was imagining it, but when the kiss ended, I was certain I almost whimpered out loud when his lips left mine.

He looked down into my eyes and smiled.

"I'm sorry," we both said in unison as we continued to dance.

"GOD, MY FEET ARE KILLING ME," I cried as I slipped my heeled shoes off and placed my feet on the cool night sand.

"Mine too," Aurora said, doing the same thing as the four of us sat on lounge chairs across from the event room where the reception was still going on.

"Are you going to walk back to our room, or am I going to carry you?" Dylan questioned, looking over at me and winking. I couldn't help but laugh as I looked over to Aurora, who smiled.

"If I have to do the fireman carry to get you back to the room, you can guarantee I'm going to want to smack your ass. Knowing how much it turns you on, I doubt we'll make it back to the room."

"Whoa, way too much information, Dylan," I said, covering my ears.

It was bad enough I shared a condo with Aurora and heard the goings on in the bedroom some nights. I didn't need to see it.

"I'm a big girl. I'll be fine." She giggled, standing up and handing Dylan her shoes.

Dylan looked over at Knox and shook his head.

"Damn, she's a big girl, but here, you can carry my shoes."

The four of us laughed as they turned toward the direction their room was in.

"Oh, good luck, man. See you guys in the morning," Dylan said, before taking Aurora's hand in his free one, shoes dangling from the other.

We watched as they walked down the beach. I sat there smiling to myself. I was happy for my best friend. She'd found her forever, something I doubted I'd ever find.

"You just about ready?" Knox questioned.

I nodded. "Maybe just a few more minutes," I said, rubbing my foot.

Knox sat down across from me, reached over and took hold of my foot, carefully straightening my leg before he wrapped his large hands around my foot.

"What are you doing?" I questioned.

"Giving you the Evans special foot rub." He grinned, digging his strong fingers into the sore part of my foot, immediately releasing some of the pain I'd felt.

I leaned back in the chair and closed my eyes as he continued rubbing my foot in all the right spots, before massaging my calf muscle with his other hand.

"Oh god, that's nice," I muttered, closing my eyes and enjoying the feel of his hands on my legs.

"Give me your other foot," he whispered as I opened my eyes.

I did not know how long he'd been staring at me, but this time I kept my eyes open as he worked my foot and leg with his hands, all the while keeping his eyes locked with mine. When he finished, he bent down and grabbed my shoes and held his hand out for me to take.

We walked down the beach hand-in-hand, passing some couples I'd recognized from the wedding. They all smiled and nodded at us, continuing on their way. As we continued, I spotted a very familiar figure coming our way and knew immediately it was Hugo and Molly.

"Great, can't they go away already?" I muttered, more to myself than Knox.

"I thought you could handle him?" Knox questioned.

When I said nothing, Knox smiled. "Is that you, admitting defeat?"

"No," I scoffed, swallowing hard the faster we approached them.

"Okay then, let's see what you got," he challenged.

My stomach twirled the closer they came when I finally squeezed his hand. "Fine, yes, this is me giving up. I can't do it," I cried.

Knox shook his head, that cocky smile of his

returning. "Lorelai, Lorelai, I guess I am going to have to teach you." He chuckled.

"Knox, please," I begged.

"Okay, princess, just stick with it," he reminded me, interlocking our fingers together.

Not a word was exchanged between the four of us as we passed. The moment we were out of earshot, Knox looked at me and grinned. "See what I did there?" he questioned.

Instead of answering him, I let out a huff and pulled my hand away from his and continued walking.

"What did you do that for?" Knox questioned.

"What did I do?"

"You let go of my hand."

I swallowed hard. I knew this was only for show. I knew once we were back in Vancouver, this was gone. Hugo would be back, banging down my door, and Knox would be back out cruising for girls, and I'd have to hear all about it from Dylan and Aurora.

I'd already made one fatal mistake by letting my guard down and sleeping with him. In my defense, my walls had been knocked down. It was drunk sex, but still it was sex with someone I'd once had feelings for, obviously still did. Something I'd internally vowed would never happen between us. Amazing, mind-blowing sex that I knew I would want again and again but knew I couldn't have. I'd never be able to have him the way I wanted him.

"Because…"

"Because why?"

I didn't answer him. Instead, I kept walking ahead of him, not wanting to have this conversation because I'd had a few too many drinks in me. We both should know full well how that turned out the first time.

I knew how it would turn out this time, too.

One look from those blue eyes, one more kiss from those lips, and I'd end up in bed with him again, only to have him run off the following morning, leaving me feeling worse than ever.

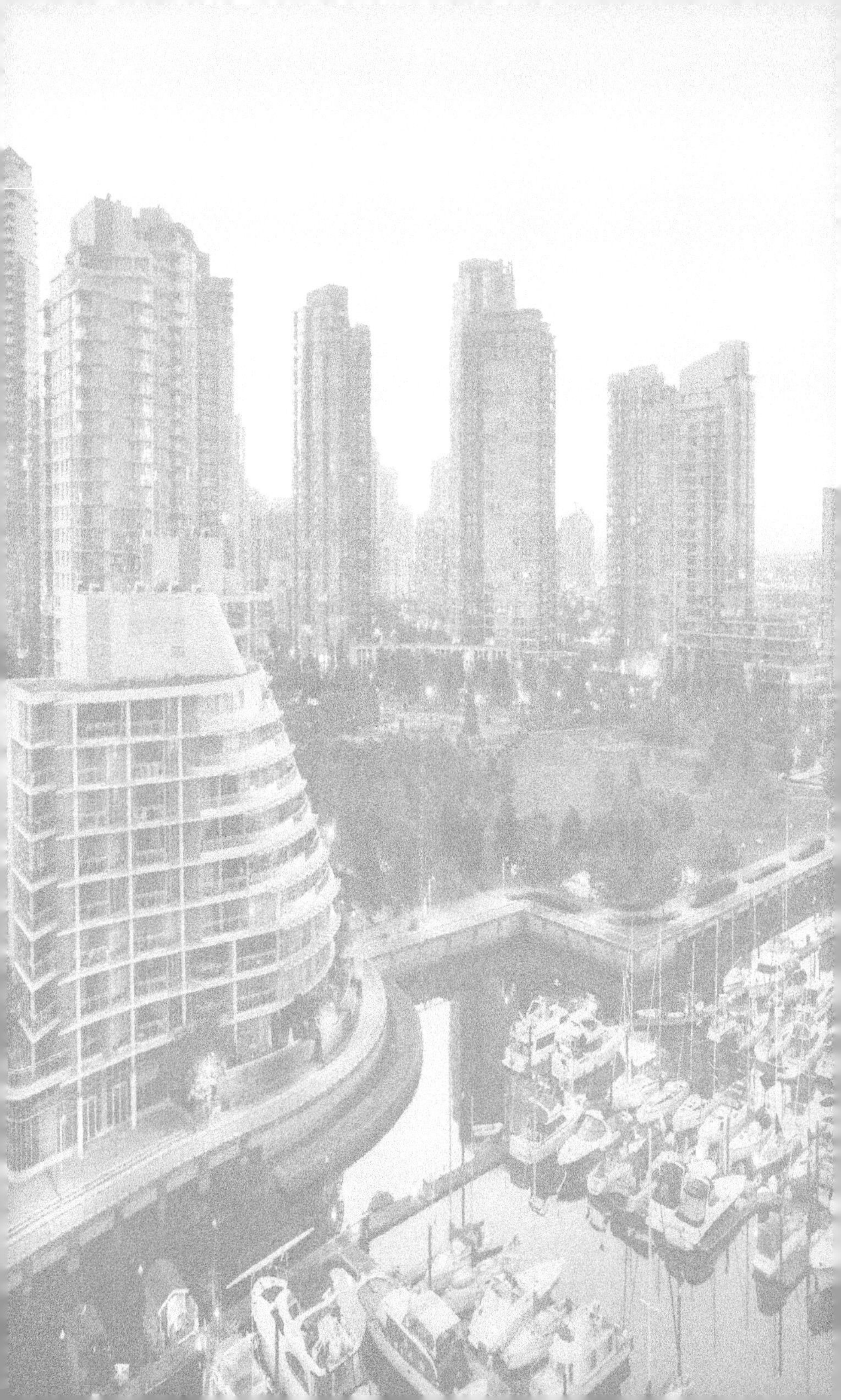

Chapter 9

Knox

"WOULD YOU WAIT UP!" I said, finally catching up to her and grabbing hold of her arm, stopping her.

She spun around and glared at me. "What?"

"I asked you a question, and I think it's only fair you provide me with an answer. Why did you pull your hand from mine?"

I watched her. She shifted foot to foot, then avoided my eyes while she chewed on her bottom lip.

"I pulled away from you because I know this is all for show."

I frowned, feeling very confused. "Okay, I'm not sure I understand."

"You are acting as if we are dating for real. We aren't, it's not. This is all just for show. All the tender kisses, the soft touches, the hand resting on my lower back every time we enter a room, the comments you keep whispering in my ear as we dance, those are all things that actual couples do, and we aren't a couple... this isn't real. This is all some form of deception to get back at my ex. Don't even get me started on that apology you gave the first night we were here."

My eyes locked with hers. Was this how she seriously felt? She couldn't see that all those things were my way of showing her I liked her, that I wanted this to be more?

Silence fell between us as we both stood there looking at one another.

"Is that why you said all those things to me this afternoon?" I questioned.

She glanced away and then turned her back to me. I hated not being able to see her eyes, to read what it was she was thinking or feeling. It was then I caught sight of her shoulders beginning to shake and she brought her hand up to her mouth.

She was crying, and I was gutted. This wasn't what I wanted. I thought I was being completely transparent with how I felt, and she thought I was only playing into the game she'd created to make her ex jealous.

I stepped up behind her and gently placed my

hands on her shoulders, hoping I was soothing her instead of making her angry. When she didn't pull away, I stepped closer, until I felt her body against mine. Then I brought my lips to the shell of her ear and whispered, "What if it wasn't for show?"

"Don't be crazy," she answered back, still not pulling away from me.

"I'm not. What if it wasn't for show? What if I were doing these things because deep down inside, I truly like you?"

She was silent. For once Lorelai Anderson did not make some snotty comment back to me. "Knox, you are crazy. Don't think you are fooling me."

I thought for a moment while she stood up against me. Then I once again brought my lips to the shell of her ear. "I am not trying to fool you. What I am trying to say is would it be so bad if I wanted this to be real?"

As the words passed my lips, I felt my stomach flip. No matter how many times this conversation had run through my head in the past twelve hours, I still felt nervous. I wanted this, I wanted her so bad.

"I don't know. I've never told you before, but you hurt me so bad all those—"

I brought my finger to her lips, silencing her.

"I know I did; I could see it. That was why I apologized. Now, I'm telling you, I want to try this with you. I'm serious, Lorelai. No jokes. I know a lot of things have happened between us in the few short days we have been here. I also know I didn't deal with them the right way. I didn't deal with them at all. I should have stepped up and been the man I've become, because the man I've become would never leave a woman the morning after."

"Why did you leave?" she questioned, spinning around in my arms and looking up, meeting my eyes.

"I was afraid of your reaction, that perhaps you'd have told me it was a huge mistake."

She nodded. "Can I be honest with you?" she questioned, her voice shaking.

"Yes," I said, wrapping my arms around her.

She looked up at me. I could see her calculating how safe she felt telling me what it was she had to say.

"The whole idea of us trying something together terrifies me."

"Why?"

"What if, like before, you hurt me."

"Despite what my actions showed the other morning, I am not the same man I used to be back then. Hell, I wasn't anywhere near to being a man, hence my apology now. I was a fucking coward then, and had I known then what I know now, I'd never treat you the way I did."

"Really?" she questioned.

I nodded. "Lorelai, I've been kicking myself over

the other morning. I swear to you, a pump and dump isn't my style. Despite waking up late and needing to leave to meet the guys, I should have immediately come to you when I returned, and I somewhat did, you just didn't know it." I shrugged.

"What do you mean?"

"Instead of coming to you, I followed you around the resort. I sat out at a bar the entire evening while you guys had dinner. Then I followed and watched you from a distance up at the patio bar while you guys danced, and when you returned to the room, I followed you all the way back, parking my ass on a lounge chair at the pool. I watched from below, until I knew you were asleep because the thought of speaking with you and confronting how I felt terrified the hell out of me."

I could see the disbelief in her eyes as she looked up at me. That was when I decided it was now or never. I slowly brought my lips to hers, devouring her mouth as I wrapped my arms around her waist, kissing her hard, dropping her shoes in the sand. I cupped the back of her head, laced my fingers through her hair as my tongue parted her lips.

"I've wanted you for so fucking long," I whispered between kisses. "Now, you are so close to being mine I can fucking taste you. Don't make me beg."

She let out a loud moan as I kissed her, gripping

her ass, letting her know I already felt that she was fucking mine. When our lips parted, Lorelai looked up at me with a dirty grin.

I chuckled. "Lorelai Anderson, are you not wearing any panties?" I questioned, studying her eyes.

She bit her bottom lip and slightly nodded, which was when I glanced around to make sure there wasn't anyone coming as I pulled her over to a bank of empty lounge chairs.

"What are you doing?" She frowned, watching as I sat down then shifted myself up onto the chair, leaning against the backrest, getting comfortable. I held my hand out to her.

"What do you think?"

She gave me a confused look, and I couldn't help but chuckle as she slid her hand into mine.

"Come here."

She went to sit down beside me, but I stopped her, shaking my head.

"Straddle my lap," I said, keeping my voice low.

"What?" she gasped, as she looked up and down the beach.

I wanted her out of her shell. I wanted her to be free with me—freer with me than she'd been with anyone else. I knew she had it in her. Hell, she'd shocked me so much the other night when she told me to rip her panties off, I almost came on the spot.

While she continued scanning the beach for signs of people, I undid my belt, then the button on my pants, followed by unzipping my zipper, adjusting myself.

"Straddle my lap," I repeated, shaking her hand. "I want to take what's mine."

"Here? On the beach?" she questioned, still looking around.

My cock ached as I watched the worry of being caught fill her face. "Yes, here. I want to meet that inner bad girl again," I said, gently tugging on her arm. "The one who belongs to me, and only me."

Just when I figured she wouldn't do it, she proved me wrong and lifted her dress a little higher as she swung her leg over to the other side of the chair.

My heart raced as she looked down at me.

"Fuck yes…there's my dirty girl," I whispered as she knelt on the edge of the chair.

"What if we get caught?" she quietly asked, hesitating.

"Well, if you don't sit the hell down and someone sees me, I'm going to be caught for indecent exposure. How do you think that will look in the sports section?"

She let out a laugh as she lowered down a little more, finally letting go of her dress, concealing what was going on.

"One second," I mumbled as I shifted beneath her

a little, digging into my pocket for the condom I'd put there earlier. When I didn't feel it, disappointment rushed through me.

"What is it?" she questioned.

"I shoved a condom in my pocket earlier. Fucking thing is gone," I muttered, feeling around on the seat beside me, praying it had fallen out. When I felt nothing, I threw my head back on the seat.

My cock was throbbing with the anticipation of being inside her again, and that was when I caught the disappointment on her face. Suddenly, I wished I'd shoved it into my wallet instead, or my shirt pocket.

She bit her bottom lip, then leaned forward and kissed me as she reached down between us.

"What are you doing?" I murmured as I closed my eyes as her hand slid over my hard cock.

"What if I told you I don't care about that?" she whispered, shifting to her knees.

As the words fell from her lips, my cock jumped, and I cupped her cheek, kissing her hard. Gripping her ass with both my hands, she lined my cock up with her entrance, and I helped guide her to sink down on me, my body shuddering with every inch her hot, tight pussy devoured.

She closed her eyes and gripped my biceps as I thrust up into her, filling her even more. I gripped her ass tight, gently guiding her motion as she rode my cock.

"That's it…" I whispered. "Just like that."

She let out a tiny whimper as she continued to ride me, her pussy clenching my cock tight. I knew she was getting close, so I shifted a little in the seat to give her even more of me, burying myself even deeper inside of her.

"Oh god," she cried, dropping her head back as I continued to guide her hip movements.

"That's it. Just like that. Keep going." I moaned, breathing hard. "I want you to come first."

She met my lips to silence her cries as her orgasm rushed through her body. The instant those cries got louder, I gripped her tight and let go too, spilling myself inside of her.

TWO WEEKS Later

I GLANCED at my watch as I made my way down the hall toward Lorelai's office. We'd been back almost two weeks, and the boys and I had been on the road practically every single day since we landed. Tonight was my only free night, and I couldn't think of a better way to spend it.

"Does she know you're back yet?" Dylan asked, walking beside me on his way to see Aurora.

"She knows we were coming back today. I didn't tell her we got an earlier flight. I wanted to surprise her."

"Big plans tonight?"

"I'm taking her to the Conservatory, then out for dinner. She'd mentioned in Hawaii how much she'd have loved to go to the conservatory there because she loved butterflies and birds, but since we didn't have time there, I figured this would be the next best thing."

"She'll love it, man. Do you think you'll be coming back to the condo later?"

I smirked. We'd been gone for two weeks. No doubt Dylan and Aurora were dying to fuck, and they probably wanted their privacy.

"Why?" I questioned, trying to keep a straight face.

"Fuck off, man, you know why."

I couldn't help but laugh as I continued down the hall, leaving Dylan outside of Aurora's treatment room. "We shall see where the night leads," I said, picking up my pace, not giving him a definite answer. I knew I didn't want to walk in and find them in the kitchen with a can of whipped cream doing some kinky shit where I'd more than likely eat breakfast in the morning.

I stopped outside her treatment room and listened hard to see if she was with someone. Then I knocked.

"Come in," I heard her sweet voice say.

I opened the door just enough to poke my head inside. She sat at her desk, face down, studying the paperwork in front of her. She looked a little more frazzled than she had when I'd left her a couple of weeks ago inside her condo, wrapped in blankets.

"So, I hear you are dating the biggest asshole on the team," I said, disguising my voice to sound a little like Coach Thompkins.

"What? What…where…" She tore her eyes from the paper and sat upright, then turned and looked at me.

"Knox, you're here?" she said, getting up and coming around the desk while I slipped inside her room and shut the door behind me.

We'd kept things hush-hush since we'd gotten back. Dylan and Aurora, Phil and Candace, Lucas and Clay were the only ones who knew about us. We'd agreed to wait a while before telling anyone else on the team.

My eyes skimmed her body as she walked over to me. She looked amazing in her favorite set of pink scrubs, and I wrapped my arms around her just as she walked up to me and threw her arms around me, nuzzling her face into my neck.

"God, you smell so good," she whispered, kissing me.

"You taste better," I whispered.

"I'm so glad to see you."

"Same here," I said, claiming her mouth one more time, loving the feeling of her soft lips on mine.

"What time are you finished here?" I questioned, looking over at the files that were scattered across her desk.

"That stuff can wait until Monday." She shrugged, glancing over at the mess on her desk.

"No, if you need more time—"

"I'm already here an hour past my time. Let's get out of here."

"WHERE ARE WE GOING?" Lorelai asked excitedly as she sat in the front seat of my car while I drove through the city.

"Well, I remembered how you'd wanted to go to the conservatory in Hawaii, and how you were so disappointed because we didn't have enough time. So, last night, I got us tickets to go to both the butterflies and the birds, then we are going for dinner."

Lorelai gave me a funny look and swallowed hard. In fact, on a second glance, she looked like she might be sick. "Birds?" she questioned.

"Yes, you mentioned one night in Hawaii how much you wanted to visit the conservatory there."

Taking my eyes off the road for a second, I looked over at her again to see her looking out the window, fidgeting with her phone.

"What is it?" I questioned.

"Just for the butterflies. I only wanted to see the butterflies," she muttered.

"What?"

"I love butterflies." Then she muttered something I couldn't make out.

"What?" I asked again.

"God, Knox, I feel terrible, but I'm terrified of birds," she said, turning to me, panic in her eyes.

I didn't mean to laugh but couldn't help it. "Seriously?"

"Yes, I'm not lying," she said, sitting there fidgeting in her seat. "I was attacked by my grandmother's chickens when I was four. It scared me for life."

"Then tonight should be interesting." I reached over, placing my hand on her thigh.

"I'm so sorry," she said, placing her hand on mine, her eyes filling with tears.

Not wanting her to be upset or worried about telling me the truth, I made a quick left-hand turn and pulled into the Sip and Stir, parking the car.

"Okay, first, no need to be upset. Second, we are going to go grab a snack," I said, wanting her to calm down before we got to the conservatory. I climbed out of the car and made my way around to the passenger's side and pulled the door open.

Together, we made our way in and got into line.

"Order whatever calms your nerves," I whispered, rubbing her lower back.

"Why?" she questioned, looking at me as if I were crazy.

"Well, I can tell you are upset about where we are going, and I don't want you to back out. Instead, I want to help you overcome your fears. Plus, I also want to know what it is you like to eat when you are upset, so I can surprise you a little more often." I winked.

She looked up at me and softly smiled. "You are too good to me."

I pulled her in and placed a kiss on her forehead just as we stepped up to the counter. "Go ahead," I urged.

"Could I get a coffee with cream and sugar and two peanut butter cookies?"

The lady smiled and then looked over at me.

"I'll take a black coffee and two peanut butter cookies as well." I smiled.

She nodded and went about gathering our order.

"I didn't know you liked peanut butter cookies, too." She smiled.

"Of course, but can I tell you a secret?"

She nodded.

"Only one of those is for me. The other is for damage control after we leave the conservatory." I winked. "You know, in case you need it."

Lorelai wrapped her arms around me and giggled. "You are the only damage control I need."

"ALRIGHT, you're sure you are ready?" I questioned as we stood inside the butterfly area.

Lorelai looked up at all the butterflies flying around. "No, I'd rather just stay in here and watch these, but if you insist."

"I do. Let's go face this fear you have."

I wrapped my arms around her and together we walked through the door into the aviary. Most birds in this section were in cages, so we took our time walking through, looking at the parrots and Kookaburra.

Lorelai clung to my hand as we continued through the aviary, now coming into a room where all the small birds could fly free. We were just about to enter when she looked up at me, fear in her eyes.

"I don't know if I can do this."

"You go outside, right?" I questioned.

"Well, yes, of course."

"Then you are going to be fine. Nothing is going to dive bomb you," I said, pulling her against me. "It's just going to be like walking through the park. Let's go."

Together we walked into the small bird area and once inside, we sat down on a bench and took a moment to look around. While Lorelai was afraid, I took the lead, pointing out all the small birds I saw, finally pointing at one of the most colourful little guys.

"Oh my god, he's so cute," she said, looking up at him.

"See, nothing to be afraid of, are they?"

She shook her head. We sat there watching them for a little longer and then got up and moved forward a little more. I glanced over to the wall to see a posting of the many birds we might see in this area and pointed it out to her.

"How about we look for the zebra finch?" I said, wanting to make it a bit of a game.

"Okay," she said, her voice still shaking, but she looked up anyway. Soon she'd wandered away from me and finally signalled for me to go to her. I wrapped my arms around her waist as she pointed out the zebra finch.

"That's my girl," I said, kissing the side of her neck. "I may just have to reward you tonight," I whispered, just as a couple of kids walked by.

"With?" she asked innocently.

I chuckled. "It's totally inappropriate to talk about in front of children," I whispered back, tapping her ass, which caused her to laugh.

Once we made it into the large bird area, I was worried Lorelai wouldn't want to continue, but she put on her brave face and followed me into the large, plant filled room. Almost immediately, she grabbed my shirt and stood behind me to hide from the parrots on our left side.

"I swear they won't hurt you," I said, just as one let out a loud squawk, which even caused me to jump a little, which made Lorelai laugh.

We continued walking, looking at the birds when we finally got to the end. I slipped my hand into hers. "That wasn't so bad," I said.

"No, it wasn't," she admitted. "Thank you for taking me. I'm sorry tonight started off so rocky."

"I can guarantee you one thing."

"What's that?"

I leaned in and brought my lips close to her ear. "It won't end that way," I whispered.

She looked up at me, her cheeks heating as she pressed a kiss to my lips.

I REACHED across the table and held her hands in mine after the server cleared our dinner dishes away.

"You really enjoyed yourself tonight?" I questioned, knowing she did as she hadn't stopped talking about the large blue bird with the funky hair she'd seen in the last part of the aviary.

"So much."

"What do you say I get the cheque and we head out of here? Go back to my place?"

I wanted to be alone with her. I wanted it to be just her and me.

She looked at me, her eyes telling me she wanted to be alone with me as well. I signalled for the cheque, and once we had paid, we made our way out of the restaurant. I'd just reached the door when I heard a woman call my name.

I glanced over my shoulder and saw a woman I'd never laid eyes on before wave at me and immediately knew this was a fan. I put a smile on my face and whispered to Lorelai to wait a moment.

"Yes, can I help you?" I questioned, making my way over to where she stood.

"Sorry to both of you, Knox, but would you mind taking a moment and signing this?" the woman asked, holding out one of my cards. "My son is a huge fan, and he will just die knowing that I ran into you here at this restaurant." She smiled.

"Sure thing," I said, taking the card and a marker from her. Once I'd signed the card, I handed it back to her. That was when I noticed she was busy watching Lorelai. I'd normally think nothing of it, but most genuine fans would take a picture to prove it was me signing the card, instead she was studying her.

"There you are," I said, holding the card for her to take.

When she didn't look at me, I loudly cleared my throat, causing her to finally pull her eyes from Lorelai.

"Your card," I said.

She gave me a funny look as she took the card from me and shoved it in her bag.

I frowned, turning back toward Lorelai, and placed

my arm around her as if I were protecting her, while I ushered her out the door. I took a quick look back and noticed the woman was still watching after us once we'd left the restaurant and waited for the valet to bring my car around.

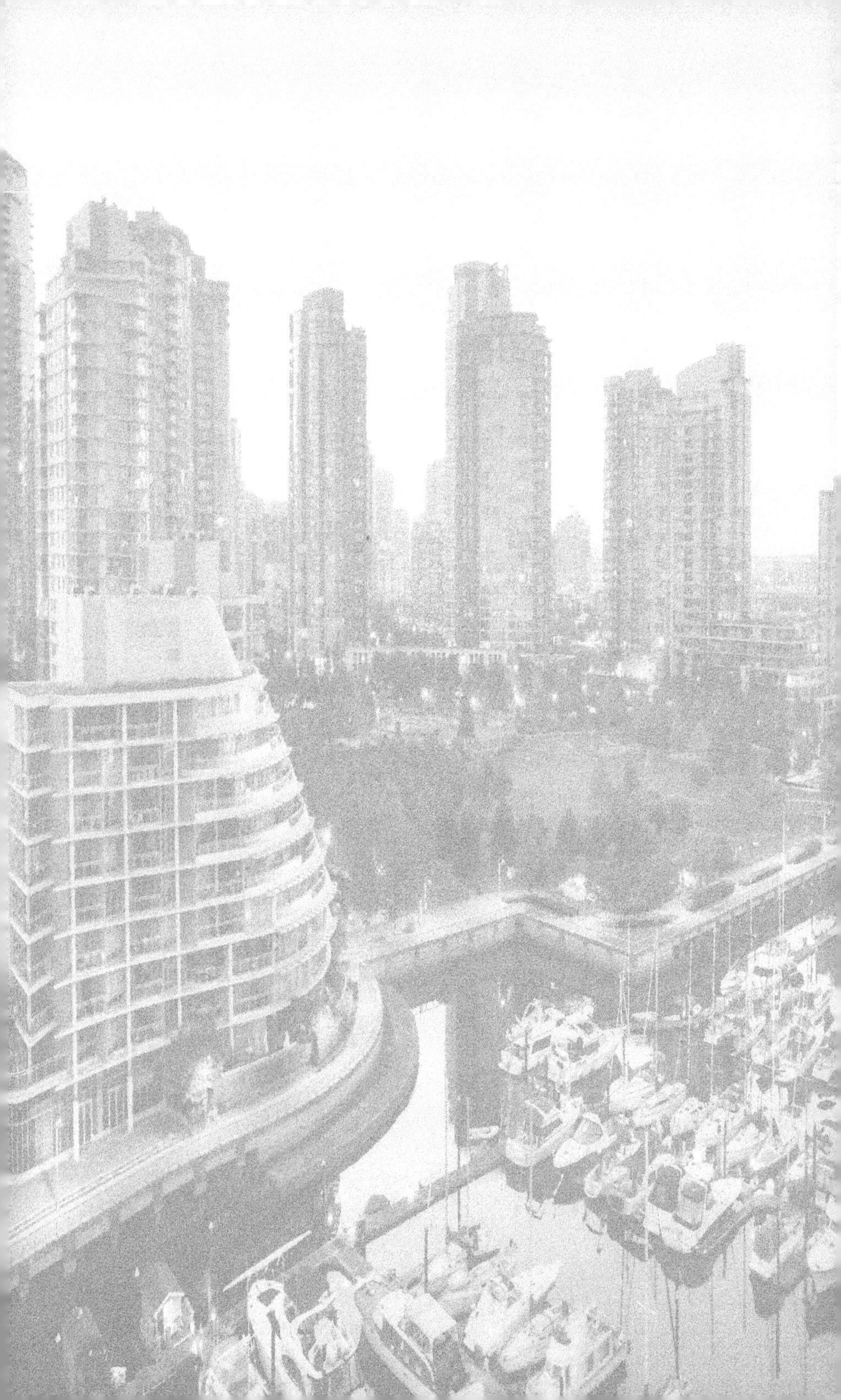

Chapter 10

Lorelai

"SORRY ABOUT THAT," Aurora said, shoving her phone back into her purse and focusing her attention on me. "How are things going with you and Knox?" she asked as I looked down at my phone once again, only to see there were no messages waiting for me.

"Hmmm, okay I think." I shrugged, shoving the last piece of steak into my mouth.

"Just okay?"

I'd been waiting for the next stone to drop. It seemed things between us were a little too good to be true from what I was used to in a relationship.

"It's hard, I know, dating someone who's always on the road."

I smiled, swallowing the last of my wine. Just as I set my glass down, the server appeared and poured each of us another glass before taking our plates away.

"If it makes a difference, it will get easier," Aurora added, giving me a soft smile.

When I didn't smile, Aurora looked at me with concern. "What is it, buttercup? Why so glum?"

My stomach did that nervous little flip, and I took a deep breath. Aside from a handful of text messages and a couple of calls since the guys had left, that was all I'd heard from him. I knew that he'd been stressed with hockey, and I'd hoped I was just reading into things a little too deep. Aside from the date last night Knox had been distant since we'd returned from Hawaii, and after the woman who approached him at the restaurant, I was now questioning things.

"I feel like something is lacking. Can I ask you a question?"

"Of course."

"It's rather personal," I muttered, feeling embarrassed for even attempting to ask her. "As if we've never shared personal information before," I added.

I looked at Aurora, then leaned across the table. "How do you guys…um…handle the intimate parts of your relationship while you're apart?"

Aurora's cheeks turned red, and she looked away from me for a second. "Ah, well, Dylan, he bought me a…he took me to a sex shop and bought me a vibrator."

"What?" I questioned, not sure now that I really needed to know the answer.

"Hell, we share pretty much everything, so why not tell you the truth?" Aurora shrugged. "Besides, I have nothing to be embarrassed about." "What about you guys?" she asked. "You haven't…have you?"

I shook my head, my stomach doing that nervous little flip again.

"We did, while we were in Hawaii."

Aurora looked at me, shock on her face. "What? You never told me that!"

I knew she was going to start asking me all kinds of questions. "Anyways, it's just now, we haven't since we've returned. I thought we would have last night, but all he wanted to do was cuddle, claimed he was exhausted."

"Maybe he really was tired. The games take a lot out of the guys, and I know Dylan has been stressed. He also mentioned Coach Tompkins had increased the length of their practices."

"I don't know."

"Has something happened?" Aurora asked, bringing her glass to her lips.

I shook my head, the words on the tip of my tongue to ask her if she ever thought Dylan would cheat on her, but I stopped myself.

"No. Nothing. What did you want for dessert?" I asked, wanting to take the eyes off myself for a moment so I could regroup.

"I'm having that double fudge chocolate cake. What about you?"

"Same." I shrugged, closing the menu, not even looking at it.

Aurora was my best friend, and she knew I loved dessert. She also knew I never chose based on what someone else was having. She looked at me with that questioning glance of hers and tilted her head to the side.

"What's going on?"

"Can I get you anything else?" the server asked.

"Two pieces of the fudge chocolate cake, extra whipped cream, please," Aurora said.

"Two coffees," I added.

Once the server was gone, Aurora looked at me, waiting for an explanation.

"Have…have…has Dylan…"

"Has Dylan what?"

"Do you ever worry about Dylan cheating on you?" I questioned.

Aurora looked at me, concern in her eyes. She

knew exactly where this was coming from. Hugo had me convinced he wasn't messing around on me, and then I'd caught him. I was certain she could understand. Hugo wasn't anywhere near as good-looking as Knox, nor anywhere near as popular. He also didn't have women falling at his feet every time he turned around. Knox did.

"Dylan cheat? No," she said, laughing, but stopped the instant she noticed I wasn't. "I don't think you need to worry about Knox."

"You don't?"

"No, I don't. Dylan and Knox, Phil, Lucas, and hell, even Clay, no matter what some might think, aren't guys like Hugo. For them, the thought of us being unfaithful to them, according to Dylan, is a worry as well."

I nodded, still not sure I believed what she was saying.

"Why do you ask? Has something happened that is making you question his loyalty?"

I shrugged, not wanting to divulge what happened last night as we left the restaurant.

"If it was some crazy fan, you better get used to them." Aurora shrugged, smiling. "They are everywhere. In my case, it wasn't a fan, but his ex. You'll probably get those as well. Apparently, some people have a hard time letting go," she said, rolling her eyes.

The server returned and slid our cake and coffee down in front of us and instantly, we both dug in.

"You are right. I guess I was just letting my insecurities get the best of me," I said, shoving the ideas off to the side and forgetting about it.

"You aren't. I remember you telling me Candace worried about that sometimes. It's probably natural, but I don't think you need to worry about it at all. Once you guys find a rhythm and start experimenting with things while they are away, you'll get a feel for just how devoted he is. Now, eat up, we've got to get to the game."

WE GOT to the arena three hours before the game, so we could get our seats and possibly see the guys. Tonight, they were doing a meet and greet with young fans.

We stepped inside, showed our passes, and made our way over to where Dylan and Knox were busy signing some things for a couple young fans.

Knox gave a small smile the second he saw me and quickly finished up with the young kid he was signing a jersey for, then turned to Pamela, whispered something to her, then got up and let Lucas take a seat.

"Where is he going?" I asked, whispering in Aurora's ear.

"Not sure, bathroom break? They have been at it for a little over an hour already," she said, glancing at her watch.

Dylan looked over at the pair of us and gave a wave before turning his attention to the young boy in front of him.

"Maybe it was a bad idea to come early?" I said, whispering to her again.

She shook her head and glanced over my shoulder, a small smile on her lips. "No, it's perfect. I enjoy watching Dylan with young kids, makes me think about having them with him one day. I think he'd make a great dad."

I looked over at her to see her all dreamy eyed as she watched him and shook my head in disbelief. I was about to say something to her when I felt a light tap on my shoulder. I turned and came face to chest with Knox. I looked up as he looked down at me.

"Been waiting for you to get here," he whispered.

"Oh?"

"Come with me for a minute. Aurora, we'll be back in a moment," Knox said, taking my hand in his, heading down the hall toward the guy's locker room.

Knox left me out in the hall while he entered the change room and in moments returned carrying something behind his back. He smiled, bent down and met my lips, and then handed me an Evans jersey.

"What is that for?" I questioned.

Knox shrugged. "I'd like to know where my girl is tonight."

I frowned. "How are you ever going to pick me out of the crowd? I doubt I'll be the only one wearing an Evans jersey."

"No, you are correct, but you'll be the only girl wearing my old jersey. Plus, it's not that hard to pick out the most beautiful girl in the stands," he said, tugging at the fabric of his old worn jersey.

"Evans…let's go," I heard Pamela's assistant call. "You have fans out here waiting for you."

Knox gave a wave, letting him know he'd be there in a moment, then rested his arm against the wall.

"However, I have my biggest fan right here," he muttered to me as he leaned down and placed a kiss on my lips. "See you later tonight?"

I loved kissing this man, and I slowly opened my eyes to see he was watching me. I nodded, softly smiled, and kissed him one more time.

"What time will you be finished and home?" I questioned, knowing it was probably going to be late since they had interviews to give tonight after the game.

"Not sure, just be in bed waiting for me. I'll come by with Dylan."

He met my mouth one more time before he left me.

"Knox?"

"Yeah?" he said, turning back to me and smiling.

"I'll be waiting, perhaps wearing nothing but this," I said, holding up the jersey.

He closed his eyes, then smiled. "I can only hope, but I can promise you I'll hurry home." He winked before disappearing out of sight.

THE BOYS WON THEIR GAME. The stands went wild as Aurora and I started climbing the stairs to exit the seating area. Out of all the games I'd seen, this one had been different. I'd not been able to take my eyes off Knox the entire night. I flinched each time he got hit or shoved into the boards. Aurora found it hilarious. She'd even covered my eyes at one point to see if I'd flip out. I did, which made her laugh harder.

"Wait up!" I yelled to Aurora, who was almost at

the top of the stairs, as a woman stepped out in front of me, stopping me.

She looked over her shoulder and nodded but continued to climb anyway.

I shoved past the woman and had just reached the top of the stairs and stopped to see if I could see Aurora through the crowd when someone bumped into me from behind.

I shrugged it off and went to step forward when I was shoved again. This time, though, the person still had a hold on me.

"What do you think you are doing, bitch?" I heard a woman's voice say behind me.

I turned around and looked up to see who had a hold of me. I was shocked to see the woman from the restaurant. Before I could say anything, she delivered the blow to my face. My head pounded as I tried to digest what had just happened.

"He's mine!" she growled, hitting me again.

I covered my face, shocked and scared, not knowing what to do, as this woman continued to hit me.

"How dare you touch my man!" she screamed, grabbing hold of me.

I covered my face, praying that someone would see, and that was when out of nowhere I heard Aurora shout, and suddenly the woman let go of me.

When I opened my eyes, I saw Aurora shove her away, and that was when I saw her, looking at me as if she wanted me to die.

"Back the fuck up!" Aurora shouted as she shoved the woman again and then came over to me.

"What the fuck was that?" I questioned, looking over at the woman who was standing there with her friends, glaring at me.

"You've just been introduced to a crazy-ass fan. Aren't they fun?"

"Not really."

Aurora grabbed my arm and was about to spin us around when the girl came back at me.

"Knox is my man! You stole him from me!" she screamed, grabbing my shirt.

Almost immediately a man stepped in between her and me and kindly separated us. "You should call the police."

I stood there, frozen, not knowing what to do, but Aurora grabbed her phone and quickly dialled the police.

Forty minutes later, we both sat in the hallway of the Vancouver Police Department waiting for the officer who had taken our statements.

"Here is a coffee," Aurora said, glancing down at her watch before sitting down on the bench beside me.

"Thanks. I can't believe what happened." I sniffled,

snuggling down into Knox's jersey a little more. I was still shaking from what had happened and my stomach was in knots.

I was cold and tired and happy to have had something a little warmer than the cute T-shirt I'd worn for dinner.

"Miss Barlowe, could I speak with you for a moment?" the officer who'd taken our statements asked as he stepped out into the hallway, looking at both of us.

Aurora looked at me, softly smiled, then got up from where she was sitting and followed the officer. When the door closed, I sat up and glanced over my shoulder through the window to see her cover her mouth. Anxiety and worry filled my body as I watched her hang her head and then make her way slowly to the door.

"What's going on?" I questioned.

"You best make that call," the officer said, coming out of the office and heading down the hall.

I glanced at Aurora. She looked like she was going to be sick as she sat down beside me.

"Aurora?"

"They have pressed charges against psycho bitch, but psycho bitch is going to be pressing charges against me."

"What for?" I questioned, sitting up, getting defensive as my best friend sat there with worry on her face.

"She is pressing assault charges on me for shoving her."

"It was self-defense!" I exclaimed.

"Not according to her."

"I think it's time we call Dylan," I said, slipping her phone from her hands and getting ready to call him.

Aurora shook her head and placed her hand over mine. "No, I shoved her."

"What about your mom, or Walker?" I suggested. "We could call them?"

"Lorelai, what is my mother going to do? She's living in that tiny little place, barely making enough to live off. I can't go to her for money."

"I have savings," I said. "I could also call Phil."

"No way, we are not calling your brother after all he's done for us. I'll just have to face the music."

Just then, the officer returned and asked Aurora to step back into his office, once again closing the door. I sat there worried about my best friend and the trouble she was in because of me. I could barely sit there knowing that she was probably going to lose her job because of me.

I looked down at her phone sitting in my hand and pulled up Dylan's number from her contacts. I hesitated for a moment and then pressed the call button, listening to the phone ring as I sat there straining to hear anything that was going on in the room behind me.

"EVERYTHING OKAY?" Dylan questioned the moment he picked up the phone.

He knew that we'd have left the game and made our way back to our condo while they were doing their interview thing. If I had calculated the times correctly, they were probably just getting showered and would leave the arena soon to come to the condo.

"It's Lorelai. Don't let on that it's me," I said.

"Hey, Aurora, what's going on?" Dylan questioned, doing as I'd said.

"Whatever you do, say nothing to Knox. We are at the police station."

"What? Food Poisoning? Is she okay?"

I knew almost instantly that this was why Aurora was head over heels for this man.

"I had a crazy fan attack me after the game, and Aurora stepped in to protect me. I'm pressing charges, but the crazy fan is also pressing charges on Aurora." I sniffled.

"How sick is she?" Dylan asked. "That bad? She just wants to sleep it off then?"

"Can you please come down here? I'm worried about her. She said she didn't want any help, she said that she did what the girl is saying, and she needs to own up to it."

"Yep, no problem. Give me half an hour?"

"Thanks, Dylan."

I ended the call, shoved Aurora's phone back into my pocket, and then sat back against the bench. A wave of nausea rolled through me as I sat there waiting for Dylan to arrive.

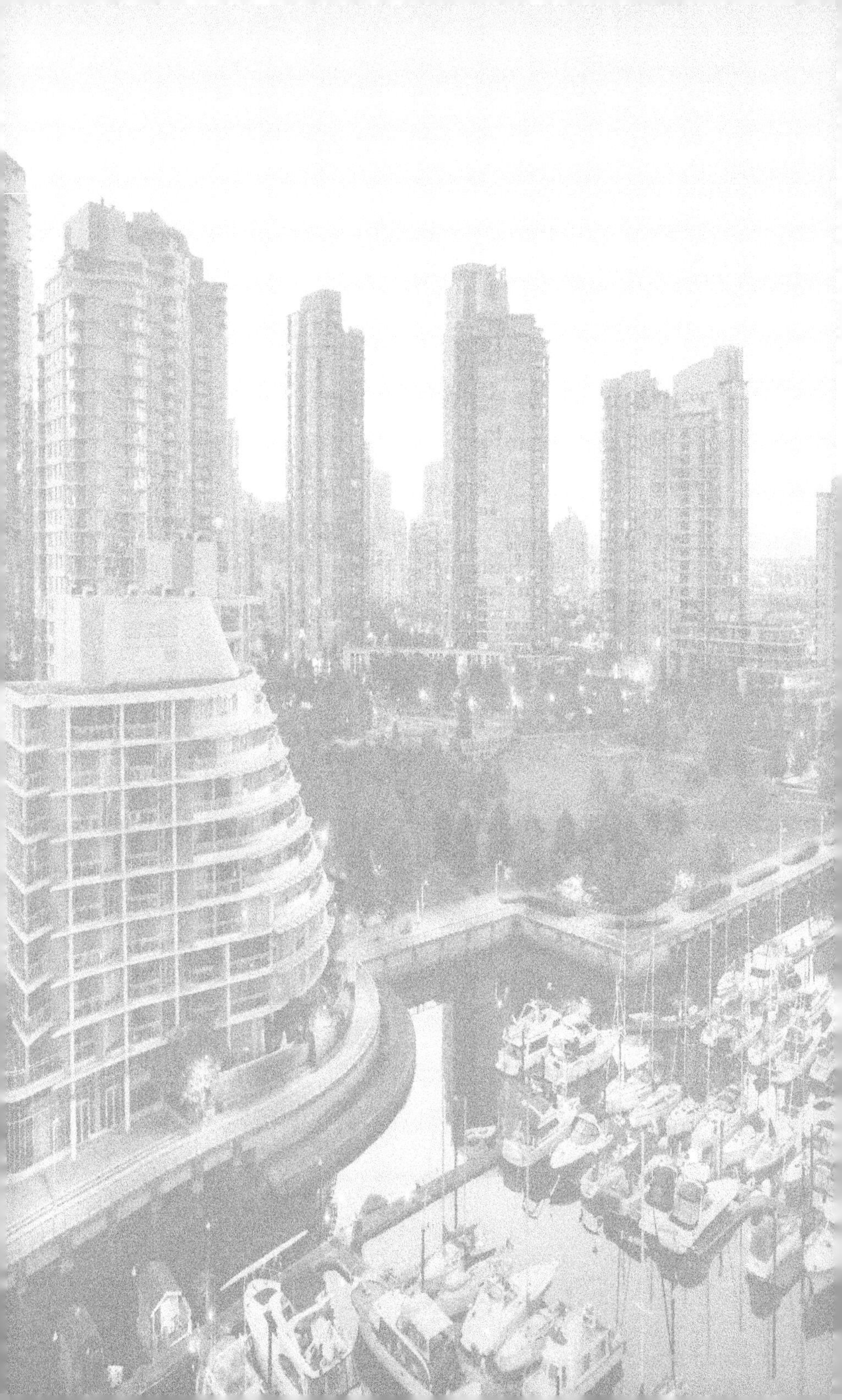

Chapter 11

Knox

I'D JUST THROWN my shirt on, grabbed my wallet and phone from my locker. Shoving my wallet into my back pocket, I quickly checked to see if Lorelai had responded to my message. Dylan had muttered something about her not feeling well. When I told him we should hurry, he said Aurora told him Lorelai was in bed and wanted to be alone. Worried, I sent her a message before I got in the shower.

She hadn't even read my message, so I locked my locker and turned in time to see Dylan slip out of the change room without me. I'd figured the least he could do is drop me at my place if Lorelai wasn't feeling well.

Yet, something wasn't sitting right with me. The moment the call came in, Dylan started acting strange. What went from a relaxed conversation turned into a race to get ready and leave. Dylan also went from being in a fabulous mood after the win to being agitated and stressed.

I glanced over at the guys and shrugged.

"Fucker didn't even say goodbye," Clay added.

"Yeah, thought we were going out to have a celebratory beer, at least that was what he'd said earlier," Lucas added.

"I'll find out," I said, taking off out of the changing room after him.

I took off down the hall, jogging to catch up to him, but he didn't slow down.

"Hey, wait up, would you?"

"Yeah, sorry," he said, taking a shortcut to the far side of the arena where we'd parked. He shoved the door open and headed toward his car. "I thought you were going to get a ride with Clay or Lucas."

"Nah, man, thought I'd go with you. I want to check on Lorelai, make sure she's okay."

"Aurora said she isn't well, man. She told me that Lorelai said she didn't want to see anyone."

"I'm not just anyone. I want to make sure she is fine."

"I know and I get that, I do, but you should respect

her wishes, man." Dylan hit the button on his key fob, unlocking his door. "You don't want to get her pissed off, do you?"

In my mind, her being pissed off with me because I wanted to check in on her when she was sick was nothing to worry about. I was worried about my girl.

"Would you stay away from Aurora if she asked?"

When Dylan didn't immediately answer me, I knew something was up, and I didn't like it. He'd been acting oddly ever since that phone call had come in. I'd been with this guy through thick and thin and I knew when he wasn't being himself. This wasn't himself.

"Most definitely," he said, glancing my way before he climbed into the driver's seat and started the engine.

"Bullshit!" I said, pulling the passenger door open and climbing in. "What's really going on? Don't fucking lie either," I said, putting my seat belt on as Dylan sped out of the parking garage.

"I knew I shouldn't have said anything. I should have just slipped out while you were in the shower and let you fend for yourself."

Now I knew something was wrong. We never left one another to fend for ourselves. I'd had his back with all the shit that Dylan went through with his ex when he'd started dating Aurora. Never once did I ever think about leaving him to fend for himself.

"Just tell me."

Dylan pulled around a corner and stopped the car in front of the Vancouver Police Department, killing the engine, then looked over at me.

"Look, don't make a big deal out of this, but some fan attacked Lorelai after the game. Aurora got involved, and the girl who assaulted Lorelai is now pressing charges against Aurora."

"What the fuck. Let's go," I immediately said, pulling at my seat belt. I'd climbed out of the car and was halfway up the stairs to the front door of the detachment when Dylan grabbed my arm.

"Look, man. She asked me not to tell you. You can't go storming in there like this."

"I can and I will. I want to make sure she is okay."

"Okay, well, just take a breath for a moment. Let me go in first."

I nodded, allowing Dylan to go ahead of me. We stopped at the front desk, and Dylan was quickly directed to the room where Aurora was while I was told I could head down the hall to my right to see Lorelai.

As I made my way down the hall, I saw Lorelai curled up on a bench, the familiar colors of the Dominator's jersey alerting me it was her. I was just about to her when she looked up.

"What…what are you doing here?" she muttered, standing.

Her hair was dishevelled, she looked exhausted, and there were bruises forming on her cheek from where the girl had hit her.

Without a word, I took a step forward and pulled her against me. I was ready for backlash, for her being angry, yet she didn't move, and then I felt her slowly wrap her arms around me, gently sobbing into my chest.

She pulled away to wipe the tears from her face and that was when I placed my forefinger under her chin, lifting it so I could look at the bruises on her tear-stained face.

"What the fuck happened to you?" I said, gently running my thumb over the bruise on her cheek. "I'm the one supposed to be full of bruises, not you," I said, meeting her eyes.

"It was awful. This girl just attacked me out of nowhere. She claimed I stole you from her," she said as I checked her face over for other signs of bruising.

"These damn fans," I muttered. "Some of these girls get seriously unhinged."

"It was the girl from the restaurant, the one who stopped you for your autograph."

Anger and irritation built inside of me at what she'd just told me, but I kept my composure. When I was satisfied she had no more bruises, I pulled my cell phone from my back pocket.

"What are you doing?" Lorelai questioned.

"Calling my lawyer."

"What for?"

"Representation. You need someone who won't stop, and who will make sure you get what you deserve."

She pulled at my hand, trying to stop me. "Please don't do this."

I looked down at her as if she were crazy. "Look, this girl could have hurt you way worse. There is no telling what she might do next. The last thing I need to be worried about is you being attacked again when I'm on the road. I want to make sure these charges stick, and the only way to do it is to get my lawyer involved. Besides, Dylan wanted me to call anyway, for Aurora."

"This is why I didn't want you here," Lorelai murmured, just as the team's lawyer answered his phone.

WE WALKED INTO THE GIRLS' condo almost three hours later. Dylan and Aurora headed to bed, while I followed Lorelai into the living room. She hadn't spoken a word to me since I'd placed the call to the lawyer and he'd arrived at the station. The entire ride home, she sat in the back of Dylan's car, with me beside her, looking out the window, ignoring me, as if I weren't even there. I'd be damned if she was going to be pissed at me over this. I'd also be dammed if we went to bed angry at one another.

"You seriously don't know how to take a hint, do you?" she said, flopping down into the chair in the corner.

I looked over at her. The bruise on her face had turned into various shades of purple, and it was now swelling bad enough that soon her entire eye would be closed. She needed an ice pack.

Ignoring her accusation, I got up off the couch and left the room, returning with an icepack I'd found in the freezer and held it out for her to take.

"What is that for?" she asked, looking at the ice pack in my hand.

"The bruise on your cheek."

"It doesn't need ice," she bit back, crossing her arms in front of her chest.

I looked at her; she knew better than this.

"Are you really going to argue with someone who might know about these types of things? How many black eyes, swollen cheeks and lips do you think I've had?"

"Why should I care?" She shoved my hand away and glared at me.

I was feeling beyond frustrated now. I did not know why she was acting out toward me, but I was tired of the attitude she'd been giving me when all I wanted to do was help.

"Look, you can be mad at me all you want, but you need ice. Your eye is going to swell shut by morning if you don't get the swelling down. Now take the damn icepack."

I dropped the pack in her lap and made my way over to the couch where I lay down, adjusting a pillow behind my head.

"It doesn't need ice," she muttered under her breath.

I ignored her. I would not continue this with her. We sat in silence for a bit when finally, out of the corner of my eye, I saw her pick up the ice pack and place it on her cheek while she glared in my direction.

"Problem?" I questioned, crossing one leg over the other.

"You think you know what's good for me?"

I closed my eyes, irritated as hell at her. "Are you looking for a fight, because I can give you one!"

"Nope, I'm just keeping our relationship in check here," she gritted.

"What?"

"Nothing."

"No, by all means, say what you are going to say. Lay it all out on the table."

I knew she was angry at me for stepping in and calling the team's lawyer, but it needed to be done. If she was pissed, I wanted to hear her say it. Not hide it from me. I knew that dating me would come with risks; however, I'd never dreamt it would have been like this.

I'd seen some crazy things with other players and their wives. That was why most of the guys never brought their wives to any games, aside from home games. For this to have happened at a home game was going to bring a whole new warning to the players on the team.

I'd felt so powerless when Dylan told me. I hadn't been there to protect her, which was all I wanted to do. So, since I hadn't been able to do it when it happened, I protected her the only way I knew I could.

"Well?" I asked. "Are you going to lay it all out or what?" I sat up, resting my forearms on my knees, waiting for her to talk to me.

Lorelai let out what sounded like a sigh mixed with a whimper, and I glanced over to see her sitting there with her eyes closed, holding her head.

"What is it?" I questioned, watching her.

"My head is pounding," she sobbed, placing her head in her hands.

Without another word from her, I got up, walked over to her, and picked her up out of the chair.

"What are you doing?" She frowned, holding onto my shoulder.

"I don't want to hear any more. You need to get some rest."

I turned and carried her down the hall to her room and gently placed her down on the bed and then made my way back to the kitchen. Moments later, I returned with a glass of water and two headache pills and handed them to her. She didn't fight me this time; she took the pills and a sip of water and then lay back in the bed.

I sat down on the edge of her bed and carefully removed her shoes, then unbuttoned her pants.

"What are you doing now?" she questioned, looking at me.

"Getting you ready for bed. Now lift," I instructed.

She lifted her butt off the bed while I slid her pants down and removed them, placing them in a pile on the floor. She sat up, reached behind her, and undid her bra.

"Could you get me a T-shirt from the top drawer?" she asked.

I did as she asked and waited while she changed into it, handing me the shirt and bra she'd had on. She slipped under the covers and rested her head on the pillow while I covered her.

"Night," I said, shutting off her bedside light and placing a kiss on her cheek. I made my way over to the door of her room and had just opened it.

"Where are you going?" I heard her quietly ask.

"I think it's best if I grab a cab and head home," I said, not wanting to start any more of a fight with her tonight. Tomorrow, once our heads and hearts had time to clear, we could talk about what happened tonight if she wanted.

I was about to pull her door closed when I heard her call my name.

"What?" I questioned.

"I um…I want you to stay," she said, rolling over to look in my direction.

I debated for a couple of seconds whether to stay or go, but the look in her eyes decided for me. She needed me, whether she wanted to admit it or not.

"You want me to stay?" I questioned.

"I do," she whispered, pulling the blankets down on the opposite side of the bed, waiting for me to crawl in.

I shut the door, walked over, slipped out of my jeans, and pulled my shirt off over my head, then crawled into the bed beside her. I'd barely had a moment to get comfortable when she shifted her body against mine.

I wrapped my arm around her waist and pressed a kiss to the side of her neck as I pulled her body tight against mine.

"I'm sorry," she mumbled.

"What are you sorry for?" I questioned, smiling to myself, knowing exactly where this was going.

"I didn't mean to get upset with you. This girl attacking me wasn't your fault. You were only trying to help me."

"I was," I quietly answered.

She spun onto her other side and moved her body closer to mine.

"Think you could forgive me?" she asked, touching her nose to mine.

I brought my lips to hers, my tongue parting her lips, washing through her mouth. I ran my fingers through her hair as she let out a soft moan.

"I think I can forgive you," I said as she rested her head on my shoulder.

"Good."

I OPENED MY EYES, blinking so they could adjust to the light that was pouring through the partially closed blinds. I shifted in bed, feeling the weight of her body next to mine. It was then I felt her hand slide down my stomach and grab hold of my aching cock.

I chuckled a little and looked over at her sleepy face.

"What are you doing?" I questioned, pushing the hair from her eyes, exposing that horrible bruise.

"This was poking me most of the night," she said, biting her bottom lip as her cheeks turned a slight shade of pink.

"That's because it knows it was you," I said, meeting her lips as she stroked the full length of my cock.

"How are you feeling?" I questioned as I lifted myself up on my forearm as she lay down partially under me.

"Better," she said, lifting the blankets to reveal her naked body.

I couldn't help but chuckle. "I see," I said, running my hand up her side and cupping her breast, running my thumb over her nipple.

She hissed as I did it again. "I love it when you do that," she muttered.

"When I do what?" I asked innocently, repeating the action once again.

Her cheeks turned a brighter shade of pink as she met my eyes.

"What do you love?" I questioned again, wanting to hear her say it.

"I love it when you play with my nipples."

I slid down in the bed and sucked one nipple into my mouth, flicking it with my tongue while my finger and thumb pinched the other at the same time.

"Oh god." She hissed. "I love that," she breathed.

I slid my way down farther, throwing the covers over my head, and placed a kiss on her bare belly, then on her hip, then on the top of her upper thigh. Lifting the covers, I poked my head out and looked up at her.

"Ready?" I asked, pushing her leg to the side, opening her to me.

I didn't wait for an answer. Instead, I slid my tongue through her centre, loving the sound she made as my tongue concentrated on her clit. I felt her fingers slide through my hair as she bucked her hips off the bed a little.

She let out a moan, then stopped.

"Why so quiet? Not enjoying yourself?" I questioned, gripping her hip.

"They will hear," she whispered, glancing toward the door.

"Fuck, let them hear. They certainly have no

shame." I winked, flicking my tongue over the small bundle of nerves.

She bucked her hips again, inhaling, but still being quiet.

"I can't hear you," I said, this time sucking it between my lips.

"Oh god, Knox…" she moaned.

My cock was hard as a rock, and I was doing everything I could to resist burying myself inside of her. I wanted to claim her every way I could think of. I wanted her to know she was mine and that she'd look for no one else.

Her hips rose off the bed, and she let out a loud moan as she fisted my hair. I wasn't letting her come down. I got on my knees, took hold of her and rolled her over, pulling her back toward me. I ran my cock through her wetness, loving the sound of her moan, and buried myself into her tight pussy.

She stilled, breathing hard, trying to adjust to me being inside of her.

I pulled her back against me, kissing the side of her neck while my fingers played with her nipples. She whimpered as I pinched them a little harder than normal and met my mouth with a hungry kiss, silencing her cries.

"I love feeling you inside of me," she whispered, interlacing her fingers with mine.

"You do not know how much I love it," I said, sucking the lobe of her ear into my mouth. Gripping her hips, I thrust deeply into her as she clenched around me. I could feel my orgasm building, the base of my spine getting tighter.

"You ready?" I whispered, thrusting into her again.

"Yes."

Gripping her hips, I slid myself back and then thrust into her, then holding her in place, I picked up the pace. Sweat poured down my back as the intensity built, and with one last pump, I felt myself tip over the edge at the same time she screamed my name.

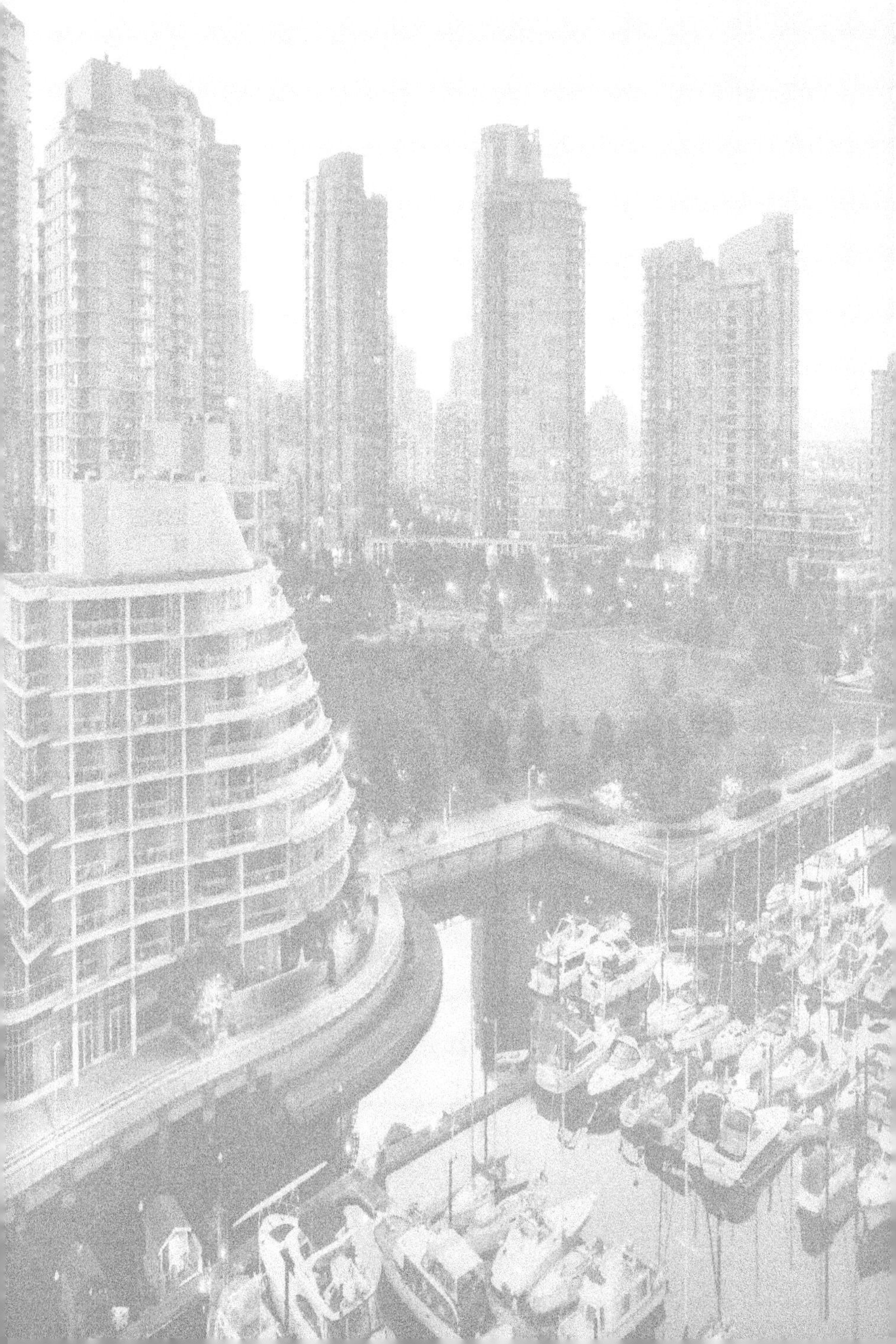

Chapter 12

Lorelai - One Week Later

"OWWWWW!" Knox yelled.

"Make sure you stretch while you're gone," I said, working to loosen his hip flexor.

"Oh god, that hurts," he said, holding his breath. "Anyone ever tell you how torturous you are?"

I looked down at him and couldn't help but giggle. His face was red, and he looked like I was indeed torturing him.

"Would you breathe?" I giggled. "It's not that bad, but if you breathe through it, it will help."

"Would if I could. It hurts like hell, and you digging around into that spot isn't helping. It's painful as hell."

"I know. I'm sorry, but that's because you haven't been doing what I've told you to do. It's all tight again."

"I have, I swear. Heat, ice, and muscle rub, which stinks by the way. Do you want to get into bed every night with a smelly man?"

"Nice try, buddy. I can tell you haven't been doing these things. Besides, repetitive injuries are the worst. It won't heal overnight, and just because you think it's better because it doesn't hurt doesn't mean you can ignore my treatment plan. It's a plan for a reason."

I massaged his hip and glute once I'd straightened his leg and smiled down at him. "There you go," I said, patting his chest and winking. "Torture is over for now."

Knox sat up and stretched, while I went over to the cabinet and pulled out another tube of muscle cream. Going back over, I placed it into his hand as he wrapped his arm around me. I met his eyes.

"Not at work," I whispered, in case someone was outside my office door. "Now, make sure you use this."

He didn't stop. Instead, he pulled me into him.

"You know, I was thinking, I won't heal if someone doesn't stop begging me to fuck her," he whispered.

I felt my cheeks heat at his comment.

"News flash, I don't beg." I winked, giving him a quick kiss before pulling away. "Make sure you're stretching. Stacey is going on this set of games with you guys, so I'll tell her what we've been doing for treatment. Perhaps a massage or two before each game as well will help," I said, going to my desk and making my notes.

"I'd rather it be you that's going," he said, pulling me backward until he had his legs wrapped around mine.

"That would be trouble." I giggled as he kissed the side of my neck before letting me go. I went back over to my desk and grabbed his file, adding a few more notes.

"What are you guys going to be doing while we are gone?" Knox asked, sliding off the table and grabbing his sweatshirt.

"Girl's night," I answered, closing his file. "Why?"

"No reason."

"Knox?" I questioned, after seeing the look on his face.

"What? I was only wondering. I'm curious like that."

"No, you are worried that what happened last weekend is going to happen again."

"Not at all," he said, leaning against my desk."

I slipped between his legs and placed my hands against his chest, glancing up at the clock.

"We've gone over this already. I know you are

worried, otherwise you would have let me come up for air this week. I promise you; everything is going to be fine."

Knox hadn't left my side the entire week. Ever since the night of the attack at the game, he'd picked me up after his morning practices and brought me in to work. He'd driven me home every night and had spent the nights at my place. This was the first time that we would be apart for a few nights, and while I knew he was worried, I needed my space as well. I didn't want him to spend every waking second worried about me.

"I can't help it. I feel responsible for what happened." He shrugged, brushing the loose strand of hair from my face.

"You aren't. We've talked about that. Now, stop being silly. I don't want you to be late, and if you don't get going, that's what will happen. Coach Thompkins won't like it either. The man hates to wait," I said, pressing a kiss to his lips.

"What time will you be in?"

"Not sure, ten maybe?" I shrugged.

"Okay, I'll call you around ten thirty."

I frowned as I studied his eyes. This wasn't the confident, secure Knox I was used to.

"Are you worried about something?" I questioned.

"No."

"This isn't like you."

He looked away from me for a moment and then met my eyes again.

"Just talk to me," I said, trying to figure out if he was worried about something else or if it was the events last weekend that were spurring this on. Only he said nothing. Instead, he hopped off the table and gave me a soft smile.

"Sorry, I should give you space," he said, getting up and making his way to the door.

"Knox, that isn't what I'm saying," I said, going to take a step forward just as Dylan appeared.

"Hey, Lorelai. Knox, are you just about ready to head down to get our gear? Coach is on a rampage. He demanded everyone be ready to head out in thirty minutes."

"Yep, we were just finishing up here. Got my muscle rub," he said, holding up the tube of cream, looking me directly in the eyes before he turned toward the door.

Without so much as a goodbye glance, Knox left my office. I walked over and called his name, but he didn't respond. Instead, I watched them walk down the hall, tears filling my eyes until they were nothing but two blurry figures heading away from me.

AURORA and I sat on the floor of the living room in our pajamas. A pizza box containing a double pepperoni and mushroom pizza sat open in between us as we watched an episode of *Big Bang Theory*.

"Can you pass me a napkin?" I asked as my phone vibrated.

I glanced down as Aurora handed me a napkin and saw Knox's name on my screen. This was the fifth time he'd called since ten thirty, not to mention the slew of texts he'd sent before the game. I frowned and flipped the phone over and took the napkin from Aurora.

"If you want to answer it, go ahead." Aurora shrugged, playing the next episode.

"It's girl's night. We never get to do this anymore." I shrugged.

"That is true. So, things are going okay between you and Knox?"

When I didn't answer right away, Aurora looked over at me and frowned. "What's going on? Everything is okay between the two of you? Right? I know last weekend really caused things to act up."

"Yep, fine," I said, picking up my phone and shutting it off just as it vibrated again.

Aurora paused the show and rolled onto her side, holding her head up with her hand, and stared at me.

"What?"

"Don't what me, what's going on?" she questioned. "He's been calling, and you are ignoring him."

I shrugged, feeling as if I could break down in tears for the way Knox and I had left things. It certainly wasn't how I'd hoped to leave them. I'd hoped he'd speak to me, talk to me about how he was feeling, but he'd stormed off.

"Is this what it's like dating them?" I questioned, wiping my eyes to stop the burning.

"What do you mean?"

"The crazy fans?"

"No, most of the time, people respect your space when you're out together. You were just the one caught in a weird incident. Sort of what happened to me in that club. Only the girl who attacked me had a reason. She didn't. She didn't even know him."

"Yeah, a weird incident that I got my best friend involved in," I said, tears once again welling in my eyes.

"It's fine. No crazy bitch is going to attack you while I'm around. Everything is fine with me. All those silly charges were dropped. Psycho bitch is the only one being charged."

"I know." I'd been so happy to find out that the

lawyers that Knox and Dylan called had quickly and quietly gotten things taken care of for her.

Aurora looked at me, questions in her eyes. I'd seen this look before. It was the same look she'd given me when I'd come to her about Hugo but didn't know how to say the words. We'd had a long talk, and she'd pried it out of me.

"Are you happy?" she asked.

"Am I happy?" I frowned.

"Yes. Are you happy? Does being with Knox make you happy?"

I didn't even need to think about that answer.

"I'd love to tell you no, but he does. Every morning since Hawaii, I wake up and pinch myself to see if I'm dreaming. I'm always afraid that one time I'll open my eyes and he won't be there. That it will all have been a dream."

"I see. Is it the sex thing again?"

I shrugged, not sure I wanted to tell her the truth and figured this might be the easiest way to continue the conversation, making it fun instead of so serious.

"It's okay, right? I mean, he makes you come and all, right."

I felt my cheeks heat at her question but nodded my head.

"Always first? Dylan will hold off until I come first every single time."

"Yes, always," I said, remembering the handful of times we'd done it so far.

"Does he cuddle afterward?"

"Yes."

"Now, for an embarrassing one, does he go down on you? I'll tell you, it's my most favorite thing with Dylan. Never liked it with Greg, but man, I'll say Dylan knows exactly what he is doing."

I remembered our very first time. The feel of his tongue on me was so vivid in my memory I could almost feel it now.

"Can I tell you a secret?"

Aurora nodded.

"I can still feel his tongue."

Aurora grabbed me, shaking me as we both screamed and then laughed.

"God, it's almost too much information we share with one another, isn't it?"

"Yes. I agree. Knox would probably kill me," I said, taking another mouthful of pizza and washing it down with some cola. I glanced at my phone, turning it on. Once it loaded, I noticed I had voicemails and let out a sigh as I flipped it back face down.

"Okay, so it's not the sex. So, tell me what is it? What's bothering you?"

I glanced up and looked at my best friend. "How

do you know that something is bothering me? We were just laughing and giggling like two schoolgirls."

"I know you well. I think you were using my suggestion as somewhat of a deterrent to what you really wanted to talk about. So, spill it."

Whatever the reason, this entire situation was paralyzing me. All I could think about was the look Knox had given me as he walked out of my office. I had enough problems opening up about things, but opening up to Knox was especially hard, given our history. It seemed perhaps he was the same.

"Today, during my treatment session with Knox, he asked me when we'd be home tonight."

"So." Aurora shrugged.

"So, he wasn't asking because he wanted to know."

"Why do you say that?"

"Just a feeling I was getting."

"Why do you think he was asking?"

"So he could call me and check up on me."

"What do you mean?" Aurora frowned.

"It felt like he wasn't trusting me."

"Lorelai, I don't think that's it."

"You didn't see it. He wouldn't talk to me. Then Dylan showed up. He never said goodbye. I tried to get his attention, but he ignored me and left." I shrugged.

"He didn't seem angry to me when I went down to see them off."

"Did he say anything about me?" I questioned.

Aurora looked at me and shook her head while she took another slice of pizza, picking off the pepperoni once it was on her plate and shoving the slices into her mouth. Ever since I'd known her, this was how she'd eaten pepperoni pizza. She said it tasted better if she removed it first.

"Did you hear me? He never said goodbye."

"I heard you."

I waited for her to say something else, but she didn't. She sat there picking off the pepperoni, shoving it into her mouth until her pizza was pepperoni-less while she watched TV.

"Well?" I asked impatiently.

"Well, what?" she questioned, finally tearing her eyes away from the screen.

"What should I do?"

"You should finish your pizza, then you should pick up your phone, head down to your room, shut the door, and call your man. Then I think tomorrow we are going to go out, get massages, and go shopping."

"What are we going to go shopping for?" I frowned.

"We are going to go to a sex shop, and we are going to buy you a vibrator, so tomorrow night you can give Knox a show he won't forget. Now go on, go down to that bedroom of yours and call your man."

I'D TRIED CALLING Knox after we'd gone to bed but his phone kept going to voicemail. I'd finally given up just shortly after midnight. Now I stood in the vibrator aisle of Intimate Treasures while Aurora handed me all the different vibrators.

"Are you girls doing okay? Do you have any questions?" the store clerk asked, making me want to die.

"Yep, we are fine," I said, holding up one box and waving it in the air.

The clerk smiled, then turned and walked away.

"Okay, so this is what Dylan got me," she said, handing me a box that contained two pieces."

"What is it?" I questioned, looking at it with confusion, then switching to another box.

"It's a panty vibrator. It has an app that he can use," she said, raising her eyebrows.

"Seriously?"

"Yep." She smiled.

"Does it work?" I questioned, looking at the tiny thing inside."

"Zero to sixty, my dear. I sometimes wear it when I'm in my room at night, then I message him before he's back in the hotel room to let him know I'm wearing it. He surprises me by giving me a little buzz here and there when he is on his way back to his room to get me worked up."

"Oh, my god," I said, feeling my cheeks heat when the realization of what she'd said came to me. "Are you telling me that wasn't a spider in your room the other night?"

Blush rose to her cheeks, and then she giggled.

"Oh, my god…seriously!"

"Yeah, you need this one," Aurora said, grabbing the box from me and shoving it under her arm. "Now, for the other one."

"The other one?"

"Yes, the other one. Let's see what we have."

I seriously wanted to die as she pulled the boxes from my hand, looking at each one of them, reading the boxes, as if we were making the most important purchase we'd ever made.

"This one!" she said, thrusting a box into my hand.

I looked down at it. "What the hell is a thrusting vibrator?" I questioned, looking at the box.

"I have this one too. I love it. Dylan can control it as well."

"What the hell goes on in your room?" I frowned, looking at her.

Aurora giggled. "Come on."

"How much are these things?" I said, following her

as she pried the other box from my hand and headed to the register.

"NOW, TEXT HIM," Aurora said, sitting behind me on the couch, looking at my screen.

"What am I supposed to say?" I said, my hands shaking as I held the phone.

"Ask him if he is in the mood for a little fun tonight."

I shook as I typed; I had never talked to a boyfriend like this before and I'd never dreamed I'd start with Knox. Once I had finished typing the words, I waited before hitting send.

"What are you waiting for?"

"What if he comes back and says he isn't. What if he comes back and says that we are over? He's never not answered his phone before."

"Maybe he was tired last night. Dylan said he was beat after the game, and he told me that Knox turned in early."

"Yeah, to call me, which I completely ignored. He probably doesn't even want to hear from me."

Aurora giggled. "You are being silly. I don't think

you need to worry about anything. I think he is going to love this. I know Dylan does. Hit send," she urged, hitting my arm.

I did as she said and then I waited. When he didn't immediately respond, I worried that perhaps he didn't like semi-forward Lorelai.

"He isn't responding," I cried.

Aurora looked at me and nodded to my phone where I saw three little dots bouncing around.

Knox: Absolutely!

I stared at the screen, not knowing what to write back.

"What did he say?" Aurora questioned.

I was sure the look on my face was one of shock that he'd responded with that answer.

Knox: See you tonight when I get home.

"Oh my god," I said, glancing to Aurora.

"What?"

"They are coming home tonight. I knew this would blow up in my face."

"Nonsense. Girl, you are going to rock this, and he is going to love it."

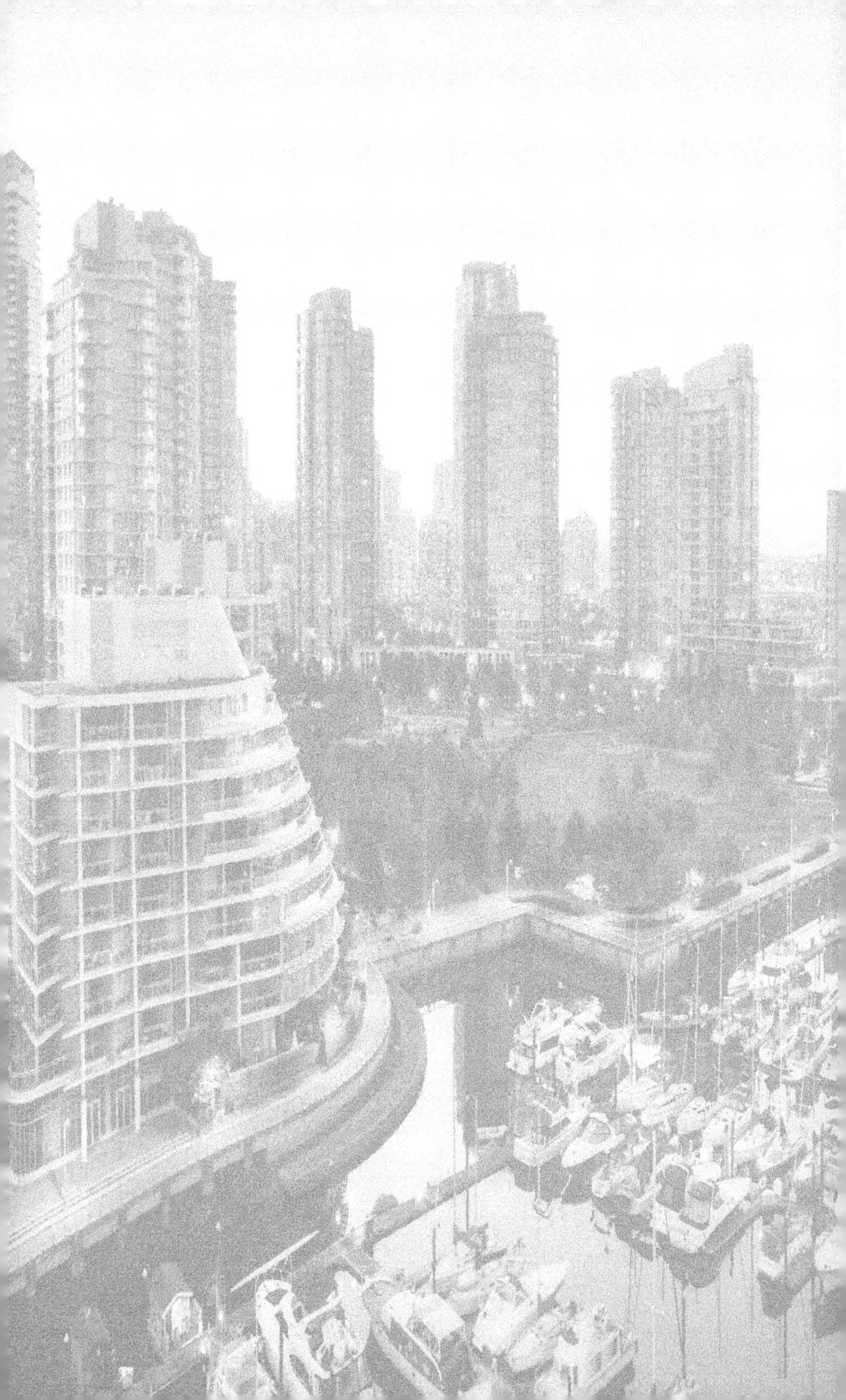

Chapter 13

Knox

DYLAN OPENED the door to the condo, both of us laughing at something he'd said as we stepped into a dark kitchen.

"Quiet, I am sure the girls are probably in bed," I whispered as he dropped his bag inside the door.

"I'm sure Aurora is waiting up for me, and if she isn't she should be." Dylan chuckled.

We'd lost our game tonight, and afterwards the team got on a flight and we made our way home. A long time ago we used to stay in the away city, go out on the town and have a few drinks after a loss. Not anymore, not only did our coach believe there was nothing to celebrate after we lost, but most of the guys on the team were now married. The days of partying it up were over.

Dylan opened the fridge and pulled out the can of whipped cream and then headed over to Aurora's bedroom. I couldn't help but chuckle. He always had been a kinky fucker.

"Oh wait, did you want this?" he questioned, holding the can of whip cream out to me.

"No, go eat your girl." I chuckled and continued down the hall to Lorelai's closed door.

She'd messaged me earlier, wondering if I wanted to have a little fun tonight. I'd be lying if her message hadn't piqued my curiosity, and I wanted to send back a message that showed a little more interest than a single-word answer, but it was a little hard to do when I was surrounded by my teammates.

I hoped she was still awake. I turned the handle of her door and slowly opened it to find her lying in bed with a book in her hand.

I walked over without a word, slipped off my joggers and T-shirt, and flopped into her bed, pulling her into me. I claimed her mouth and within seconds, she was already straddling my lap with her naked body.

The moment our lips parted, I brushed her hair behind her ears and met her eyes. "I missed you," I whispered. "Sorry we left things the way we did."

"Me too, and I missed you too."

She brought her lips to mine, this time kissing me so gently her lips felt like feathers.

"So, what did you have in mind for tonight?" I questioned.

As I studied her face, her cheeks heated. She bit her bottom lip and shook her head, giving me a shy look. "It was nothing." She shrugged.

I wanted her to say it. I wanted to hear the words fall from her lips.

"No way, it was something. Tell me, babe. I want to know what you had in mind."

Again, she was quiet. "What if you don't like it?" she questioned, her cheeks turning pink, still not telling me what had been on her mind.

"Listen to me, with you, there isn't anything I don't like. Trust me," I urged.

I studied her, waiting, hoping she would tell me.

"God, this is so dumb," she muttered, reaching over to the drawer of her nightstand and opening it.

"I thought we could…have some fun with…uh… these," she said, dropping not only one but two sex toys down on the bed, immediately piquing my curiosity.

I'd heard some of the guys talking about this stuff, and I knew Dylan and Aurora were into this shit as well. I'd only hoped that Lorelai might be open to things like this, and to say right at this moment I wasn't hard as a rock would be a lie.

When I looked at her, she covered her face with her hands.

"Sorry, stupid Aurora and her dumb ideas. Don't worry about it. It was more for when you weren't here anyway. Something about an app…and giving me a little buzz on the way back to your room…. just stupid."

I sat forward and pulled her against me, meeting her mouth. This shit was hot as fuck, and I wanted nothing more than to try these out when I wasn't here.

"Babe, I can't wait to try these out. However, I am here now, and there is no way I'm letting a piece of plastic satisfy my woman when I am able, willing, and ready."

WE WERE GEARING up for another set of days on the road, so I'd decided to celebrate with Lorelai tonight before I left. I'd made reservations at The Lighthouse, the oldest restaurant in Vancouver.

I watched her from across the table as she looked over the dessert menu. She looked stunning in the black dress she'd gotten for tonight. She'd curled her dirty-blond hair and those large, soft curls cascaded over her shoulders, framing her face perfectly.

"Have I told you how amazing you look tonight?" I questioned, taking her hand in mine.

Glancing up at me, she shyly smiled as she bit her bottom lip. "Yes, I almost think you need to stop." She giggled.

"I can't, it's true. I also hope you know how sorry I am for leaving the way I did last time."

"It's okay, and we have already discussed things. That won't happen again because we agreed our stubborn asses need to be less stubborn." She smiled.

I had no idea what I had done to deserve another chance with her, but I was almost certain I was falling in love with her. Each time I saw her, she became more beautiful, including when she was all fired up mad. I was certain it was my favorite thing about her.

She looked down at her menu again, running her finger down the list of desert options, and all I could do was sit there and stare at her. When she looked back up and caught me staring, she gave me a sexy smile.

"What are you thinking about over there?"

"Nothing."

"Well, it might be nothing, but it looks like you are up to trouble." she said as she looked at me, shook her head and giggled as her cheeks turned a slight pink.

"What is it?" I questioned, smiling over at her.

"Did you happen to check your phone before we left?" she questioned, looking back down at her menu.

I frowned, not sure what it was she was talking about, but I was curious, so I grabbed my phone from my suit pocket. There on the screen sat an invitation from Lorelai.

"What is that?" I questioned.

She played with her napkin, twirling her fingers into the fabric and looked over at me. "An invite for an app for that panty vibrator I bought. I thought I'd install it before we came out for dinner tonight," she said nonchalantly.

I felt my cock jerk and immediately wondered if she had it on now.

"Is that so?" I said, quickly installing the software onto my phone and accepting her invitation.

Our eyes locked as she twirled a piece of her hair around her finger, watching me. Her eyes told me everything I needed to know. She was wearing it alright, and I knew she was waiting for me to use it.

"Ready?" I asked, my voice low as I glanced over at the table beside us.

She nodded, reaching across the table and taking hold of my hand. Our eyes locked and that was when I hit the button.

Her eyes opened wide, and she stared at me. "Oh god," she murmured under her breath as I watched her wiggle a little in her seat and close her eyes. I let it go for a second or two before shutting it off.

When she finally opened her eyes and met mine, I smiled.

"Did you like that?"

She was just about to speak when I flipped it on again, this time turning the vibration up a little.

She jumped a little, and her cheeks flushed as she looked at me. Her eyes were full of want. I let it run for a second or two before I shut the thing off and looked over at her.

"Did you want dessert?"

"Huh?"

"I said, did you want dessert?" I said, flipping it back on.

She gripped the edge of the table this time and looked over at me, her eyes pleading with me to stop.

"You better turn it off," she said, breathing harder.

"Why?" I smirked, watching her as she gripped the table tighter, her knuckles turning white.

My cock was hard as a rock. I loved the look in her eyes as she sat there, breathing hard, her cheeks flushed.

"You know why," she said, her teeth clenched.

I shut it off as I noticed the server approaching.

"Anything for dessert?" he asked.

"You know, I think we are going to take the berries and cream to go," I said, glancing over at Lorelai. "If you could kindly bring the check when you return as well, that would be appreciated. I've got a flight to catch shortly," I said, glancing at my watch.

"Sure thing, Mr. Evans," he said, hurrying away.

I looked over at Lorelai and once again smirked. "How'd that feel?" I questioned, my cock still straining against my suit pants.

She was about to answer me when the server returned with our dessert to go and the bill, which I quickly paid, then pocketed my phone. We got up from the table and made our way to my car. I opened the door for her, then made my way around the driver's seat and climbed in. I shoved my phone in the console and was about to put my seatbelt on when Lorelai in one quick motion, straddled my lap, kissing me hard. She reached her hand down between us and ran it over my hard cock.

"I need this," she said, meeting my eyes. "Now."

"Yeah?" I said as I reclined my seat back to give her a little more room. I didn't think it was possible to be harder than I was earlier, but she'd just proved me wrong.

"Yes," she said, pulling at my belt and unzipping my pants, reaching inside and stroking my cock.

"Ride me," I murmured, running my fingers through her hair as I looked at her.

"Here?"

"Yes," I said, running my hands up her legs, gripping her ass as I slid her skirt up. "Pull your panties to the side and slide down on my cock," I whispered. "Just try to leave that little vibrator in place."

She rose onto her knees and did as I asked, lining my cock up at her entrance. A loud moan erupted from her throat as she slid down onto my cock. As she rode me, I reached over and grabbed my phone, turning on that little vibrator as she bounced on me.

She bucked her hips as I gripped her ass.

"Knox, turn it off." She moaned into my ear as she ground down on me.

"No way," I said, breathing hard, my orgasm building faster than I wanted.

I could feel her tightening around me as she rode me a little faster.

"God…" She moaned as she tipped her head back.

I reached up and grabbed her breast, gently rolling her nipple between my fingers.

"Knox, I'm going to come…" She panted, grinding her hips down on me once again.

"Come, baby," I whispered, meeting her lips to silence her cries as she clenched around me.

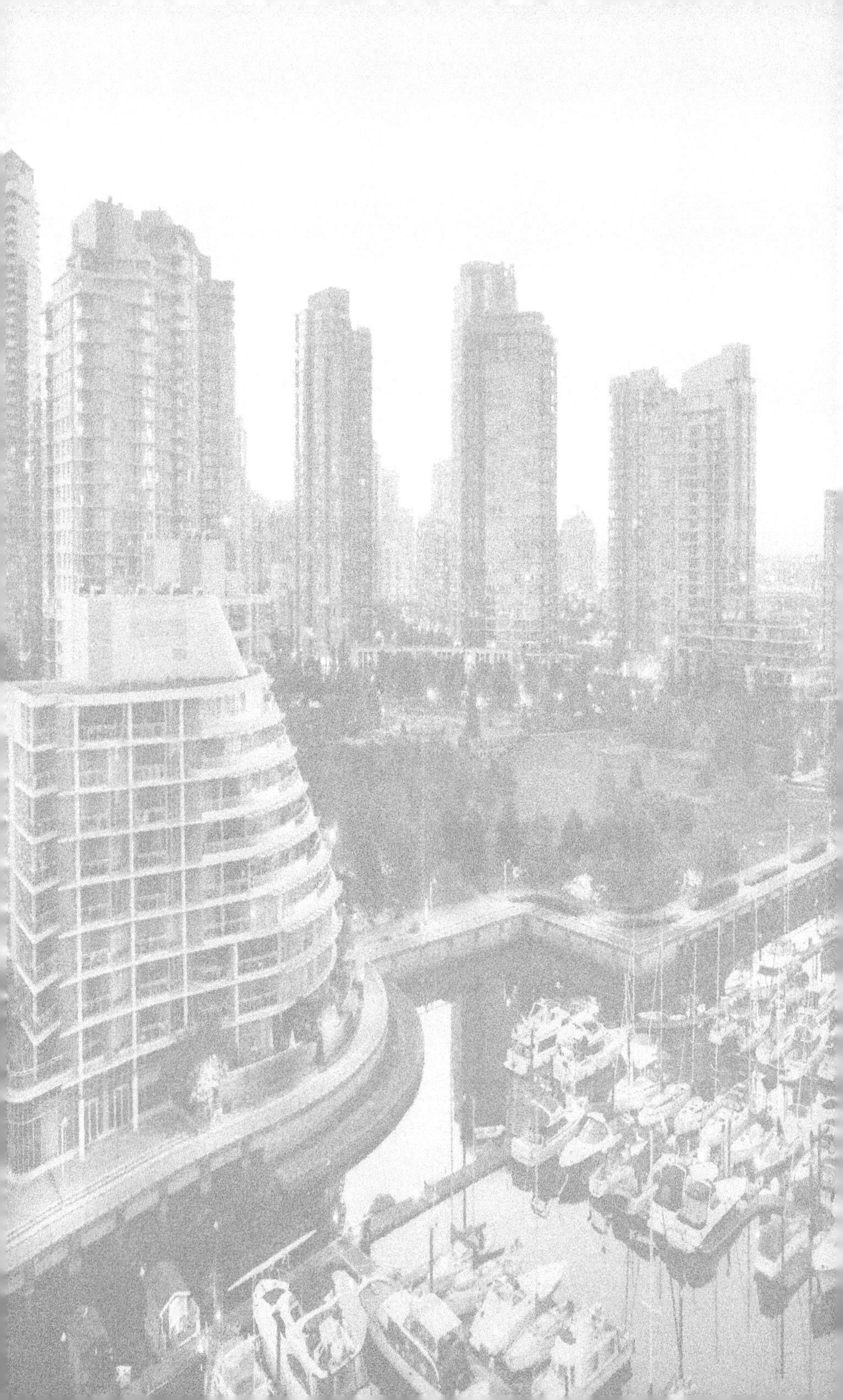

Chapter 14

Lorelai

I WANDERED down the hall and poked my head into Aurora's office. "Ready for lunch?" I questioned.

"Am I! I'm starving. Honestly, I feel as if I didn't have breakfast this morning, the way my stomach has been grumbling."

Aurora and I normally had lunch with Dylan and Knox when they were here, but they were once again travelling. Their schedule lately had been heavy with away games. They were nearing the end of the season, and in a few weeks, they'd be home for the summer. I was excited about that.

We headed out of the arena and climbed into

Aurora's car, then we drove over to Sip and Stir for lunch. We ordered our usual and then made our way over to the booth we'd claimed during school. It was almost like the restaurant had saved it for us.

"I'll be right back, need to use the washroom," Aurora said, heading away from the table.

I sat down and checked my phone for messages, then took a bite of my sandwich which I quickly put down. My stomach turned as I read the article on my screen.

"Sorry about that," Aurora said, sliding into the seat across from me. "What are you looking at?"

When I said nothing, she glanced up. I'd opened up the sports app, the one I used to follow the guys. It had been a mistake to open it because there, on the main page, was an article, and in it was not only Knox's mentioned but me as well.

"Lorelai?"

I looked up and then swallowed hard, passing Aurora my phone. She looked down at the screen and then back up at me.

"What the hell is this?" she questioned, sinking down into her seat across from me.

"That is what I'd like to know."

"Hockey Player's Girlfriend: Disgusting History as a Cheater," Aurora read out loud, then stopped as she read the article.

Fire built inside of me until I felt as if I could explode. I knew who'd done this. There was only one person, and to think I'd once thought I'd loved him.

"Aren't you going to eat?" Aurora questioned as she looked over at me, shoving the last of her sandwich into her mouth while she continued reading the article.

"I'm not hungry," I murmured as I took my phone back and stared down at the article. I wanted to cry. I wanted to beat Hugo within an inch of his life, and I was certain Knox would too when he found out that it came from Hugo.

"You need to eat. Don't worry about that gossip rag," Aurora said. "It's just that they will trash talk any player if they think they can."

I knew this; I wasn't a stranger to being in a sports family. It just hurt and hit home when the article was about you.

"I know," I mumbled.

"You think it was Hugo, don't you?" Aurora questioned.

I blinked away the tears that were clouding my vision and nodded, trying to force a bite of my sandwich down.

"I know it was," I whispered, shoving my tray to the side. There was no point in trying to eat. I'd just end up throwing it all back up, anyway.

"Things were going so well between us while he

was home." I muttered, wondering how this was going to affect us moving forward.

I wanted to text him, to warn him this was out there, but I was in such shock I couldn't. I looked at the plate of food in front of me and shoved it off to the side, my stomach turning.

"You really should eat," Aurora said, looking over at my uneaten lunch. "Don't let him win."

"You know, I think I am going to go home. I'll call the arena and just tell them I must have eaten something that didn't agree with me."

"Lorelai," Aurora said.

"I think I need to be alone."

"Lorelai, really, this isn't anything to get upset about. It will all clear up with a call from the PR department. You know this. That gossip column is always after dirt and they twist words around like crazy."

"Yes, I know. What I don't know is how this will affect Knox and me. So, regardless, I'm gonna go. Just go back to work," I said, dialling the arena.

"At least let me take you home. I don't know if I want you wandering the city alone in this state. Knox would kill me."

I shook my head. "Well, good thing for you Knox isn't here. I'll be fine. Go. I'll grab a cab. I won't do anything crazy."

Aurora looked at me with worry as I called and told them I was heading home with a migraine. Then we said our goodbyes. Once she was gone and I'd calmed down enough, I called a cab and made my way home.

I'd never been so glad to step into my own space. I shut the door and locked it and then slid down to the floor, burying my face in my hands at the thought of that article. This would affect Knox; it might even harm his career. It was affecting me, and somehow deep inside I knew it would affect our relationship, which was something I'd never wanted to happen.

I sat on the floor and cried until no more tears fell, then I got up off the floor and headed down to my room where I curled up in bed and cried all over again until I fell asleep.

I SLOWLY OPENED my eyes and looked around my room. My eyes were dry, my chest hurt from crying. I had no idea how long I'd been asleep, but it was dark as I stared out the window and looked at the twinkling lights of the city.

I normally loved looking out the window at night,

the city all bright with lights. Tonight was different though; it had somehow lost its magic.

I glanced at the clock and slipped from my bed. My feet sank into the soft, plush carpet as I made my way to the bathroom. I shut the door and started running a bath, dumping about three cups of Epsom salt into the running water. Then I added a few drops of lavender essential oils before turning and looking at myself in the mirror. My makeup was smudged from crying and my hair was a mess. My body felt heavy, and I couldn't wait to crawl into the warmth of the bath. It was the only comfort I could find.

I could hear the clanging of pots and pans down the hall and knew Aurora was probably making dinner. I'd been sleeping so soundly I hadn't even heard her come home.

Grabbing my phone, I placed it on the edge of the tub and slipped out of my clothes and then climbed into the hot tub, welcoming the warmth against my aching body. I closed my eyes, and that was when I heard my phone vibrate against the edge of the tub. I wasn't sure I wanted to face any more bad news today and had a mind just to shut it off, but when it went off again, I decided to look.

I closed my eyes and inhaled deeply, the smell of lavender calming me, and then reached for my phone. Knox had messaged me.

KNOX: All I'm going to say is I am going to kill Hugo!

I stared down at the message, swallowing hard. This wasn't good. Knox already hated him, and judging from how things went in Hawaii, I knew without a doubt he'd follow through with harming him if given the chance. No one would ever understand how happy I was that Knox wasn't in the same country at this point.

LORELAI: You are going to have to beat me to it.

I typed, then watched the screen. I felt sick again. The three little dots bounced around for what felt like forever.

KNOX: I shouldn't have started out that way. What I really want to know is, are you okay?

LORELAI: Yeah, I think so. I wasn't earlier. I was upset. I really wished you were here when I saw that article.

KNOX: Why didn't you message me?

LORELAI: I choked, I didn't know what to do. I was so angry, so hurt, there were so many emotions flooding me I couldn't sort through them. I'm worried about us, you, how this will affect things for you.

KNOX: You aren't the only one who was angry. When I get back there, I'll take care of it. As for us, we are fine, something like this has no impact on our relationship. I have to go get ready for the game.

Coach is screaming…again…I'll message you later, tonight.

I stared down at the screen, at his words, knowing full well he meant what he said about Hugo. There was no way I could let him near him now. As I sat there reading over his words, a part of me did question the us part, and the worry started all over again.

LORELAI: Talk later.

Once I got out of the tub and got dressed, I tiptoed down the hall to the front door. I wanted to sneak out without Aurora seeing me; I had to take care of this. I'd just slipped my shoes on and had quietly grabbed my keys from the closet when they slipped out of my hand, clanging to the floor.

"What the hell!" Aurora shrieked.

I turned around to see her watching me from the living room, where she was eating and watching the game.

"Sorry about that. Didn't mean to scare you."

"Where have you been? I was worried sick."

"I was sleeping in my room."

Aurora gave me a confused look, then sort of giggled. "I didn't check there."

"Oh well, that was where I was. Now, I'm going out. I'll see you later."

I slipped through the door before she could question me any further and took off down the hall, hitting the elevator button.

THERE WERE two cars parked in the driveway in front of the little bungalow I'd hoped to see again. This house held too many terrible memories for me, including the worst night of my life. The night I'd come home from school to find Hugo in the shower with the woman he'd been having an affair with.

It looked like he was up to his old tricks, I thought to myself as I watched a woman other than Molli step out the front door. She turned, gave him a long kiss on the lips before getting into her car and pulling out of the driveway. Hugo looked around before heading back inside. Once she was gone, I got out of the car and made my way to the front door.

Anger flooded me as I stood there waiting for him to open the door. It was better if I confronted him than Knox. It wouldn't look good for his image if he was up on assault charges.

I heard the lock flip and then the door open. The slimy smile that Hugo wore ignited a raging fire inside of me. Before I could stop myself, I slapped him across the face.

"What the hell, you bitch?" he yelled, holding his cheek.

"Don't start! Stop ruining my life!" I screamed.

"It's not your life I want to ruin," he said, still holding his cheek.

"Stop pretending like that hurt. I didn't hit you that hard, but I am sure Knox will…so you better toughen up," I gritted, clenching my fist.

"Don't hit me again."

"Why does it bother you so much that I am happy?"

Hugo looked at me, smirked, and then shrugged his shoulders. "You can't possibly be all that happy? The guy is gone all the time!"

"I am happier than I have ever been, and I am happier than I ever was with you. I know you can't stand it. You proved that when we were in Hawaii."

"Yeah, whatever you say. That entire thing was a charade. I could see it written all over your face."

I crossed my arms over my chest and stepped closer to him. "The only charade there was you, begging and pleading for me to come back. You don't want me back. You never wanted me in the first place."

He stood there staring at me with disbelief. "I loved you," he said.

I rolled my eyes. "Listen, you chose to be with your mistress, so what happened between us, is on you. I see you haven't changed all that much, seeing what left your house this evening. Does Molli know? Does Molli know you were begging me to come back?"

"I don't know what you are talking about," he said, clearing his throat, the same nervous stance he'd taken so many times when he was lying to me.

"The woman who left here about ten minutes ago. I saw it. Don't bother trying to deny it. Does Molli know?"

Hugo shifted from foot to foot, then cleared his throat and swallowed hard.

"I can already tell she doesn't, so you can save the lies," I said, staring at him. "You know what I think?"

"What?"

"I think perhaps Molli should get a phone call tomorrow."

"Lorelai!" Hugo said, raising his voice to me.

"Don't you dare raise your voice to me. You better retract what was said in that article, otherwise I know that when a certain someone gets back into town, he's coming for you."

"He wouldn't dare."

"Oh, he would. I also know that if that statement doesn't get retracted, Molli is going to get a phone call from me," I said, turning around and making my way down the walkway.

"You wouldn't dare call her."

I turned around and looked at him. "Maybe I would, maybe I wouldn't. Just remember, if shit gets ruined, it's on you again. It's all on you. No one else."

I walked down the driveway and opened the driver's side of the car, getting in. I looked at the house to see Hugo still standing on the front step, watching me. I didn't wait around. I pulled away from the house and drove down the street, pulling over once I'd rounded the corner.

I took a deep breath and tried to calm my beating heart. Then I grabbed my phone and dialed Knox's number. Of course he didn't answer, so I left him a voicemail letting him know that I'd hopefully taken care of the situation.

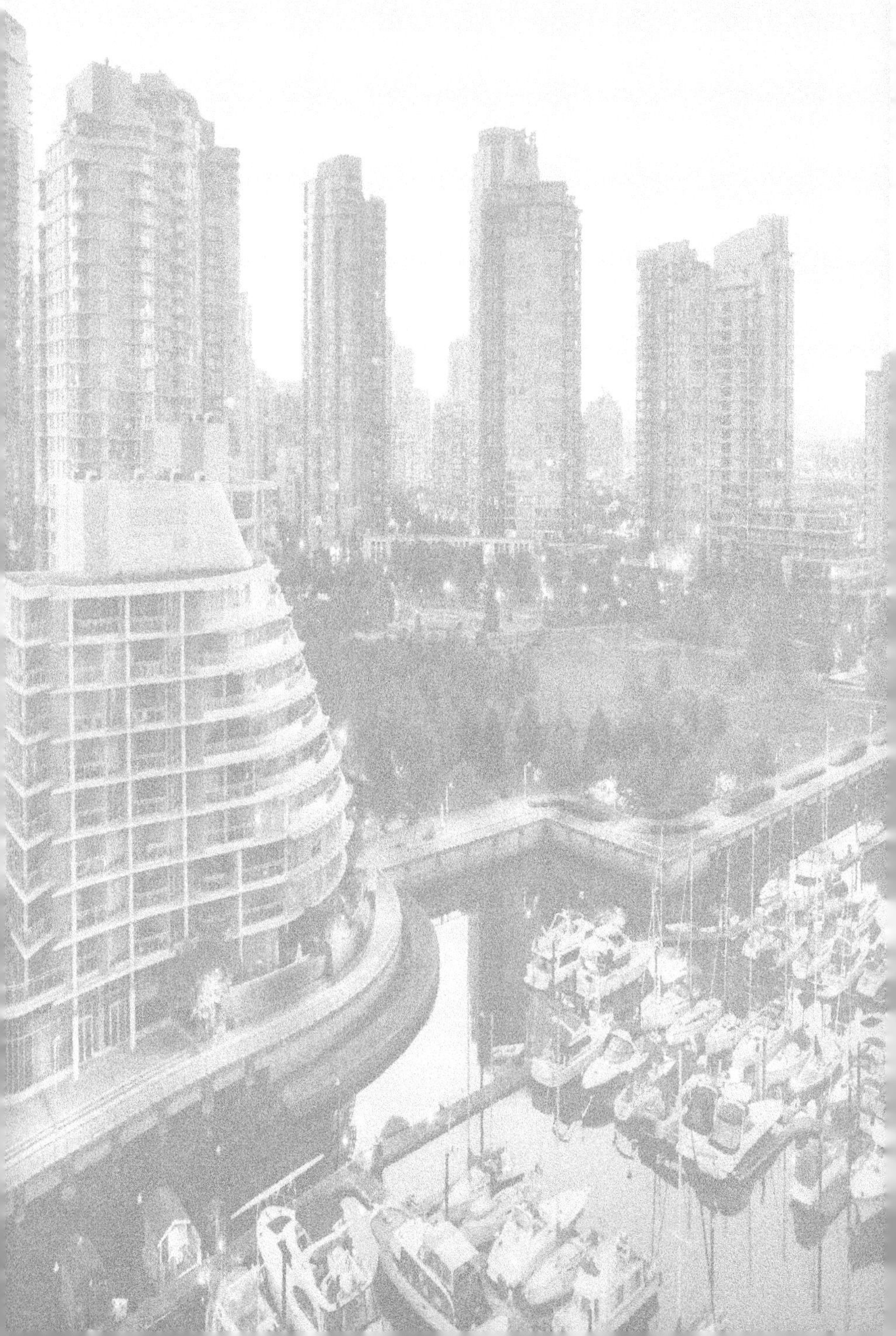

Chapter 15

Knox

I WALKED into the locker room before the game and threw my shit off the bench and down onto the floor. I was glad I was the only one in here. I didn't need razzing from the guys tonight. My phone hadn't stopped going off with notifications and emails. It seemed every damn sports blog in the world had gotten word of the article about Lorelai, and now they were smearing both of us all over the place.

"Hey, man, how you doing?" Dylan asked, walking into the room and dropping the bag he was carrying on the floor.

"Don't want to talk about it," I said, taking a seat

on the bench I'd just cleared in the centre of the room and stretching out my hip.

"That bad, huh?"

"Yes, it is that bad. Guess you didn't see the latest?"

Dylan shook his head. "No, I was with Aurora last night and most of today, since she had the day off."

I pulled my phone from my back pocket and showed him the newest article that had come out. Dylan studied the screen, his brow furrowing.

"Shit man, get PR on this."

I glanced down at the screen and read the headline again, *Knox Evans - cheater extraordinaire, now beat at his own game.*

I remembered when the media had gone down the cheating rabbit hole with me when I'd been single. Every chance they got to share a picture of me with another woman, they had. This was why I protected Lorelai every time we'd been approached in public. I didn't want this to come to her, but it appeared it had.

"They are, trust me." I threw my phone down on the bench and continued stretching.

"Did you go over to see Hugo?" Dylan questioned.

"Nope, she refused to let me. Absolutely put her foot down."

"Probably for the best. The last thing you need on top of all of this is to beat the hell out of someone and have charges pressed against you."

The door to the locker room opened and John, Pamela's assistant, stood there. "Evans, can I see you for a moment?" he questioned.

Dylan looked over at me. "What the hell could PR want?" Dylan questioned. "He looks pissed too."

"Who the fuck knows?" I said, throwing my water bottle down on the floor. "I do know, I'm fucking sick of it." I muttered as I pushed the door open and stepped out into the hall.

"What!" I barked.

"I just got off the phone with the clothing line that just signed you for representation."

I could already see what was coming. I was going to lose the contract because of all the shit floating around. This was the biggest contract I'd signed.

"Okay?" I said, swallowing hard.

"They are going to hold off for now."

There it was, exactly what I expected.

"What?"

"Unfortunately, because of the shit in the media right now, they are going to hold off for now."

"They are cancelling?"

"Not cancelling, just waiting to see what happens, I guess. They aren't sure you are the right one to represent them. We are in talks."

Anger boiled inside of me. If Lorelai thought I was going to stand by and let Hugo ruin my career, she was wrong. He needed to be taught a lesson, and I needed to be the one to give it to him. I glanced at my watch, noticing I had fifty minutes before we needed to be on the ice. I didn't have time to go take care of anything right now.

"Don't worry, Knox, we are gonna take care of this for the both of you. Now, go play your best game," John said, turning around and heading down the hall away from me.

I stood there, anger almost boiling out of me. Go play my best game? Easy for him to say. I turned to go back into the locker room, but before I did, I took a punch and slammed my fist into the locker just outside the door.

THE GAME WAS GOING for shit. My mind wasn't on it. It was on everything but. Dylan passed me the puck, and that was when the largest player on the opposing team rammed me into the boards. Adrenaline shot through my body as I fought to regain the puck, and when I did, another player hooked my foot with his stick, sending me flying.

The ref called it, and just as I got up, the same

player got into my face. I wasn't backing down; I needed to get rid of the rage that had built inside of me, and I took a swing at him and missed. He fought back, taking a swing at me, clocking me right in the jaw. I grabbed him and gave him a couple hits to the ribs just before I felt the ref grab me and pull me back, sending me straight to the box.

Tonight, hadn't been my best game. This was the type of player I'd been before, always getting into fights on the ice, but the older I got and when I'd come to the Dominators, I'd calmed that side of me, until tonight.

Dylan punched me in the shoulder as I skated past him over to the box, where I'd already spent most of tonight.

My hip was killing me from the shove into the boards and the trip, and just as I was getting to the door of the box, the coach stopped me.

"Evans, come here!" he yelled.

"What?"

"You're done. Get out of here," he gritted.

"No way, coach," I shot back, getting into his face. "That was an unfair play, fucking hooking me."

"What the hell was the fight with the other player then?" he yelled.

"That was justified," I spat.

"I'm not telling you again. You're out of here

now!" he said, getting right into my face, not backing down for a moment.

"I won't."

"Evans, I'm not fucking around. Get out of here now. Get your fucking head screwed on and don't make things worse for yourself. Now go!" he said, pointing down the hallway toward our locker room.

I glared into his eyes ready to take him on but luckily thought twice. Throwing my stick down, I proceeded down the hall on my way to the locker room, shedding my gear as I went.

Instead of heading to the locker room, I made my way to the medical area. My hip was now on fire and throbbing from being smashed into the boards. It was also the same leg they hooked, so no doubt I'd done some sort of damage to something that was already fighting to heal. Stacy immediately came over, giving me some ice, and had me lie down, taking pressure off that side, while she examined me.

I groaned as she moved my leg in different ways and closed my eyes to try and take my mind off the pain. The moment she finished I lay there for a moment then opened my eyes to see Lorelai, watching us. She softly smiled at me and then came in, cautiously approaching me.

"Are you okay?" she questioned, placing her hand on my cheek and looking down into my eyes. She then bent down and kissed me gently on the lips before whispering to Stacy to leave us for a few moments.

"Not really. I lost my shit out there." I said, running my fingers through my hair.

"That you did. I saw it all on the screen in my office. So, I figured I'd come down here and see how you were."

"It's just everything with the gossip blogs and the articles got inside my head. Right before the game I found out the largest deal I've ever signed wanted to hold off, to make sure I am the ideal representative for their brand."

Lorelai studied me for a moment before she bent down and met my lips with the softest of kisses. As she pulled away from me, I caught this unsettling look in her eyes.

"It will all blow over. Just give it time," she whispered against my lips. "Now, let's look at this hip."

I lay there as she examined me as well, feeling uneasy about the look I'd caught in her eyes, her words said one thing, but that look said something completely different.

AFTER SHE DID a little work on my hip, I hobbled to the locker room where I showered and changed, then I met her outside in my car. We both climbed in, and I drove over to her place.

She'd been quiet the entire drive there, including the elevator ride up to her condo. She unlocked the door, and we stepped inside where she flipped on the lights over the island in the kitchen.

"Want anything to eat or drink?" she questioned, opening the fridge and looking inside.

I didn't want anything to eat or drink. I wanted her in my arms, so I went to make my way over to her, but she shut the fridge door and slipped out of my grasp, moving over to the pantry and opening it, looking for something to eat there.

I took a couple steps and went to grab her hips, only she once again slipped from my grasp, going to the opposite side of the kitchen opening the cupboards.

"Is something wrong?" I questioned, clearing my throat.

"Nope. Crackers?" she asked, pulling down a box from the cupboard.

I shook my head and studied her eyes.

"What is it?"

"Nothing." She shrugged, shoving a cracker into her mouth.

I made my way over to her only to have her move to another spot in the small kitchen.

"If it's nothing, why won't you let me near you."

She avoided my eyes, looking down at the floor.

"Lorelai, what is it?" A knot was forming in my stomach.

She looked up at me, tears in her eyes, and shook her head, still refusing to tell me.

I wasn't sure if I should go to her or stay where I was, so I followed my gut, not moving, waiting for her to tell me what the problem was.

Tear-filled eyes stared back at me. "I think it's time we take…" She inhaled deeply, wiping her eyes. "A break from each other."

Her bottom lip trembled as she looked at me, and my stomach twisted in knots. I didn't want this, not in the slightest. I did my best to calm myself.

"Why is that?"

"You know why."

"I don't."

"Look at everything that is going on. Our names are being smeared all over the front page of every sports blog, magazine, and app there is because of me. You are losing contracts because of me," she said, pointing to her chest, her breathing uneven.

"It's not because of you," I answered.

"Yes, it is. If it weren't for me, you wouldn't face

losing these contracts. Your name wouldn't be smeared."

"First, I'm a big boy, I can handle it. Second, it's not because of you. It's your ex-boyfriend. Not you."

"He may have caused it, but I am the one who caused everything else. If it hadn't of been for my breakdown on the plane to Hawaii, we'd never be involved, which again, is because of me and my inability to stand up for myself."

I wasn't losing her. I also wasn't going to stand here and listen to her completely belittle herself and blame herself for someone else's doing. This was ridiculous. I pushed myself off the counter and made my way over to her, pulling her into my arms.

"I think for tonight, we should just head down the hall, crawl into bed together, and go to sleep, look at everything with fresh eyes in the morning."

When she didn't wrap her arms around me, I knew she'd decided. She was done. There wasn't anything I was going to say or do to change her mind, either.

"I think it's better if you just leave," she said, her voice shaking. She pushed herself out of my arms and stood there staring at me.

Fuck, this wasn't what I wanted. This wasn't why I'd shared with her what had happened tonight, for her to blame herself more. Yet this was the result of that.

I'd made her feel like it was her fault, when that wasn't what I was saying.

"If that is what you want, then fine."

She started to sob. "It is."

I backed away from her and grabbed my keys off the counter. I opened the door to her condo but before leaving I turned and looked at her tear-stained face one more time, before I slipped into the hallway and closed the door behind me. I stood there in the hallway, listening to her sobs, then turned and walked down the hall with my head down. I hit the button for the elevator and stood there waiting. When the door opened, I was about to step inside when I heard Dylan's voice.

"Where the hell are you going?" he questioned.

I looked up to see both Aurora and Dylan standing there, looking at me, confusion on their faces.

"She wants to take a break," I muttered, my heart feeling like it was going to break into a million pieces any second. I'd never felt like this before, and I knew I had to get out of here before it happened.

"What?" Aurora questioned, glancing down the hall toward their unit. "What do you mean?"

"Don't worry about it, if she needs a break that's fine. I'm heading home. I'm going to give her some space and see how it all pans out."

I stepped into the elevator and hit the lobby button,

putting on what I imagined was a real smile, when in fact it was probably pitiful, as both Aurora and Dylan watched me. When I got downstairs, I felt my phone vibrate in my pocket, and without looking at the message that was left, I turned the power off, climbed into my car, and made my way home.

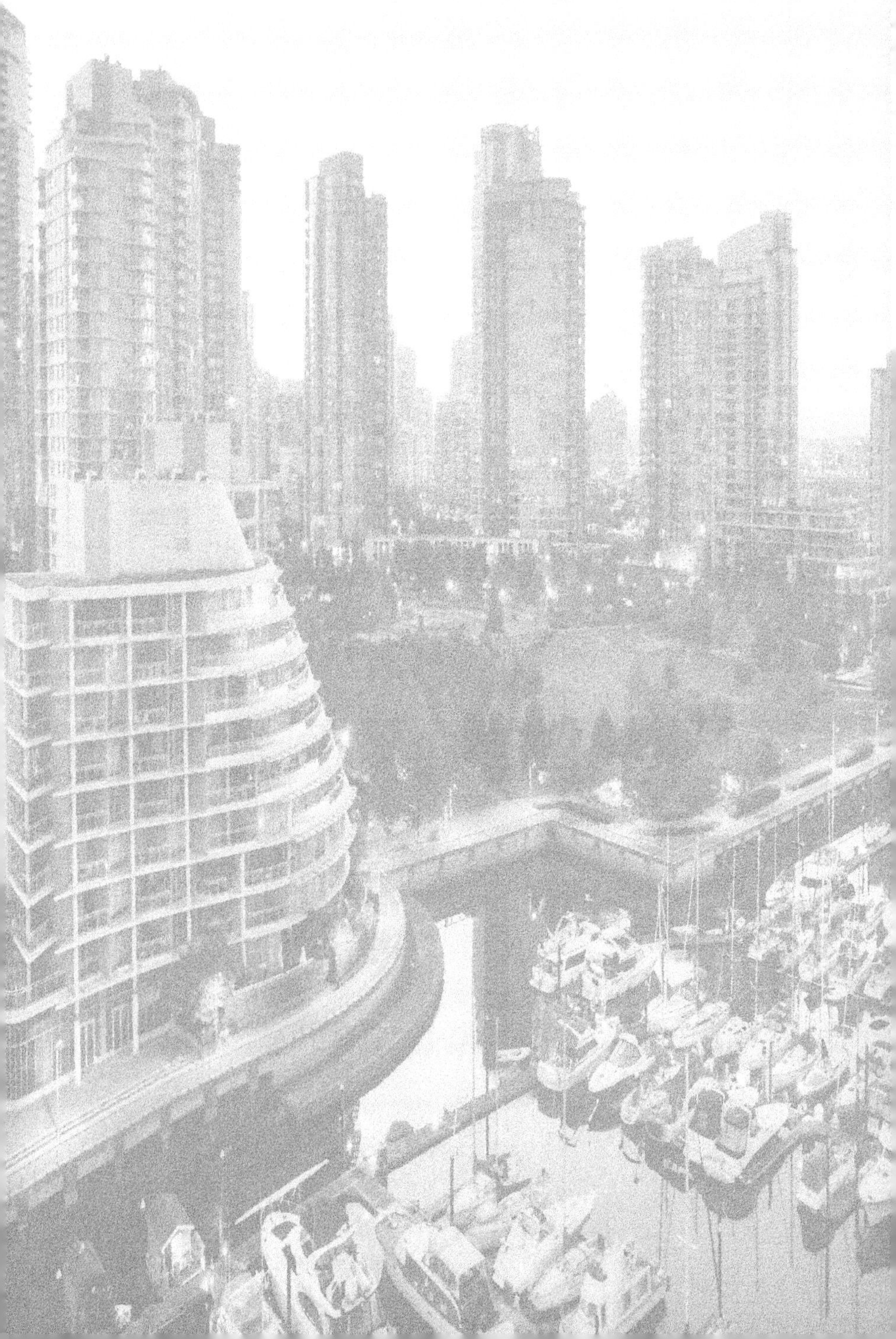

Chapter 16

Lorelai - 1 Week Later

I SAT in the living room watching TV, drowning my sorrows in the remaining pint of Ben and Jerry's ice cream, when Aurora came into the living room.

"Really? Is this all you've done today?" she asked, looking around at the dark room with disgust.

I'd called in sick for the entire week. The place was a disaster with pillows and blankets all over the floor. The kitchen was piled with dirty dishes; I hadn't done laundry or showered in days. I looked around. "What?"

"Knox called again, and he asked about you yesterday at work."

Ignoring what she'd just said, I shoved my spoon back into the container and scooped out more ice cream.

"You haven't gotten dressed or showered in days. This room hasn't seen sunlight in about as long, and this place is like a dungeon," she said, bending down and picking up the pillows off the floor before making her way over to the window and opening the blinds.

"Hey!" I yelled as the bright light from the sun hurt my eyes.

"I've had enough. You can't continue this. Why don't you call him back?"

My eyes burned with tears. "I told you to tell him to leave me alone."

"I'm not telling him. If you want to tell him that, go ahead. Just remember you chose this," she said, putting her hands on her hips and staring at me.

I got up and pulled the blinds shut again before looking at her.

"Look, I can do what I want. You go to work, spend all your time with Dylan, do what you want to do," I said, flopping back down and picking up the container of ice cream.

"What I want is to have my friend back!" Aurora said, staring at me, waiting for some sort of reaction. When I didn't give her one, she came around and stood in front of the TV. "Have you even tried to contact him?"

I dropped my spoon into the container with force and looked at her, my eyes burning with tears at her question.

"You haven't, have you?" she asked.

"We aren't talking about him. I've told you to tell him to stop asking about me, to stop thinking about me. I'm not good for him."

"Oh no. We are talking about him. I've also told you I'm not being your voice." She bent down and grabbed the remote, shutting off the TV. "I'm done. You have been unbearable. You ended it with him and look at what it has caused. This place is a mess, and you stink."

"I did what I had to do. Now let me wallow in my own self-pity."

"Oh my god, you are impossible. You didn't have to do it. You are being ridiculous over the entire thing. The articles have been retracted. If you had been at work one day over the past week, you'd have gotten your emails and know that the PR team has lined you up for interviews to clear your name. Hugo retracted everything."

"It still doesn't matter. The damage has been done, and it's damage I have caused, just like I have caused with each relationship I've had. I'm always the cause."

"Are you serious right now?" Aurora questioned, placing her hands on her hips.

I nodded. "I am."

"How on earth do you think you caused the end of your relationship with Hugo?"

I shrugged. "Probably didn't give him enough attention."

"What about Bill?"

Bill and I never had an ounce of anything in common. It was a brief relationship which simply faded away. There hadn't been a cause at all. I looked at her and shrugged.

"Maybe I should have been more interested in his stupid cars."

"Oh my god, get over it already. Lorelai, the only relationship you are the cause of ending is this one. The man adores you, he'd do anything for you, I'd even put money on it that he is in love with you, and here you are treating him this way…why?"

"He loves me? That is funny. Do you realize that aside from you and Dylan, Lucas and Clay, no one knows about us? The other players, he hasn't even mentioned it in interviews."

"So, most of them are that way. Remember how long it took Phil before he mentioned Candace?"

"That was different."

"How?"

"Candace didn't bring all the adverse publicity to him. My ex-boyfriend and my past are ruining his career, and I can't be the one to do that. It's better if we part ways."

It was the way I'd felt when he looked at me the night in the treatment room and as he stood here in the kitchen. However, the more I thought about it, the more I missed him, the more I realized I'd made a huge mistake. I wanted to be with him more than anything, and as things started to settle and return to this new normal, the more foolish I'd felt. So much, in fact, I'd made myself sick every morning for the past week knowing what I'd lost.

Aurora stood there looking at me, then she shook her head. "If you believe that, you are crazy. You didn't tell Hugo to take out that article. He did it because he is an awful person. So, if that is the case, then perhaps I shouldn't be dating Dylan then either."

I frowned. "Why is that?"

"Well, he doesn't speak with his father anymore. I caused that, so perhaps it's time I tell him to take a hike."

"What are you saying?" I questioned, sitting forward, feeling the world spin out of control at the thought that my best friend would give up something so wonderful for her.

She pulled her phone from her pocket and texted.

"What are you doing?" I asked again, trying to grab her phone.

"Texting Dylan. Telling him we're over. I can't have him not speaking with his father because of me," she said. "It will just lead to more problems down the road when he realizes what a mistake he's made."

"Don't you dare. I'm going to text him and tell him to ignore your messages," I said, looking around for my phone.

"Stay out of it, Lorelai," she said, as she feverishly typed away.

"Aurora, stop it. This will just be something else I have to add to my list of what I've done."

"What you've done? Nope, this is all on me. I had the one-night stand, he ended up being my stepbrother, and even though our parents split, Dylan still doesn't speak with him, all because of me."

"He did that. Not you. Why would you even consider doing something like this when he makes you so happy," I begged, still watching as she continued typing.

"Because I can." She shrugged. "There…finished, now to send it."

I got up and grabbed her phone from her hands, stopping her from making the dumbest mistake she could ever make. "I won't let you do it!" I screamed.

"It's my decision," she said, reaching for her phone,

only I pulled it back out of her reach. "Just like it was your decision to end things with Knox."

I shook my head, not believing what she was planning to do. She couldn't end things with Dylan. I turned my back to her and looked down at her screen. I'd planned to change every word she'd written, only when I began reading what she'd written, I found nothing, it was a pile of nonsense written in the body of an email. I turned and looked over my shoulder at her.

"This doesn't even make any sense," I said.

"Yep, you are right. It doesn't." She shrugged. "None of it."

I looked back down at her screen. "Why would you…"

"To prove what an ass you are being," she said, going over and opening the blinds, then grabbing my ice cream and some of my dirty dishes and heading into the kitchen. "You can't control what others do, Lorelai. You are not the cause of your relationships ending, nor are you the reason behind any of the shit that has gone on in the media. Stop blaming yourself for things out of your control."

"I can't help it. It just seems people always get hurt when they get involved with me."

"The only person I see getting hurt is you," Aurora

said. "Don't help it. Call him. Make yourself happy for once, because you aren't happy."

She pulled me into her and hugged me tight. She was right; I was being ridiculous. I was the only one hurting myself by blaming myself for everyone else's actions. "I hate that you are right. I know ending things with Knox wasn't my finest hour."

"Well then make today your best hour and go call him." Aurora said, giving me one more hug before letting me go.

I smiled. "Thank you. Leave all this. I'll clean everything up," I murmured. "I have a phone call to make first."

"Go get him!" Aurora yelled as I made my way down the hall to my room.

Two weeks later

I STOOD in front of my bedroom mirror. I'd chosen a champagne-coloured dress for the Dominator's benefit gala tonight for Kids' Cancer Research.

"I think these shoes will go better," Aurora said, coming in with a pair of heels.

"Oh goodness, I don't know." I looked down at the black five-inch heels in her hand.

"Seriously, just try them on. Dylan loves these shoes. I'm sure Knox will feel the same way," Aurora said, smiling up at me.

I knew the look on her face. She'd turned into a sex maniac after she got together with Dylan, and I really didn't want to know anything about what had gone on with those shoes.

"Okay, fine. I'll try them on, but please, spare me the details," I said, grabbing one and slipping my foot into it, followed by the other.

"What details. He just really likes it when I wear them while—"

"Uhhhh…what part of I don't want the details did you miss?" I laughed, looking over at my friend's mischievous smile.

Aurora laughed, then gave me a once-over when I stood up. "Those are perfect."

"You girls ready to go?" we heard Dylan call from down the hall.

"I think I am going to have to request they give us our key back," I said, rolling my eyes as I grabbed my matching clutch from my dresser and carefully walked down the carpeted hall.

"We are ready," Aurora said.

I'd just come around the corner and caught sight

of Knox dressed in an all-black, perfectly tailored suit. I softly smiled and made my way over to him, placing a kiss on his lips.

The last two weeks had been perfect. I'd been so afraid to contact him that afternoon, but soon my fears were eased. He'd come to me the moment he finished practice, and we'd barely parted until he had to leave for a set of away games.

"Don't you look fucking hot," he said, taking my hand while I did a full spin.

"Thank you, as do you," I said, meeting his lips once more.

"Now, before we head out. The two of you are good, right?" Dylan questioned, looking over at us.

I nodded and then glanced at Knox.

"Knox?" Dylan asked. "We don't need some major fight or argument tonight. That goes for you too, Lorelai."

"Yeah, we're good. Things have blown over with the media, and with us. Tonight, it's all about appearances and making people aware that we are in love. Something that should have happened ages ago," he said, wrapping his arm around me, pulling me back against him and kissing the side of my neck. "We should go, before I peel this dress off you and make you mine again," he whispered in my ear.

Excitement flooded me at the thought. We'd made up for the lost time over the last couple of weeks.

"We need to go." I giggled, taking his hand and leading him to the door.

WE'D HAD dinner and had been mingling around for the past two hours. Knox had given a couple of interviews on the advice of the PR team, and now we could enjoy the rest of the night. He led me out onto the dance floor where he pulled me into his arms. I closed my eyes and rested my head against his chest.

It had been a bad four weeks. The only thing I was grateful for was the fact that, with everything that had gone on, we'd become stronger.

"You doing okay?" he asked me quietly.

I nodded, snuggling against him. "I am trying. I'm still really mad about everything, but I'm working on letting it go."

"We are going to have to let it go," he whispered, placing a kiss on my forehead.

"He is just such a piece of shit. One that I actually thought was good for me."

Knox held me tighter. "Listen, we all make mistakes in our lives. We enter into relationships that we think are healthy. Then something happens and we find out that the person we thought they were is the exact opposite of who they truly are. It's not your fault."

I looked up at him and smiled softly. "I know. I'm just happy that you gave me a second chance."

"Second chance? Babe, I never let go of the first chance." He twirled me around the dance floor, making me smile as he pulled me into him.

"You about done with tonight?" he questioned.

I nodded. "Very much so. The pictures, the watching eyes. I'm over it already."

Knox chuckled as he pulled me closer to him.

"Honestly, I don't know how you do it every day." I sighed. "It's exhausting."

"Well then, what do you say to getting out of here?" he asked just as the song ended.

"Will we be missed or needed for anything else?" I questioned.

"Nope, I already told Pamela I was at my interview quota for tonight, so even if they wanted to ask me a question, they can't."

I looked over at Dylan and Aurora, who swayed to the song that had just started. She had her eyes closed as they danced together.

"Do you think we should let Dylan and Aurora know, or Lucas and Clay?"

He chuckled. "Dylan and Aurora look perfectly comfortable together. Lucas is off talking with some other guys, and Clay, well I saw him leave with some girl over twenty-five minutes ago."

I giggled. "Did it look serious?"

Knox let out a laugh. "Clay serious about a woman? I highly doubt it. He'll be serious for tonight. Tomorrow he won't even remember her name."

I slid my hand in his as I laughed at what he said and followed him out of the event area. We made our way to his car where he opened the door for me and waited for me to get in before closing my door and making his way around to the driver's side. Once in, he buckled up and started the engine.

WE'D STOPPED on the way home and grabbed a couple slices of pizza, and now, an hour later, we sat on the floor in his living room, him in a pair of shorts and me in one of his T-shirts, surrounded by pillows and blankets, each of us eating the last bite of our pizza.

He rested his head on his hand and watched as I wiped my mouth with a napkin before taking a drink.

"Can we talk about something?"

"Sure. What would you like to talk about?"

"Life, us."

I nodded, beginning to feel a little uneasy. The last few weeks hadn't been easy, and even after we'd made up, I worried this was coming.

"Okay, so what about life?" I questioned.

"Well, where do you see yourself in, oh, say, five years?"

I thought for a moment. "Um, I think I'd like to own my own place by then. Don't tell Aurora that, by the way. I think she thinks we are going to be roommates forever." I giggled.

"Okay, noted," he said, winking at me. "Cross my heart."

I smiled. "I'd also like to get married one day. Have a couple of kids, a dog, and a house over off the water and surrounded by nature."

"Not in the city?" he questioned.

"No, I still want to be close to it, but I don't want to be in it like I am now."

"Makes sense."

"What about you?" I questioned.

"I gave it some thought the other day and I want the same thing. It's taken me time to realize that I want a family. I always thought that because my job demands most of my time, that it wouldn't be something that was in the cards for me. However, now I know that's not a reason to not follow through with that want. It will be hard for them, but it will be as equally hard on me," he said, meeting my eyes.

"Just so you know, I've never found you to be unattentive, here or when you are away. You give everything you have. Whoever the woman is who ends up with you, she will be one lucky lady. I could only ever hope to have someone like you as my forever."

I swallowed hard. I had no clue how much further he wanted to take things with me, and I didn't want to assume I'd be his forever. Again, all I could do was hope.

Knox shifted and stretched his legs out in front of him, then turned to me.

"Where do you see this going?" He questioned, taking a drink of his water.

"What?"

He was silent for a moment, then met my eyes.

"Us?"

I thought for a moment before responding. I knew where I wanted it to go but was not sure about his feelings.

"Just be honest with me," he said, reaching out and

taking my hand in his. "Don't be afraid of telling me to take a hike." He winked.

Almost immediately, my heart felt like it might burst. Don't be afraid to tell him to take a hike? What was that? Was Knox feeling vulnerable right now? If so, this was a side of him I'd never seen before.

"I'm wanting to take things further with you," I said, swallowing hard, feeling that fluttery feeling in my stomach as the words settled between us.

He nodded, his blue eyes locking with mine.

"What about you?" My voice shook as I asked him because all I could think about was the night I'd turned him away and told him we were over.

He exhaled before he began. "Lorelai, my feelings for you have grown faster than I'd imagined, and I think it's time that we take this to a more serious level, if that is what you are asking me," he said, still holding my hand in his.

My eyes burned with the tears of happiness that were forming. Here I thought he was going to tell me to take a hike, or that perhaps he really wanted to end things with me, especially after he told me not to be afraid to tell him to go away. Yet here he sat, telling me he wanted to take things further with me.

Almost immediately, I got on my knees and straddled his lap, meeting his lips in a frantic yet passionate kiss. As his tongue washed through my mouth and his arms wrapped around me, I knew in that moment that here in his arms was exactly where I wanted to be.

"My mom and my sister are coming into town for the weekend. I want you to meet them," he said as he held me.

"I'd love to," I said, meeting his lips again.

"You know what I'd also love?" he asked.

"What's that?"

"You, in my bed, now," he whispered, between kisses.

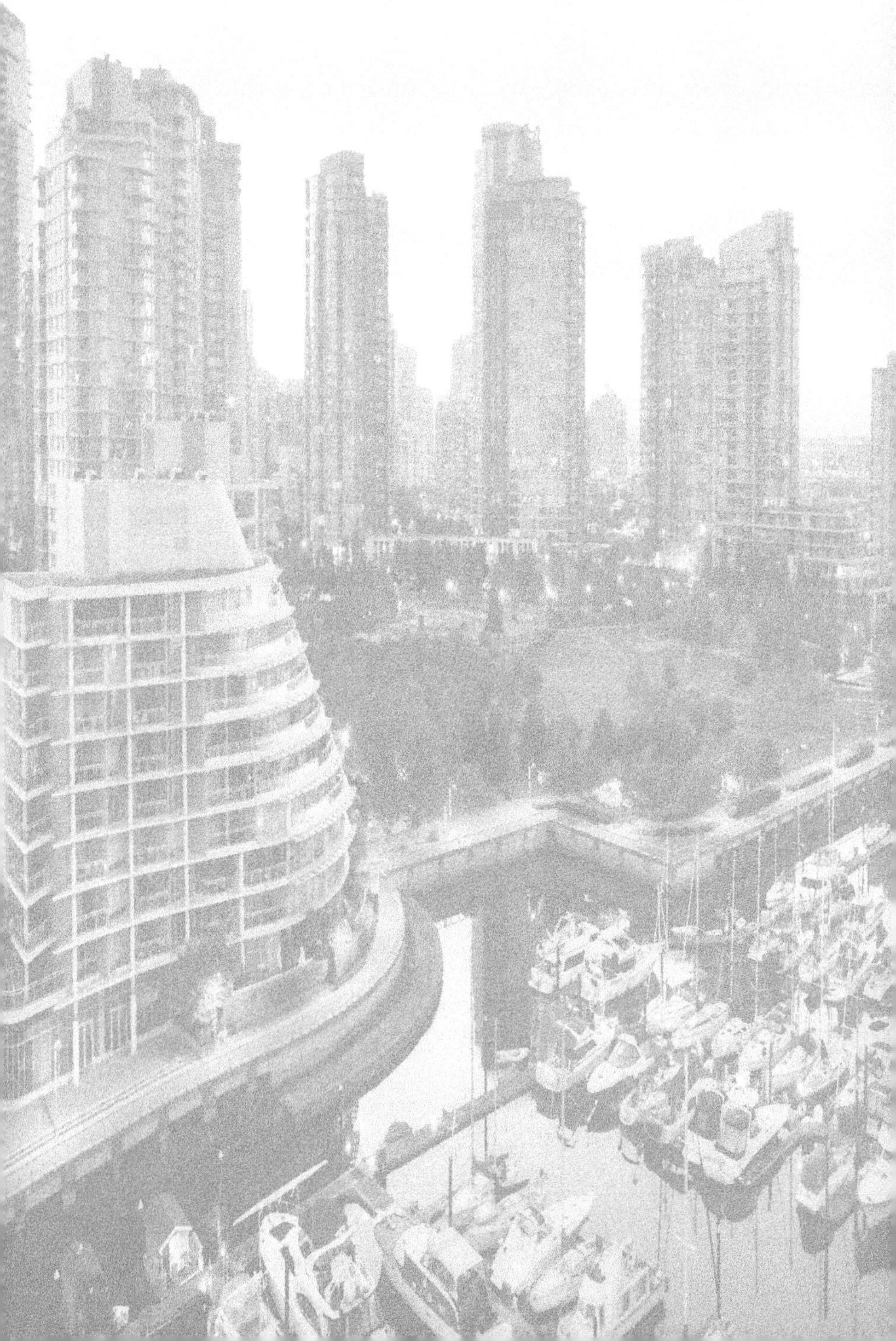

Chapter 17

Knox

LORELAI WAS SUPPOSED to come with me to pick my mom and sister up from the airport, but at the last second, she'd gotten a call from Candace who needed help with something. She hadn't divulged what it was, she just said it was important. So, after I dropped her off, I headed toward the airport and had just pulled up outside when I saw my mom and sister waiting. I climbed out of the car and waved.

"Hey, Mom! Peyton!" I yelled.

They looked over and waved, then made their way to the car. I hugged them both, then threw their luggage into the trunk of my car while they hopped in.

"How was the flight?" I questioned as I pulled away from the curb and headed back toward home.

"Fine."

"It wasn't fine, Mother. It was hell."

I glanced in my rearview mirror at Peyton. "Did something happen?" I questioned.

"Nothing happened, Knox. Peyton is just being Peyton."

Peyton was only twenty-one, thirteen years younger than me, and my half-sister. After my mother and father split, my mother stayed single for a long time and then got involved with an asshole of a man. She got pregnant and he split.

"Mother, please," Peyton whined.

"How's school?" I questioned, not wanting to listen to her whine anymore.

I knew my mother could never afford to send Peyton to university, so I'd paid for her to go. Mom worked a full-time job but struggled each month to make ends meet, so along with paying for Peyton's schooling, I also sent money home monthly to make things a little easier for her. It wasn't something I told people. Hell, the guys on the team didn't even know, but it was my way of giving back to her. She'd sacrificed so much for me when I was growing up. It was the least I could do.

"Tell him," my mother said from the front seat.

I glanced in the rearview mirror again to see Peyton glaring at my mother. "What do you need to tell me?" I questioned, putting my eyes back on the road.

"It's nothing," Peyton mumbled.

"Peyton, you promised."

"Fine. Fine. I've had some problems with my professors and, well, last week…"

"Last week what?" I barked.

Peyton got quiet in the back seat, and I looked over at my mother to see her watching me.

"They kicked her out of school. I'm at the end of my rope with her, Knox. I don't know what to do anymore."

I pulled into my driveway and got out of the car. I had nothing to say now, especially not to Peyton. She'd always been irresponsible. I grabbed the bags from the back of the car and carried them to the front door.

"Knox, say something," Peyton said as she stepped up beside me while I unlocked the front door.

"I have nothing to say to you right now," I gritted, opening the door and stepping inside. "Peyton, you know where you normally stay. Take your bags," I muttered, grabbing Mom's bag and taking it down to the second guest room. "Get settled, then we will head out for breakfast. I need to go cool off," I said, running my fingers through my hair.

MOM and I sat on a bench outside one of the stores Peyton wanted to go into. I took a drink of water while Mom sipped on her iced cap.

"I'm at a loss, Knox. I should have told you before we came out here, but she's out of control. She got involved with this guy, and the moment it happened, all hell broke loose."

Peyton had always been impressionable. She'd gotten involved with a bad crew in her last year of high school. The school year ended with her not graduating and having to spend her entire summer taking classes to graduate.

"What do you think you want to do about it?" I questioned.

"Well, the school refuses to take her back. She didn't even want to come on this trip, to be honest, but I forced her. I figured getting her away from Tor might be the best thing."

"Tor?" I asked.

"Yep, that's his name."

I shook my head and watched Peyton from where I sat. She was an attractive girl, smart, and I knew if she only took things a little more seriously and focused on school, she'd do well for herself. However, she also needed to do a lot of growing up.

"Leave it with me, let me sleep on it. I'll figure something out," I muttered as Peyton came out of the store and made her way over to us.

"So, where is your girlfriend?" Peyton questioned, sitting down beside me.

"Yes, I've been wanting to meet her," my mother said, smiling at me. "Why isn't she here with us now?"

I chuckled. "Her sister-in-law needed help with something. Plus, I think she might've been a little nervous about meeting you. She said she wasn't, but I think she was just saying that. Our relationship has been tested over the last bit, and I didn't want to overwhelm her."

"Well, that is a pile of crap," Peyton said, looking my way.

I frowned. "What?"

"It's crap and you know it. You went to high school with her and her brother. You play on the same team as he does."

My mother looked at me. "Is that true?"

I let out the breath I was holding and tried to come up with a way to explain things. "Look, it's true, but it's a difficult thing to discuss. Things are good, I adore her, and our relationship is finally in an amazing place. You will meet her while you are here."

Peyton scoffed.

"What?" I questioned, growing annoyed as I turned my attention to her.

"What about all the gossip blogs?" she questioned. "Is what they are saying true?"

"What part?" I questioned, not sure what was going to come out of her mouth next.

"The attack."

"Attack?" my mother questioned, putting her hand on her chest.

"A fan attacked her at the end of a game. It was horrible, but everything was taken care of. She is fine."

"I don't know how you put up with all this, Knox. I really don't. How horrible it must have been for her."

"It was, but I promise you she is fine."

"What about the part that she's a cheater?" Peyton questioned.

When I looked over at her, I saw the same smirk on her face that she'd had in the car. I seriously wanted to wipe it off her face. How dare she bring this up? I knew my mother didn't read gossip blogs, but I should have known Peyton would be all up in that.

"Don't believe what you read in that trash," I said.

"Well, they say that you don't fall very far from that path yourself."

"Peyton!" my mother exclaimed. "That is enough."

Anger flooded my body. I may have had fun over

the years with different women, but I wasn't and never had been a cheater; it wasn't in my blood. I'd seen what it had done to my father and mother, and I swore that when I saw the hurt it had caused my mother I'd never be the same sort of man.

"Look here," I said, turning toward Peyton, ready to grab hold of her.

"Whoa, calm down there, so uptight." Peyton smirked again. "I was joking."

"Peyton, it's enough," my mother scolded.

"It's enough," she mimicked.

I turned to my mother, ignoring Peyton completely. "Lorelai has done nothing of the sort. Don't worry, it was a report to the blogs to get back at me."

"Who would have done something like that to you?" My mother frowned.

"I'll be back in a moment," Peyton mumbled.

I was glad she'd taken off into the store. I didn't want to divulge this to her just yet. Something was off about her, her behaviour. Never had she acted this way when she'd visited. I suspected my mother was right, this Tor person had gotten into her head.

"Knox, are you going to answer me?"

I turned and looked at my mother and smiled. "Mom, I'm telling you this in confidence. It was her ex."

"What on earth? Knox, did you get in between the

two of them?" my mother questioned, looking at me with disappointment.

"No, Mom. They were over long before we got involved. He's just a bitter man."

"I see. He must be to do something so hurtful. Have you told her you love her yet?"

I knew my mother knew I loved her, and I'd been prepared for her to ask me this question, she'd always been able to read me like a book. I looked at my mother, who was waiting for my answer, and shook my head.

"I'm in love with her, Mom, but I haven't told her yet."

"Ahhhh…" she said, grabbing me and pulling me in for a hug. "I knew it. I think it's about time you tell her."

Yeah, it was, she was right. Now I just needed to figure out how to tell her.

I wrapped my arms around my mother, and that was when the alarm went off in the store Peyton had gone into. Mom and I both looked up to see Peyton rushing our way.

"We've got to get out of here, now!" she said through clenched teeth.

Mom looked panicked. However, I didn't move. I grabbed Peyton by the shirt and held her there, looking directly into her eyes.

"What have you done?" I growled as security came around the corner and approached us.

I LAY IN BED, the house quiet, trying to de-stress after the day I'd had. After the alarms had gone off and Peyton had wanted to flee, I'd refused. I'd grabbed hold of her and waited until security arrived. She'd tried to lift a pocketful of makeup, along with some jewelry.

After everything, we'd come home, and she'd spent the rest of the night in her room. I didn't want to see her, and my mother was so disappointed she'd spent the evening in tears. I'd felt bad, but I'd done what needed to be done by making her stay and face the consequences, she needed to own up to her mistakes, and if this was the way it had to be done, I was glad to do it.

My phone vibrated on the bed. I let out a sigh as I picked it up and looked at the screen to see Lorelai had messaged. For the first time in hours, a smile came to my lips.

KNOX: Hey

> LORELAI: How are things going? Thought I'd give you a little time with your mom and sister, how are things going?

I stared at the phone. How I wished she was here with me right now.

> KNOX: Not going well.

> LORELAI: What do you mean? Is it your mom?

> KNOX: No. It's Peyton. She got kicked out of school and today she shoplifted.

> LORELAI: WHAT? Oh my god, Knox.

> KNOX: Tell me about it. I had to stand there, hold on to her and let security have at her just to teach her a lesson.

I didn't want to paint my sister as some sort of criminal, but I needed to talk about it.

> KNOX: It was awful. I had to stand there and listen to her cry, beg and plead for help. My mom is a mess and doesn't know what to do with her. Apparently, she is involved with some guy my mom doesn't like and he is turning her life upside down.

LORELAI: Sounds like you did the right thing. Sounds like maybe she needs someone like you right now.

KNOX: I hope you are right, because I feel like she is never going to talk to me again.

LORELAI: She will appreciate it one day. As for the bad news guy, she'll outgrow that too.

KNOX: Doesn't feel that way right now.

LORELAI: I know.

KNOX: How is everything with Candace?

LORELAI: Okay. Her and Phil had a huge fight, she just wanted someone to talk to.

KNOX: You staying there tonight?

LORELAI: Yeah, I don't want to leave her. Which means I'll probably be late for dinner tomorrow night.

I tapped the edge of my phone. It was the last day I had with my mom and sister, and given the situation, I wasn't sure it was wise for Lorelai to meet them right now. I wanted them to meet under better circumstances—when my mom wasn't a mess, and my sister wasn't trouble.

> KNOX: Don't take this the wrong way, but how about you meet them next time? They will be back for Christmas. Plus, Candace needs you.

I waited as she typed her response, watching those three dots appear and disappear, then appear again.

> LORELAI: Don't worry about me. We will meet up with your mom and sister another time. Right now, it's important you are together and work through whatever is going on. I understand and want you to know I'm thinking of you.

My heart almost burst at her answer. I'd never had a woman I was dating to understand any family issue I'd had. She was the first one ever to understand that my family was important to me. She also knew it was important for me to be with my mom and sister.

> KNOX: Thanks babe, see you soon. Night.

> LORELAI: Night Knox.

I COULDN'T BELIEVE the weekend was over already. We stood just outside the airport, my mother hugging me tightly.

"I'll see you at Christmas."

"I know, Mom. I look forward to it," I said, pressing a kiss to her forehead.

As she pulled away and blew her nose, I turned to my sister.

"Peyton, don't hate me," I said, wanting her to speak to me at least one more time before they got on the plane. I'd heard her sneak out last night, and I'd seen the lights from the cab she'd taken pull into the driveway when she returned. I had watched from the crack through my bedroom door as she staggered down the hall and fell into bed. She was clearly on a path of destruction, and I hoped it would end before it got more serious. When my mother had mentioned her being so tired this morning, she'd looked my way as if she knew I'd seen her, but I didn't let on.

"Thanks for nothing," she said.

I shook my head. "Peyton, one day you will thank me."

"Don't think so," she said, turning to our mother.

"Mom, I'm not coming back at Christmas. I don't want to see him ever again."

"Peyton, it's enough," my mother said, looking at me, seeing the disappointment in my eyes.

"No, it's fine. If she would rather be with Tor, shoplifting and getting into trouble, that is fine."

Peyton grabbed her bags and made her way inside the airport, leaving me and my mother outside. She placed her hand on my cheek and looked at me.

"I'll deal with her, don't you worry. I can't wait to meet Lorelai, and I cannot wait to see you at Christmas. Good luck with the finals. I love you."

"Love you too, Mom. Just watch her, and if you need me, call me."

"I will."

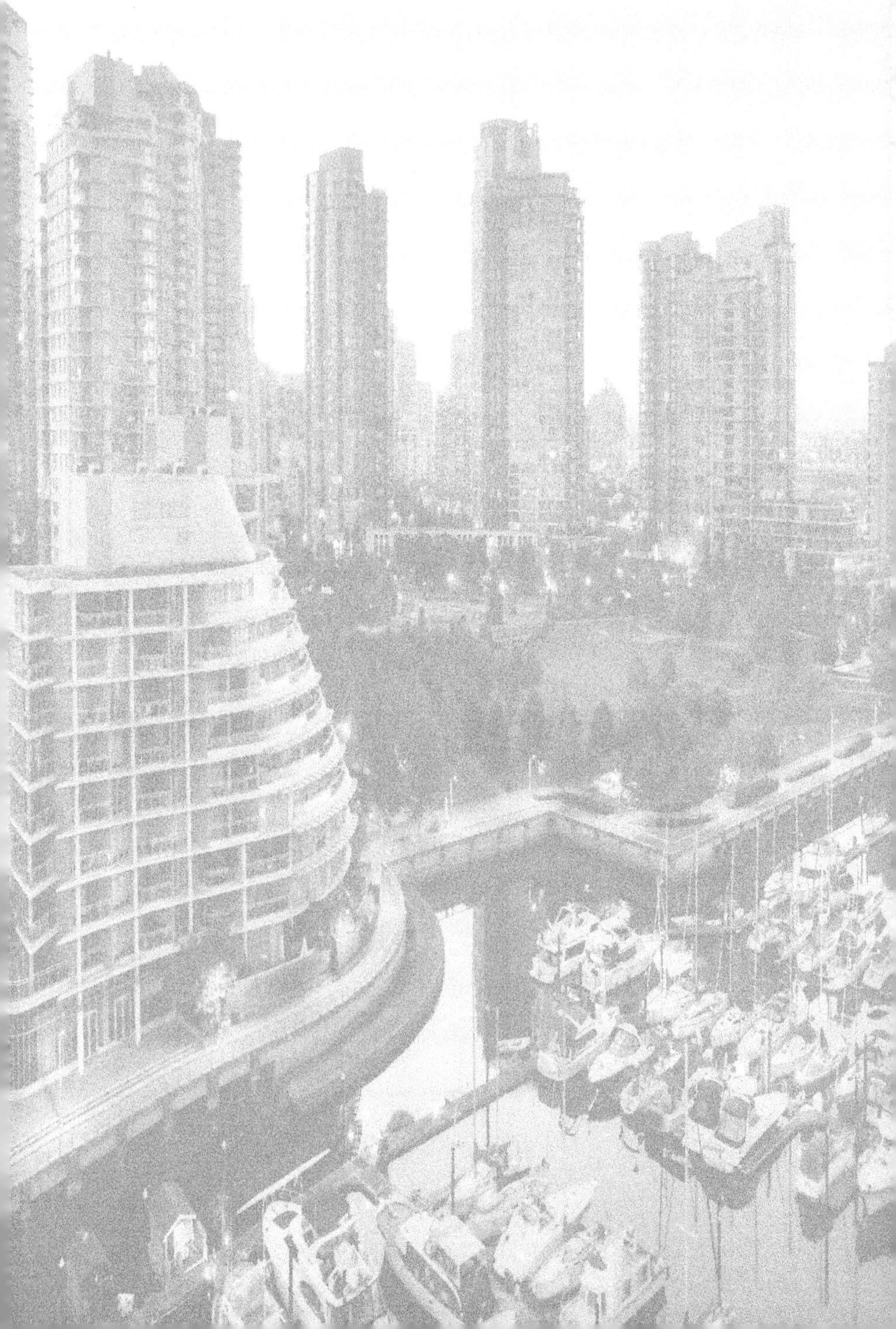

Chapter 18

Lorelai

I SAT in the lounge at the arena waiting for Joanna, head of PR, to come and get me for the interview I'd promised I'd give to set the story straight about the cheating. I had no choice; I needed to clear Knox's name and my own and should have given this interview weeks ago. However, now was a good time too.

I'd just grabbed a cola from the fridge and sat down, flipping the television on, when my phone vibrated. I glanced at the screen, happy to see Knox's name.

> Lorelai: Hey babe. How are things?

Knox: Okay now, everyone is finally on their way home.

Lorelai: I'm sorry the visit didn't go as planned.

I'd decided to give him space with his mom and sister after everything that had happened while she was here. I'd hoped things would be repaired by the time they left today.

Knox: It's okay. I just felt bad. I really wanted you to meet my mom.

Lorelai: There is always next time, like we discussed.

Knox: Dare I say, I'm embarrassed by my sister's behaviour.

Lorelai: We all make mistakes Knox. She'll grow out of it.

Knox: I doubt it. She is on a collision course. I just fear that the next collision will be one lesson that can't be fixed easily

Lorelai: Let's hope not.

Knox: Have you had the interview yet? How did it go?

> Lorelai: Have not had it yet. Joanna should be here shortly.

> Knox: Okay. I'll meet you at your place in a couple of hours.

> Lorelai: I'll be ready and waiting. I've missed you.

> Knox: Missed you too and thank you for being so understanding.

> Lorelai: No problem, just wanted to give you the space you needed.

It was then the door to the lounge opened and Joanna walked in. "Lorelai, you ready?"

I smiled. "I am."

"Let's do this, shall we."

I got up off the couch, pocketed my phone, and followed Joanna down the hall to her office.

"I'm a little nervous. I've never done this before."

She smiled. "It's okay. It's easy really. I have all the questions they are going to ask right here on this sheet. So, all you need to do is answer them, and if they try to ask something that isn't on this sheet, you just decline to answer."

She slid the piece of paper over to me and I glanced at it, trying to read everything. Was this what Knox and the guys went through every interview? My stomach turned. What happened if I made a mistake, or if I panicked and couldn't find the question on the paper and declined to answer one question that was on the sheet?

"Ready?"

I swallowed hard. "Can I ask you one question before we get started?"

"Of course." She smiled.

"What if I make a mistake and accidentally decline to answer a question on the sheet?"

Joanna smiled. "I'm going to be right here the entire time. You have nothing to worry about. Plus, you are having an interview with someone who I know personally. There is no worry about any funny stuff. Just relax and be yourself."

I closed my eyes and took a deep breath as she dialed the phone. In a matter of minutes, questions were being asked and then the real question poured in.

"So, Lorelai, tell me what happened between you and your ex."

"He cheated on me in our shared home."

"How horrible for you. What happened? How did you find out?"

"I'd been staying with my best friend Aurora while we were in school in Victoria. Hugo and I had plans on moving in together once I'd graduated. I'd come home during the holidays in my first year to surprise him. It had been hard. I was focused on getting good grades so I could get in with the Dominators, and he had been working a lot, so our relationship had sort of been put on the back burner.

"Well, it was a few days before Christmas. I came over to Vancouver and took a cab to the house. I had been planning this surprise for a month. Anyway, he wasn't supposed to be home until ten, but to my surprise, his truck was parked out front. I thought nothing of it and entered the house.

"The house was quiet, and I could hear the shower running down the hall, so I made my way down to surprise him. I got to the door and was about to throw it open when I heard a woman's voice in the throes of passion. I didn't know what to do, so with my heart in my throat, I turned and ran. The moment I was outside, though, and I realized I had nowhere to go, anger grew inside of me. He could have broken up with me, but he chose not too, and now he is painting me as the bad one because he is angry that I am happy."

"Wow, Lorelai, thank you for being so upfront about this. We are sorry to hear this has transpired."

"Thank you. It's disheartening, to say the least. He already created enough hurt in my life."

"No doubt. Now, why don't you tell me, how is your relationship with Knox Evans?"

I glanced over at Joanna, who gave a slight nod then scribbled 'keep it brief' on the paper.

"I'm happier than I have ever been," I said, which made Joanna smile and mouth 'perfect.'

"Glad to hear it. Well, thank you for your time, Lorelai. I really appreciate it," the interviewer said, finally ending the call.

Hanging up the phone, Joanna looked over at me and smiled. "That was perfect. Now, I will make sure I see the article before it goes out. I will also consult both you and Knox and add in anything that you want before it goes to press."

"Thank you."

"You are welcome."

I left her office, walking down the hall toward the exit. I'd never felt better than I did right now, and I couldn't wait to see Knox tonight.

I STOOD IN THE BATHROOM, a towel wrapped around me as I put my makeup on. I'd just finished with the last coat of mascara, put the tube away, and made my way into my bedroom when I came around the corner and saw someone in my closet and screamed.

"Sorry, didn't mean to scare you. I wanted those heels I loaned you the night of the gala," Aurora said as she dug through my closet.

"They should be there on the left," I answered, moving to the end of my bed and grabbing the dark, wine-colored dress I'd chosen for tonight. I quickly slipped into it, removing my towel, and then turned just as Aurora stood up, heels in hand.

"Zip me up?" I said, holding my hair up off my neck.

I felt her pull the zipper up the back of my dress and then, without a word, she made her way to the bedroom door.

"Everything okay?" I questioned, taking in the worried look on her face.

She turned, giving me her best fake smile, and then turned to leave the room.

"Wait a minute," I said, walking over to her and grabbing her arm. "What is wrong?"

"Nothing. Why does something have to be wrong?" she questioned.

"There doesn't, but I can tell from the look on your

face that there is. At least something is going on in that head of yours. Is everything okay with you and Dylan?"

Aurora nodded, still giving me the look of gloom and doom.

"Okay, are you sick?"

"No."

"Pregnant?"

"God no!" she exclaimed.

"Does Dylan want to try things in the bedroom you aren't down with?"

"I'm down with whatever he wants to try," she said, laughing, which caused me to laugh as well.

"Then what is it?" I asked.

I watched as Aurora avoided my eyes for a few moments. She only did that when she had something to say she didn't want to tell me. So, I knew whatever it was, it was important.

"I'm waiting. Don't make me guess again."

"Don't be mad," Aurora said, making her way over to my bed and sitting down.

"Okay."

I sat down beside her and got comfortable as she took my hand in hers.

"You know you are my best friend, right?"

"Yes," I answered. "At least, I better be." I laughed.

"I know I promised you a lot when we moved into

this place, and I feel absolutely awful coming to you now that we are now in a committed lease with this place."

"You're moving?" I questioned, disappointment beginning to flood through me.

She nodded and then met my eyes. "Don't hate me," she begged.

I knew I could play this the long way, or I could just let her off the hook.

"You're leaving me for Dylan?" I questioned.

She softly smiled, then nodded. "He asked me a while ago, and at first it didn't feel right leaving you, but now…"

"You want to be with him every chance you get," I answered.

"Yes."

I looked at the floor, trying to figure out if I could afford the place on my own or if I'd have to get a new roommate.

"Are you angry?" she asked, squeezing my hand in hers.

I shook my head and softly smiled. "No, I'm not angry. I'm happy for you. I'm sad for me, but so happy for you," I said, wrapping my arms around her.

"Are you sure?"

"If you don't call Dylan right now and tell him you are moving in, I will forbid you to move out." I giggled.

"Okay!"

I watched as she left the room, then I let out a sigh. I wasn't sure I could afford the place, and I knew that there was no way I could break the lease.

I'll figure it out, I thought to myself. *It will be fine.*

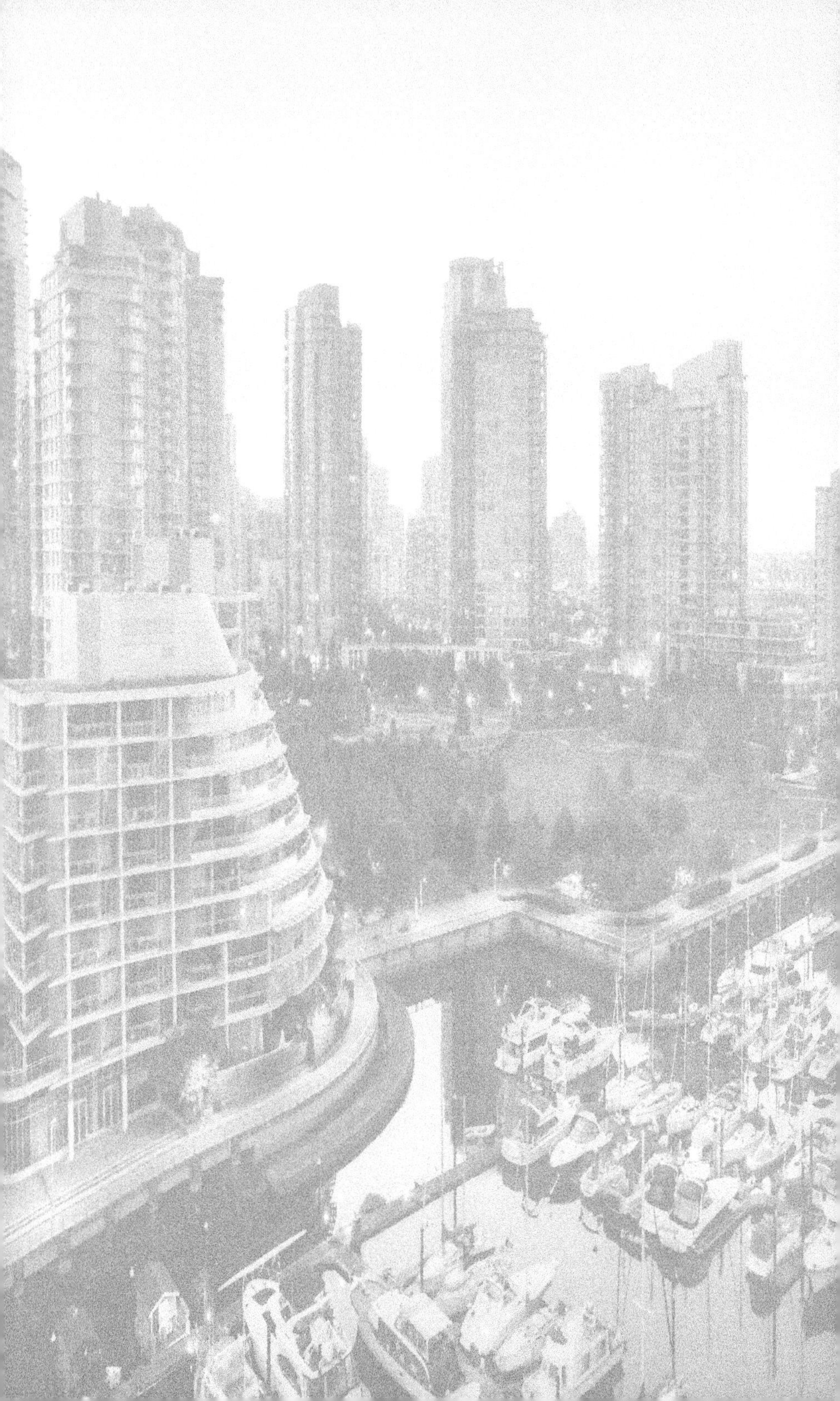

Chapter 19

Knox

SHE SAT ACROSS FROM ME, looking over at me with a gentle smile. I couldn't believe how lucky I was to have a girl like Lorelai in my life. I now regretted telling her to take a hike all those years ago. We'd wasted so much time not being together that now I didn't want to waste another moment. I was so thankful that she'd given me a chance.

"Dinner really was great," she said, picking up her glass of wine and taking a sip.

"That it was," I said, still unable to take my eyes off her.

She softly smiled, then looked up at me, a hint of worry lining her eyes.

"What is it?" I questioned, taking her hand in mine.

"Nothing," she said, shaking her head.

"Was it the interview? You said it went fine, or are you now having second thoughts?" I questioned, ready to march into Joanna's office in the morning and give her a piece of my mind.

"Oh no, it went well. Very well, actually. Joanna was great, and supportive. I'm not worried about that in the slightest."

"Good. Then what is it? I can tell there is something on your mind."

I watched as she shifted in her seat, then raised her eyes to mine. "Ah, just something between Aurora and I." She shrugged.

"Let me guess, the move?"

"You knew?" she questioned.

"I did. Dylan let it slip when we were on the road last time. He apparently asked her a long while ago, and she refused because of the new place, but I guess now that things are more serious between them, they've been talking about it more."

"I can't blame her." Lorelai shrugged again. "However, I'm a little concerned about the rent."

I nodded, knowing full well that would bother her.

"I just don't know how I am going to afford the place."

I smiled, taking her hand in mine and bringing it to my lips.

"What if I told you I don't see it being a problem?" I asked, fully prepared to pay her rent in full for the entire time she carried out the lease, if that was what she wanted.

Lorelai shook her head. "Knox, you will not help me pay rent," she said, pulling her hand from mine.

"Hey, look at me," I said as she looked away from me.

Finally, she brought her gorgeous brown eyes up to mine.

"I've been thinking a lot about us."

"I know. You told me that the other night."

I let out the breath I was holding along with the tension in my mid-back. This conversation had been weighing on my mind for days. I just hoped she was ready for it.

"I know I did," I said, looking around at the full restaurant. I was glad I'd paid the bill. I really didn't want to have this conversation here in the middle of the restaurant. "Want to get out of here?" I questioned.

She smiled and nodded.

I stood up from the table and waited for her to take

my hand. We made our way out of the restaurant and down to my car, where we both climbed in and took off toward my place.

When I pulled into the driveway, Lorelai looked over at me.

"We didn't need to come all the way to the outskirts of the city. I thought we were spending the night at my place?"

"We were, but I decided this might be better," I replied. I climbed out of the car, made my way around to her side and opened her door. Then we went into the house. Once inside, I grabbed us each a drink from the kitchen, and then I took her hand in mine and pulled her down the hall toward my bedroom.

"Knox, already?" She giggled.

I smiled and looked at the shock on her face when I stopped outside of one of the spare rooms. I'd told her I used for storage, and I had up until three weeks ago. I shoved the door open and flipped the light on. Her jaw dropped as she looked inside.

"What is this?" she questioned, stepping inside the room.

I followed her in and watched as she took in everything. I'd had the entire room done up in different shades of purples. There, against one wall, was a purple couch, complete with a purple throw and large pink pillows. In front of the picture window, I'd had a wooden desk placed, complete with a new computer. She walked over and ran her hand over the desk, then turned to the large bookshelves. I'd purchased a few collections from her favorite authors and had arranged them on the shelves, leaving most of them empty for her to place her own things.

"What is this?" she repeated, looking up at me in confusion.

"Do you like it?"

"Like it? I love it, but…Knox…seriously, this is way too much," she said as she made her way over to the bookshelf, taking in the books that I'd purchased.

I leaned against the wall, taking her in. It wasn't too much; it was what I wanted. I wanted her here. I just didn't know how to tell her.

"I am not sure I understand, though," she said, turning and frowning at me.

I smiled, reaching for her hands. "There is nothing to understand. When Dylan told me he was going to ask Aurora to move in again, it got me thinking. We spend so much time apart because of my travel schedule. I miss you so much while I'm gone, I don't know what to do with myself. Then when I am here, or I come home, I normally have to share you with Aurora. So, I thought that maybe you'd like to move in here with me."

When she lifted her eyes to mine, I could see tears already forming.

I wiped at her cheek as one tear slipped from her eye. "I hope those are happy tears."

She threw her arms around me. "They are."

"Good. So, this is your space. I wanted to make sure you had a space you could call your own. Sort of your own decompression space. You can decorate it however you want, add little touches to it to make it your own," I said.

"It's perfect already," she murmured. "It's honestly the most romantic thing anyone has ever done for me."

I wrapped my arms around her and pulled her into me, bringing my lips to hers. Then I grabbed her and picked her up, making my way over to the couch in her new room and sitting down, with her straddling my lap.

"What are you doing?" She laughed.

"Think it's time we break in this new couch," I said, raising my brows.

She got up off my lap and headed toward the door.

"Where are you going?"

She looked at me over her shoulder and then lifted her hand, wagging her finger in a come here motion. Like the lovesick puppy I was, I got up and followed her down the hall. Just outside my door, she shed her shirt, then turned to face me, undoing her pants, dropping them to the floor.

I could feel myself getting harder by the second as she reached behind her, unclasped her bra, and dropped it to the ground too. Once inside my room, she removed her panties and then sat down on the edge of my bed.

I made my way over to her, running my fingers through her hair as she pulled gently at my belt, undoing it, dropping my pants to the floor.

I placed my finger under her chin, lifting her face up, then bent and took her mouth with mine with a slow and gentle kiss.

"I'm falling in love with you," I whispered as our lips parted.

I didn't want to wait another moment to tell her. I wanted this to be our first time together when our feelings were on the table.

"I think I've always been in love with you," I said as I cupped her cheek, bringing my lips to hers.

"I love you too," she whispered, running her fingers through my hair, kissing me again.

We moved to the centre of the mattress, where I pulled her close to me and held her tight.

"I want us to go slow tonight. I want you to feel every inch of me while I drown myself in you."

I took her mouth with mine and buried myself deep inside of her, my body responding to her moans.

WE COLLAPSED against the mattress in exhaustion. We'd spent the entire weekend locked in this bedroom together, only taking a break to eat, use the washroom, and shower. We ignored our phones, the door, and the entire world, and it had been the best thing we'd done.

Making love to her was so different, and honestly, it was my favourite thing in the world to do.

"You have to leave soon." She giggled as she snuggled against me.

"Don't remind me," I said, kissing her bare shoulder.

"Are you going to have enough energy to make it through practice?"

I chuckled. "I hope so. Coach will kill me."

She rolled over and rested her head against my chest, looking up at me with a serious expression.

"What is it?" I asked, brushing a strand of hair from her face.

"I love you," she whispered.

"I love you too," I said, just as my phone vibrated

against the table, letting me know it was time for me to head out. "Just hold that thought for when I get back, okay?" I winked, slipping out from under the sheets.

"Always," she said, resting her head down on my pillow and closing her eyes. "I only have plans to be here today. Hurry back."

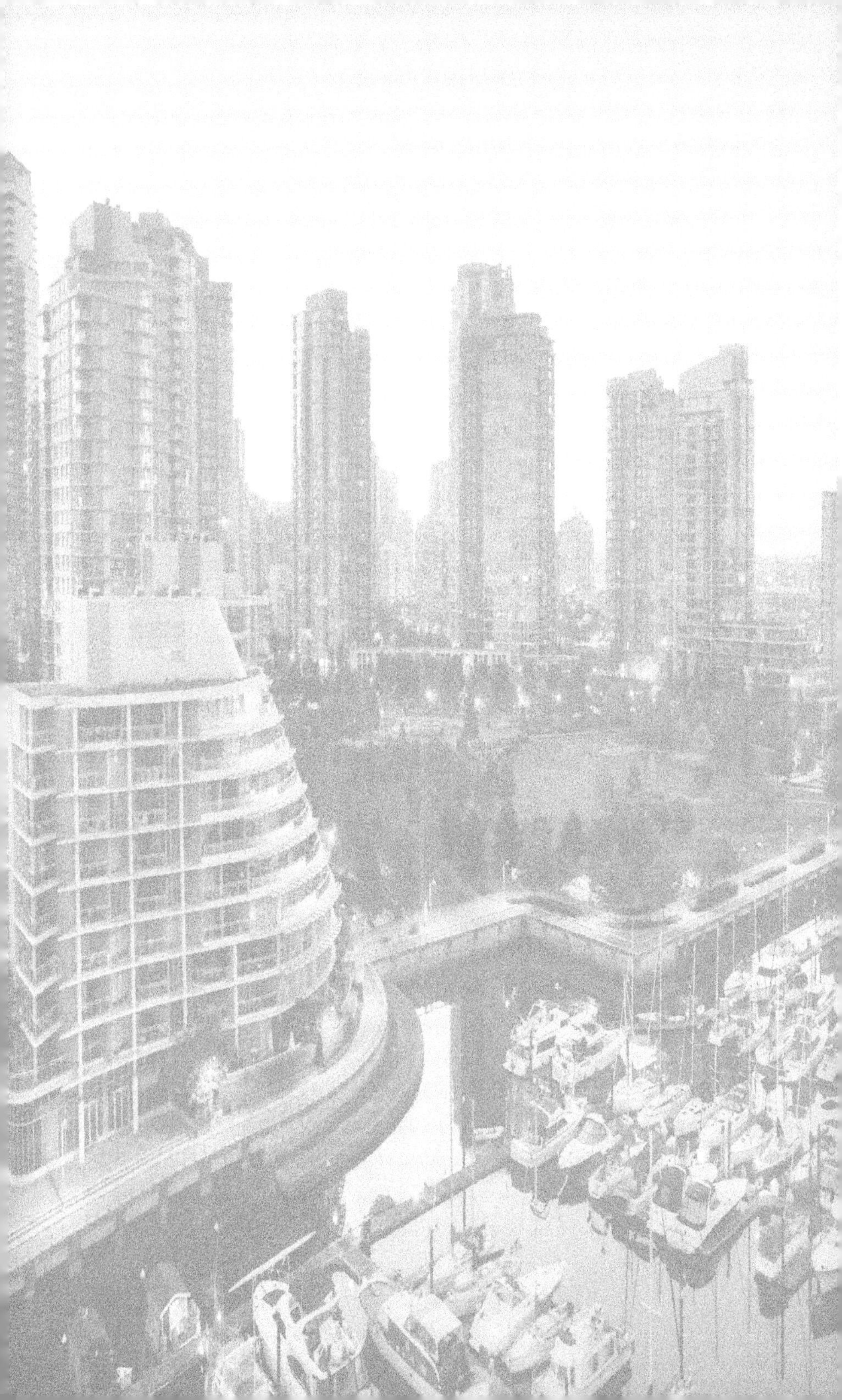

Chapter 20

Lorelai - Three Days Later

"I'M GOING to run over to Sip and Stir," I called out from the front door of our condo. "What for?"

"Coffee!" I lied.

"Can you grab me a cinnamon scone?"

Alarm bells went off. A cinnamon scone was her go-to when she was stressed, but I shouldn't talk. I wasn't only going over there for coffee. I was going for half a dozen peanut butter cookies. Yet, I frowned and slowly made my way back to her bedroom door. She sat in the middle of her room, going through a bunch of boxes.

"Everything okay?" I questioned.

"Oh yes. Just packing," Aurora said, looking over her shoulder at me. "You?"

"All good." I nodded. I still hadn't told her that Knox had asked me to move in. It still hadn't registered that it had happened. It had only sunk in that we'd finally admitted our feelings for one another, which I was sure was why I needed those cookies.

"You sure you are okay with it? I can always tell him we will wait until you find a new roommate. It's the least I can do." She shrugged.

I smiled. This was why I truly loved my best friend. She'd always taken my feelings into consideration, no matter what, just the way I'd done with her.

"No need. Really," I said, still not ready to divulge that I was moving in with Knox.

"You're sure?"

I nodded.

Aurora frowned. "Is there something you aren't telling me?"

When had she gotten so perceptive? This wasn't normally like her, and I wondered if perhaps Knox had mentioned something to Dylan already. He had already gone to our landlord and was in negotiations to get me out of my lease, another thing I really wasn't ready to divulge.

"No," I lied.

"Lorelai, you should know that you can't get away without telling me things."

I let out a little giggle, trying to suppress my smile.

"Fine. Knox, um…he asked me to move in with him on Friday," I replied, clearing a space on her bed and sitting down.

"WHAT!!!!! OH MY GOD!!!!! THAT IS AMAZING!!!!" Aurora said, getting up off the floor and dancing around the room.

I couldn't help but laugh as she grabbed me and hugged me.

"Okay, one cinnamon scone and no coffee, because you clearly need no caffeine." I laughed, getting up and heading to the door. "I'll save that for me."

"Did he wear you out?" Aurora questioned.

I couldn't help but giggle. "Not at all. Just need a little pick-me-up."

WITH MY HEAD DOWN, looking at my phone reading a message Knox sent with an update on the condo situation, I pulled the door open and walked into the coffee shop. I had just taken a step inside when I banged right into someone.

"Oh god, I'm terribly sorry," I muttered, shoving my phone into my pocket and looking up to see Hugo standing there in front of me.

"Watch where the hell you are going," he barked.

"Oh, Lorelai."

Immediately, his body language changed, as well as the look on his face.

"Hugo," I bit out, walking past him and over to the counter where I quickly placed my order. I wanted to get out of here, and at the last second, I changed my order from six cookies to a dozen.

"Sorry about that," I heard behind me.

I looked over my shoulder to see Hugo standing there watching me.

"What do you want?" I asked, hoping he'd just leave the building and leave me alone forever.

"Could we talk?" he questioned.

"That is not a good idea," I bit out.

"Why, is the protector around?" He chuckled, glancing over his shoulder.

I closed my eyes, ignoring him. *Hugo should be lucky Knox isn't anywhere near Vancouver right now*, I thought to myself.

Ignoring his comment, I grabbed my coffee, cookies, and the cinnamon scone from the counter and made my way over to the station where I could add cream and sugar. He, of course, followed me over and stood there waiting for me to acknowledge him.

"What do you want, Hugo?" I questioned.

"Look, I wanted to talk to you about the article."

I clenched my jaw. If only he knew how he'd made my life hell once again for an entire month, almost causing me to end things with the man I loved. He was taking his life into his hands, and if Knox had been here, I knew he'd be sorry forever for bringing it up.

"You are kidding, right?" I questioned.

Hugo shook his head, looking at me with that stupid, smug smile on his lips. Fire ripped through me as I stood there, dumping not one but three sugars and two creams into my coffee.

"You know, just when I thought you couldn't sink any lower. I can't believe you had the audacity to have that printed about me. How the hell can you act like I'm the one in the wrong when all I ever did was love you? You broke my fucking heart," I said under my breath.

"For almost an entire year and a half, I thought I wasn't good for anyone. I blamed myself for your actions, and until recently, didn't realize that I wasn't the cause of every horrible thing that happened in my life."

"Look, I'm sorry. I tried to tell you that," Hugo said.

"Yeah, after I found out. The least you could have done was come clean, tell me that things weren't where you wanted them to be with me, and let me go. Instead..."

I stopped. I'd never mentioned to Hugo that I'd caught him that night. Instead, I'd made some story up about seeing him in public with another girl. Well, it wasn't exactly made up. I had seen him with my cousin once, which I learned he had put the moves on her as well. I couldn't even bring myself to confront what I'd walked in on. Perhaps if I had, maybe I would have found out sooner that I really wasn't the issue, that it was him.

Hugo looked at me. Some form of sympathy was behind his eyes. "I told you, I ended it with her after you saw us in public. When she came to me claiming to be pregnant, that was when I ended it with you," Hugo said, still not knowing the whole truth.

I'd give it to him. He was at least consistent with his lie, yet I wondered how long he'd keep up with that story. I'd have thought he'd falter by now.

"Well, Hugo, I hate to break it to you, but that isn't my problem, and regardless, you screwed me over."

"I screwed you over? How do you think it felt to see you in Hawaii with Knox? I wanted another chance with you, especially after I found out the pregnancy thing was a lie."

"And I thought we were going to spend the rest of our lives together. It sucks when we can't get what we want, doesn't it?" I bit out, turning on my heel, going to make my way to the door.

"It ripped my heart out," Hugo said, causing people to turn and look our way.

I turned back around and looked at him. He was pathetic standing there, and honestly, I didn't care if I'd ripped his heart out, stomped on it, and then put it back in his chest. He now knew how I felt that very second I walked in on him.

I walked back over to him and met his eyes.

"Well, Hugo, all I can say is that now you know how I felt the night I walked in on you and found you in the shower with her, listening to you say the same words to her that you said to me over and over, every time we'd done it."

He stopped, his face turning ashen.

"What girl? What night?" he questioned, panic hitting his eyes.

"Two weeks before Christmas, when we broke up. I didn't see you out in town with another woman. I lied, well sort of, I mean I did see you with my cousin. Regardless, I came home from school to surprise you. You weren't even supposed to be home. Only the surprise was on me. You were in the shower with her."

I could see him thinking, the wheels turning in his head.

"I um, I can explain," he muttered.

"No need. The explanation was done, and you didn't need to say a word. I am going to tell you, though, that I am happier now than I've ever been, and if you dare want to start any more shit, be prepared to face a lawyer this time. You and, oh gosh, I forget her name…deserve one another. I hope the two of you are very happy together."

Without another word, I spun on my heel and headed out of the Sip and Stir, feeling lighter than I had in almost a year and a half. It was amazing what confronting the events of that night had done for me. I no longer blamed myself, and I felt more amazing knowing that I had a man standing behind me, one who supported my dreams and loved me unconditionally.

MY PHONE VIBRATED against the table in the bathroom as I soaked in the large tub.

KNOX: What are you doing?

LORELAI: Soaking in the tub...you

KNOX: Sort of the same. My therapist told me I should after a long practice.

LORELAI: She sounds like a smart girl ;) You should probably keep her.

KNOX: I plan on it ;)

LORELAI: How was your day?

KNOX: Good, we are going for the cup, baby!

LORELAI: Seriously???

At that news, I wished he was here to celebrate with me, instead of thousands of miles away.

KNOX: Seriously! Best part, the last three games of the year will be on home ground.

LORELAI: I cannot wait.

I wanted to cry; I was so excited. This meant I'd be able to watch the games from the arena, not from the comfort of the living room. I'd be able to be there when they won, to be wrapped in his arms at the end of the game, the adrenaline coursing through everything. I couldn't wait.

> KNOX: Neither can I. How's everything coming with the packing?

>> LORELAI: Good. I started tonight, got a few things ready. It's going to be a change.

> KNOX: Sure will be, but a great one at that.

>> LORELAI: Oh, I ran into Hugo today.

> KNOX: really? And?

>> LORELAI: He won't be bothering us again. I also confronted the truth.

> KNOX: How did that go?

>> LORELAI: Better than I could have imagined. Facing it, freeing it from inside of me, has made me extremely excited about the future.

> KNOX: I'm glad. I'm excited as well. I can't wait to have you all to myself.

>> LORELAI: How is the hip?

KNOX: Must we, I'm doing as you say,
and if you must know, I hate taking
baths, I'm more of a shower guy.

LORELAI: Baths are great, and yes,
we must.

KNOX: If we must, then once I tell you,
you best be ready for what I want.

I squinted at my screen, wondering what on earth he meant. I let out a sigh, wondering if I dared continue with the conversation, but then shrugged and continued typing.

LORELAI: How is the hip ;P

KNOX: It's getting there. Summer will
be a good time to relax it.

LORELAI: No summer will be a good
time to get it into shape for next
year ;P

KNOX: We will see about that.

LORELAI: Yes we will. Now what do
you want?

KNOX: Pictures.

LORELAI: Pictures of what?

> KNOX: You, in all your glory, in that tub of yours, with that wonderful little toy I got for you last week.

Immediately, my cheeks heated as I re-read his words. This was Knox, this was my life, and I was so damn grateful that even if he were thousands of miles away, he wanted me, and only me.

> LORELAI: Get ready ;)

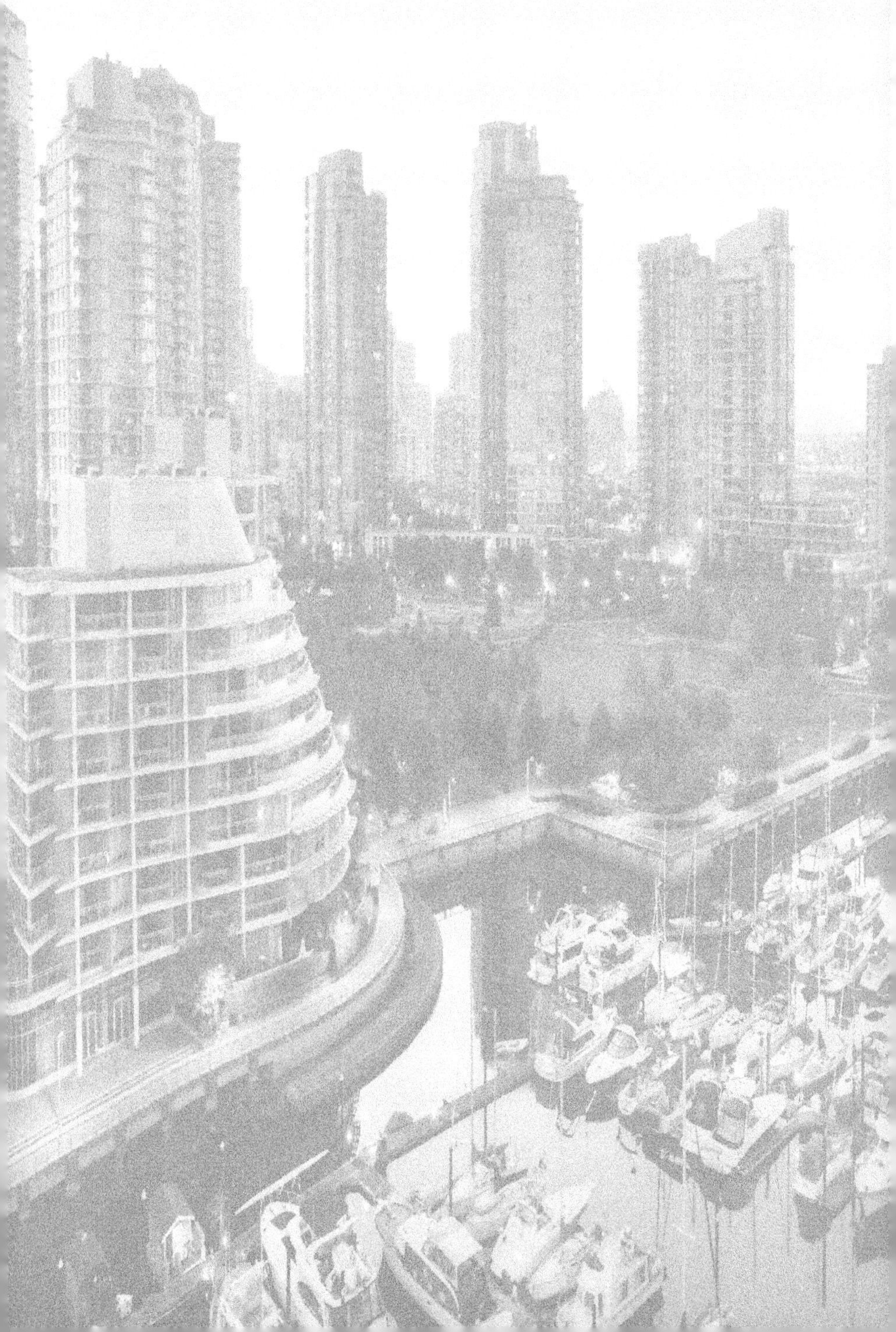

Chapter 21

Lorelai

IT WAS as if the entire crowd in the arena was holding their breath as we watched Knox hit the puck. It travelled down the ice and right past the goalie into the net, and that was when the timer went off.

The stadium erupted in cheers as the guys skated around, the other players hopping over the boards and coming out onto the ice, colliding with the others.

Aurora jumped up and wrapped her arms around me, and confetti fell from the roof of the arena, down into the audience. She grabbed my hand, pulling me from our seats and down the stairs to the edge of the ice, where Dylan and Knox came skating over, huge smiles on their faces.

They both grabbed us, hugging us tight as the crowd roared even louder as cameras landed on the four of us, projecting our private moment onto the large screen in the centre of the arena.

Knox met my eyes, and together we ignored the entire world as he pressed a kiss to my lips. "Ready to celebrate?"

I rested my forehead against his and nodded, kissing him again.

WE LAY IN BED, wrapped in sheets.

"I'll be back in a moment," he whispered, pressing a kiss to my shoulder.

I watched his naked ass as he walked away from the bed. *I'll never tire of that view*, I thought to myself. Once he was gone, I dropped my head to the pillow, closing my eyes, my body relaxed and warm. I was just about asleep when I felt the bed dip and opened my eyes to see him sitting there holding a box.

"What is that?" I questioned, recognizing the box almost instantly.

"A little treat from Sip and Stir." He smiled.

I shifted and sat up, taking the box from him and opening the lid to see one peanut butter cookie in the box's bottom with the words *'Will you'* written on it in icing.

I smiled as I leaned over and kissed him on the lips.

"How did you know I could use a cookie?" I questioned.

"A hunch." He shrugged, turning on the bedside light.

"I'm confused though, what is with the writing?"

Knox shrugged and shoved the box toward me.

I smiled, reached in and broke the cookie in half, and was just about to bring it to my mouth when something reflected in the light.

"There is something…" I frowned as I broke the half of the cookie in half one more time over the box.

I looked down at the cookie in my hand and back up to Knox as I looked down at the ring that hung halfway out of the cookie.

"Knox?" I questioned, my voice shaking.

"Lorelai, I don't want to wait."

"You don't?" I asked, swallowing hard.

"No, baby, I don't. I was planning to do this tomorrow, once we got to the cottage, but I don't even want to wait that long. Will you—"

I wrapped my arms around his neck and hugged

him tight to me. "Yes, baby, I will!" I cried, meeting his lips.

I felt him pull the cookie from my hand and drop it back into the box, then he placed the box over on my nightstand as he lay me down, kissing me the entire time.

LIFE COULDN'T GET BETTER than it was right now, I thought as I watched the replay of the winning shot over and over on my phone while waiting for Knox to finish getting dressed. We were going over to Dylan and Aurora's for a celebratory drink before we headed away for the weekend.

I giggled as I saw the look on Knox's face in the video. He'd been so surprised that the puck went into the net with only seconds to spare, he'd contorted his face into this half win smile, half loose pout.

"Don't tell me you are you watching that again?" I heard him ask as he made his way into the living room.

I looked over at him and smiled. "You look so cute in this video."

"I look ridiculous." He chuckled, trying to remake the same expression they'd caught on film.

I couldn't help but laugh. "You are ridiculous," I said, getting up and pocketing my phone as I made my way over to him.

He took my hand in his. "You all packed?"

I nodded. "Yep, all ready to go. I even put my bag in the car."

"You did," he said, running his finger over the ring that I now wore on my finger.

I nodded, kissing him. "Yep."

"We should get going. Dylan gets a little irritated if we are late," he said, kissing me deeper this time.

I laughed as his hands travelled to my ass. "We won't go anywhere if you don't stop." I giggled, pulling at his hands.

"That might be my idea." He winked, stealing one more kiss before grabbing his keys from the hook inside the door.

Twenty minutes later, we walked into Dylan's condo. The place was full of players on the team, their wives, girlfriends, or significant others. We stepped into the kitchen to see Lucas, Clay, Dylan, Phil all there talking about the game.

"Speak of the devil. Here he is, the guy who scored the winning fucking goal," Dylan said giving him a high five.

Knox smiled and shrugged. "It was no big deal."

"Fucker, no big deal? It was a damn big deal. If I

were you, I'd revel in the praise. Next year, we may only refer to you as the old guy on the team." Dylan chuckled. "Especially with that hip of yours," he said, smacking him on the back.

I laughed, then shook my head.

"Just being a team player," Knox replied, grabbing a beer and handing me one.

I wrapped my arm around his waist and looked up at him. "Dylan is right, take it. Not every day these guys idolize you." I winked.

"Now there is a girl who gets it," Dylan said, winking at me and holding out his fist for a fist bump.

I couldn't help but laugh as I hit his fist, especially when Knox looked down at me once again trying to make the face that was in the video.

"Are you saying I'm old?"

That made me laugh even harder. "No."

"Better not be." He winked, pulling me in for another kiss. "Or I'll have to teach you a lesson tonight."

"Give it a rest already." Clay gagged.

"Shut up over there. When you find a girl, you'll want her lips permanently attached to yours as well," Knox said, pointing at him.

"Not a chance! I'm not a one-woman guy. Your asses should know that."

Lucas laughed. "Not until he's forced to be."

That caused all the guys to break out in laughter.

"Not a chance in hell is that happening to me."

"It will if you don't start wrapping it." Dylan chuckled, punching him in the shoulder.

"Alright, this conversation has gone downhill fast. I think I'm going to go find Aurora," I said to Knox.

"Babe, you better get used to all the guy talk."

"Not sure I want to." I giggled as he smacked my ass and kissed me before I left the room.

"Alright, boys! What's on the agenda for summer?" I heard Knox ask as I made my way down the hall to see Aurora standing in her bedroom.

"Hey, you," I said, stepping into her bedroom. "What are we doing this summer?" I questioned, looking forward to spending time with her and the guys at our place out by the pool.

She glanced up at me, a funny look on her face. I ignored the look and held my hand up to show her my ring.

"What on earth?" she said, grabbing my hand and looking down at it.

"He asked last night." I shrugged.

She glanced at the bedroom door just as the guys started laughing at something that was said.

"Close the door."

"Oh, being secretive." I giggled. "Did you get a

new toy I'm going to have to try out? I'll admit, I'm curious to know what it is."

When I turned back to her, I saw nothing but panic in her eyes.

"Aurora? What is it?"

She lifted her hand to reveal a large diamond ring as well.

I ran back over, grabbing her hand and looking down at the ring.

"When did this happen?" I questioned.

"Last night, after the game."

I couldn't help but giggle. It was exciting to me we had both gotten engaged the same night. When we were younger, we'd dreamed this would happen and now it was.

"Oh, my god!" I said as I wrapped my arms around her. "So exciting. Did you guys set a date yet?"

She shook her head and then sat down on the end of her bed. She didn't look happy, she barely even looked excited.

"What is it? I'd have thought you would have been thrilled."

"I am," she mumbled, holding something tight in her other hand.

"Care to show me what you are holding on to?"

She rolled whatever was in her hand and then looked up at me, her eyes glistening.

"We were supposed to be going away for the summer. Dylan and Knox had it all planned…Knox wanted to keep it a surprise from you, now, I'm not sure it will even happen."

I frowned. I didn't know the four of us were going anywhere, but then Knox had mentioned something about some sort of surprise for the summer.

"Aurora?"

I walked over and sat beside her as she opened her palm. A pregnancy test with two little blue lines stared back at me. I swallowed hard as I looked at my best friend.

"Oh wow, Aurora," I cried.

I wrapped my arms tightly around her, but she didn't make a peep. Instead, I was certain I heard her sniffle.

"Aren't you happy?" I questioned.

She nodded. "I am. I guess it's a bit of a shock."

The door opened and Dylan stood there looking at the two of us, questions in his eyes. I got up and made my way over to the door, patted him on the chest, and then looked back at my friend and winked.

"Congratulations," he said to me. "Guess we have a summer of wedding planning in store for the four of us."

"I'm going to join my man," I said, turning and looking at Aurora. "Tell him," I mouthed before I smiled and, without another word, I headed to the kitchen, only to be congratulated on our engagement by every member of the team.

An hour later, Dylan and Aurora emerged, and we had more news to celebrate. The entire teamed, our new family, all celebrated not only the guys' win, our engagements, but also the announcement of a new baby Dominator being born in the coming months.

KNOX SNORED beside me as I lay awake. I watched as he slept, completely at peace. It had been a crazy ride with him so far, and I couldn't wait to experience more with him. I moved closer to him, resting my head on his chest, and closed my eyes. I'd never tire of this man, although if you'd asked me a few months ago, I'd have told you the opposite.

I laughed as I thought back to before we were together. How angry he made me simply by being in the same room. When Aurora and I finally sat down tonight, she claimed she'd always known I'd crushed on him. She said she could hear it in my voice whenever I brought up his name. I'd laughed it off, but I knew it was probably the truth.

Knox Evans started out being the most obnoxious man I'd ever known and, sometimes, still was, but I was happier than ever knowing that he was now going to be my husband and I couldn't wait until we said I do.

Ready for more Vancouver Dominators

Preorder
Two Minutes for Holding
Coming March 2025

https://geni.us/TwoMinutesforHolding

GET A FREE BOOK

Sign up for my newsletter and I'll send you a free book.

https://geni.us/NLSignupBackMatter

What is coming next from S.L. Sterling

Summer Nights and Fireflies
Coming Soon
Preorder Here: https://geni.us/SummerNightsFireflies

The Christmas Card (Willow Valley)
December 2024
https://geni.us/TheChristmasCardWV6

ACE (Vegas MMA)
January 2025
https://geni.us/AceVegasMMA

Follow S.L. Sterling

Did you know that bookbub has a feature where you can follow me and it will send you an alert when I release a book or put a title on sale? Sign up here and make sure you stay in the loop.

Bookbub:
https://geni.us/SLSterlingBookbub

Website
https://www.authorslsterling.com

Facebook
https://geni.us/SLSterlingFB

Twitter
https://geni.us/SLSterlingTwitter

Instagram
https://geni.us/SLSterlingInstagram

Tiktok
https://geni.us/slsterlingtiktok

Reader Group

Follow S.L. Sterling

https://geni.us/SapphiresReaderGroup

Goodreads
https://geni.us/SterlingGoodreads

Newsletter
https://geni.us/NLSignupBackMatter

About the Author

USA Today Bestselling Author S.L. Sterling was born and raised in southern Ontario. She now lives in Northern Ontario Canada and is married to her best friend and soul mate and their two dogs.

An avid reader all her life, S.L. Sterling dreamt of becoming an author. She decided to give writing a try after one of her favorite authors launched a course on how to write your novel. This course gave her the push she needed to put pen to paper and her debut novel "It Was Always You" was born.

When S.L. Sterling isn't writing or plotting her next novel she can be found curled up with a cup of coffee, blanket and the newest romance novel from one of her favorite authors.

In her spare time, she enjoys camping, hiking, sunny destinations, spending quality time with family and friends and of course reading.

To be notified of new releases or sales, join S.L. Sterling's private Mailing List. https://geni.us/NLSignupBackMatter

Get even more of the inside scoop when you join S.L. Sterling's private Facebook group, Sterling's Silver Sapphires: https://geni.us/SapphiresReaderGroup

Other Books by S.L. Sterling

It Was Always You

On A Silent Night

Bad Company

Back to You this Christmas

Fireside Love

Holiday Wishes

Saviour Boy

The Boy Under the Gazebo

The Greatest Gift

Into the Sunset

Letting You Go

The Spencer Brooks Diaries

Our Little Secret

Our Little Surprise

Our Little Wedding

The Malone Brother Series

A Kiss Beneath the Stars

In Your Arms

His to Hold

Finding Forever with You

Vegas MMA

Dagger

Doctors of Eastport General

Doctor Desire

Doctor Right

All I Want for Christmas (Contemporary Romance Holiday Collection)

Willow Valley

Memories of the Past

The Holiday Dilemma

Letters from the Heart

My Darling Christmas

Scars on my Heart

The Happy Holidates Series

Champagne and Fireworks

Summer Nights and Fireflies

Vancouver Dominators

Inside the Penalty Box

Ten Minute Misconduct